PART ONE

"From his brimstone bed, at break of day,
A-walking the devil is gone,
To look at his little snug farm of the world,
And see how his stock went on.

A lady drove by, in her pride,
In whose face an expression he spied,
For which he could have kissed her;
Such a flourishing, fine, clever creature was she
With an eye as wicked as wicked can be."

—From *The Devil's Walk*
by Robert Southey, 1799

May 1810

My very dear Eve,

It was a great pleasure to receive your last letter and to hear that you and my cousin Rowarth are having such a splendid time on your wedding tour. I owe you particular thanks for the present of the beautiful negligee you sent me from Paris—Dexter likes it extremely!

You mentioned that you were curious to know all the news from Fortune's Folly, and there is much to report. I fear that Sir Montague continues to inflict all manner of greedy and grasping taxes upon us under the terms of the medieval law. There are now only three unmarried heiresses left in the village, for all the others have embraced matrimony in order to escape the Dames' Tax! My good friend Alice Lister tied the knot with my cousin Miles Vickery a month or so past. You will remember Miles, I feel sure. It is perhaps a blessing for the friendship between him and Rowarth that he always preferred blondes and so never sought your favor! However, he is quite reformed now. It is most amusing to see so shocking a rake hopelessly in love with his wife rather than with someone else's.

Lord Stephen Armitage jilted Miss Mary Wheeler practically at the altar. A lucky escape for her, I feel. The other match is between Miss Flora Minchin and Lord Waterhouse. They are to wed in a few weeks. It is not a love match. His title for her money—you know the sort of thing. Though I have the strangest feeling matters may not go quite to plan....

NICOLA CORNICK

**is an international bestselling author and a
RITA® Award finalist. Her sensational and sexy
novels have received acclaim the world over.**

"A rising star of the Regency arena."
—*Publishers Weekly*

"Nicola Cornick creates a glittering, sensual world of
historical romance that I never want to leave."
—Anna Campbell, author of *Untouched*

"Ms. Cornick has a brilliant talent for bringing
her characters to life, and embracing the reader
into her stories."
—*RomanceJunkies*

Praise for Nicola's previous HQN titles

"A powerful story, rich, witty and sensual—
a divinely delicious treat."
—Marilyn Rondeau, Reviewers International Organization,
on *Deceived*

"Cornick masterfully blends misconceptions, vengeance,
powerful emotions and the realization of great love into a
touching story."
—*Romantic Times BOOKreviews,* 4 1/2 stars, on *Deceived*

"If you've liked Nicola Cornick's other books, you are sure
to like this one as well. If you've never read one—what are
you waiting for?"
—Lynn Lamy, *Rakehell,* on *Lord of Scandal*

"RITA® Award-nominated Cornick deftly steeps her latest
intriguingly complex Regency historical in a beguiling
blend of danger and desire."
—John Charles, *Booklist,* on *Unmasked*

NICOLA CORNICK

❦ THE BRIDES OF FORTUNE ❦

THE
UNDOING
of a
LADY

HQN™

Recycling programs
for this product may
not exist in your area.

ISBN-13: 978-0-373-77395-4

THE UNDOING OF A LADY

This edition published by arrangement with Harlequin Books S.A.

www.HQNBooks.com

Printed in U.S.A.

For Tony, Judy and Clare, with love.

THE UNDOING
of a
LADY

CHAPTER ONE

The Folly, Fortune Hall, Yorkshire—June 1810
A little before midnight

IT WAS A BEAUTIFUL NIGHT for an abduction.

The moon sailed high and bright in a starlit sky.
The warm breeze sighed in the treetops, stirring the
scents of pine and hot grass. Deep in the heart of the
wood an owl called, a long, throaty hoot that hung
on the night air.

Lady Elizabeth Scarlet sat by the window,
watching for the shadow, waiting to hear the step on
the path outside. She knew Nat Waterhouse would
come. He always came when she called. He would
be annoyed of course—what man would not be irritated to be called away from his carousing on the
night before his wedding—but he would still be
there. He was so responsible; he would not ignore her
cry for help. She knew exactly how he would
respond. She knew him so well.

Her fingertips beat an impatient tattoo on the stone
window ledge. She checked the watch she had pur-

loined earlier from her brother. It felt as though she had been waiting for hours but she was surprised to see that it was only eight minutes since she had last looked. She felt nervous, which surprised her. She knew Nat would be angry but she was acting for his own good. The wedding had to be stopped. He would thank her for it one day.

From across the fields came the faint chime of the church bell. Midnight. There was the crunch of footsteps on the path. He was precisely on time. Of course he would be.

She sat still as a mouse as he opened the door of the folly. She had left the hallway in darkness but there was a candle burning in the room above. If she had calculated correctly he would go up the spiral stair and into the chamber, giving her time to lock the outer door behind him and hide the key. There was no other way out. Her half brother, Sir Montague Fortune, had had the folly built to the design of a miniature fort with arrow slits and windows too small to allow a man to pass. He had thought it a great joke to build a folly in a village called Fortune's Folly. That, Lizzie thought, was Monty's idea of amusement, that and dreaming up new taxes with which to torment the populace.

"Lizzie!"

She jumped. Nat was right outside the door of the guardroom. He sounded impatient. She held her breath.

"Lizzie? Where are you?"

He took the spiral stair two steps at a time and she slid like a wraith out of the tiny guardroom to turn the key in the heavy oaken door. Her fingers were shaking and slipped on the cold iron. She knew what her friend Alice Vickery would say if she were here now:

"Not another of your harebrained schemes, Lizzie! Stop now, before it is too late!"

But it was already too late. She could not allow herself time to think about this or she would lose her nerve. She ran back into the guardroom and stole a hand through one of the arrow slits. There was a nail on the wall outside. The key clinked softly against the stone. There. Nat could not escape until she willed it. She smiled to herself, well pleased. She had known there was no need to involve anyone else in the plan. She could handle an abduction unaided. It was easy.

She went out into the hall. Nat was standing at the top of the stairs, the candle in his hand. The flickering light threw a tall shadow. He looked huge, menacing and angry.

Actually, Lizzie thought, he *was* huge, menacing and angry, but he would never hurt her. Nat would never, ever hurt her. She knew exactly how he would behave. She knew him like a brother.

"Lizzie? What the hell's going on?"

He was drunk as well, Lizzie thought. Not drunk enough to be even remotely incapacitated but enough to swear in front of a lady, which was something that Nat would normally never do. But then, if she were marrying Miss Flora Minchin the next morning, she would be swearing, too. And she would have drunk herself into a stupor. Which brought her back to the point. For Nat would *not* be marrying Miss Minchin. Not in the morning. Not ever. She was here to make sure of it. She was here to save him.

"Good evening, Nat," Lizzie said brightly, and saw him scowl. "I trust you have had an enjoyable time on your last night of freedom?"

"Cut the pleasantries, Lizzie," Nat said. "I'm not in the mood." He held the candle a little higher so that the light fell on her face. His eyes were black, narrowed and hard. "What could possibly be so urgent that you had to talk to me in secret on the night before my wedding?"

Lizzie did not answer immediately. She caught the hem of her gown up in one hand and made her careful way up the stone stair. She felt Nat's gaze on her face every moment even though she did not look at him. He stood aside to allow her to enter the chamber at the top. It was tiny, furnished only with a table, a chair and a couch. Monty Fortune, having created his miniature fort, had not really known what to do with it.

When she was standing on the rug in the center of the little round turret room Lizzie turned to face Nat. Now that she could see him properly she could see that his black hair was tousled and his elegant clothes looked slightly less than pristine. His jacket hung open and his cravat was undone. Stubble darkened his lean cheek and the hard line of his jaw. There was a smoky air of the alehouse about him. His eyes glittered with impatience and irritation.

"I'm waiting," he said.

Lizzie spread her hands wide in an innocent gesture. "I asked you here to try to persuade you not to go through with the wedding," she said. She looked at him in appeal. "You know she will bore you within five minutes, Nat. No," she corrected herself. "You are already bored with her, aren't you, and you are not even wed yet. And you don't give a rush for her, either. You are making a terrible mistake."

Nat's mouth set in a thin line. He raked a hand through his hair. "Lizzie, we've spoken about this—"

"I know," Lizzie said. Her heart hammered in her throat. "Which is why I had to do this, Nat. It's for your own good."

Fury was fast replacing the irritation in his eyes. "Do what?" he said. Then, as she did not reply: "Do *what,* Lizzie?"

"I've locked you in," Lizzie said rapidly. "I promise that I will release you tomorrow—when the hour of the wedding is past. I doubt that Flora or her parents will forgive you the slight of standing her up at the altar."

She had never previously thought the Earl of Waterhouse a man who made a display of his emotions. She had always thought he had a good face for games of chance, showing no feeling, giving nothing away. Now, though, it was all too easy to read him. His first reaction was stupefaction. His second was grim certainty. He did not even stop to question the truth of what she had said. If she knew him well, then the reverse was also the case.

"Lizzie," he said, "you little *hellcat*."

He turned and crashed angrily down the spiral stair, taking the candle, leaving her in darkness but for the faint moonlight that slid through the arrow slits in the wall. Lizzie let her breath out in a long, shaky sigh. She had only a moment to compose herself, for once he realized that there really was no escape he would be back. And this time he would be beyond mere fury.

She heard him try the thick oak door—and swear when it would not even give an inch. She saw the candle flame dance across the walls as he checked the guardroom and the passageway for potential exits. The swearing became more colorful as he acknowledged what she already knew—there was no way out. The tiny water closet opened onto the equally miniature moat and was far too small for a six foot man to squeeze through. The room in which she stood had a trapdoor that led up to the pretend battlements but she had locked it earlier and hidden the key in a hollow tree outside. She had wanted to make no mistakes.

He was back and she had been correct—he looked

enraged. A muscle pulsed in his lean cheek. Every line of his body was rigid with fury.

When he spoke, however, his voice was deceptively gentle. Lizzie found it more disconcerting than if he had shouted at her.

"Why are you doing this, Lizzie?" he said.

Lizzie wiped the palms of her hands surreptitiously down the side of her gown. She wished she could stop shaking. She knew she was doing the right thing. She simply had not anticipated that it would be quite so frightening.

"I told you," she said, tilting her chin up defiantly. "I'm saving you from yourself."

Nat gave a harsh laugh. "No. You are denying me the chance to gain the fifty thousand pounds I so desperately need. You know how important this is to me, Lizzie."

"It isn't worth it for a lifetime of boredom."

"That is *my* choice."

"You've made the wrong choice. I'm here to save you from it." Lizzie kept her voice absolutely level despite the pounding of her blood. "You have always cared for me and tried to protect me. Now it is my turn. I'm doing this because you are my friend and I care for you."

She saw the contemptuous flicker in his eyes that said he did not believe her. Lizzie's temper smoldered. She had always been hot-blooded, or perhaps just plain belligerent depending upon whose opinion one sought. It seemed damnably unfair of Nat to judge her when she had his best interests at heart. He should be *thanking* her for saving him from this ghastly match.

Nat put the candle down on the little wooden table beside the door and took a very deliberate step toward her. He was tall—over six-foot—broad and muscular. Lizzie tried not to feel intimidated and failed.

"Give me the key, Lizzie," he said gently.

"No." Lizzie swallowed hard. He was very close now, his physical presence powerful, threatening, in direct contradiction to the softness of his tone. But she was not afraid of Nat. In the nine years of their acquaintance he had never given her any reason to fear him.

"Where is it?"

"Hidden somewhere you won't find it."

Nat gave an exasperated sigh. He flung out an arm. "This isn't a game, Lizzie," he said. She could tell he was trying to suppress his anger, trying to be reasonable. Nat Waterhouse was, above all, a reasonable man, a rational man, and a *responsible* man. And she supposed it was *un*reasonable of her to expect him to see the situation from her point of view. She was in the right, of course. She knew that. And in time she was sure he would acknowledge it, too. But at the moment he was annoyed. Disappointed. Yes, of course. He would be angry and frustrated to lose Flora's fortune. He had cultivated the heiress, courted her and flirted with her, which must have been a dreadfully tedious business. He had invested time and effort in landing his prize. And now she was queering his pitch. So yes, she could see that he would be cross with her.

"What you are doing is dangerous," Nat said. He still sounded in control. "You have locked yourself in with me. Is this some ridiculous attempt to compromise me so that I am obliged to marry *you* instead of Flora?"

Lizzie's temper tightened another notch. She was starting to feel genuinely angry now in addition to feeling afraid. She was infuriated by his presumption in thinking she wanted him for herself. "Of course not," she said. "How conceited you are! I don't want to wed you! I'd rather pull my own ears off!"

Nat's smile was not pleasant. "I don't believe you. You have deliberately compromised yourself by locking us in together."

"Rubbish!" Lizzie said. "I don't intend to tell anyone. I only want to keep you here until it's too late for the marriage to take place, and then I will let you go."

"Handsome of you," Nat said. "You wreck my future and then you let me go to face the ruins."

"Oh, do not be so melodramatic!" Lizzie snapped. "You should not have become a fortune hunter in the first place. It does not become you!"

"There speaks a woman with fifty thousand pounds and a judgmental attitude," Nat said. "You know nothing."

"I know everything about you!" Lizzie flashed. "I have known you for over nine years and I care about you—"

"You aren't doing this out of disinterested friendship, Lizzie," Nat interrupted her scathingly. "You are doing this because you are selfish and spoiled and immature, and you do not wish another woman to have a greater claim on me. You want to keep me for yourself."

Lizzie gaped. "You are an arrogant pig!"

"And you are a pampered brat. You need to grow up. I have thought so for a long time."

They stood glaring at one another whilst the tension in the room simmered and the candle flame flickered as though responding to something dangerous in the air.

Somewhere inside, Lizzie was hurting, but she cut the pain off, cauterized it with the heat of her anger.

"When have I been spoiled and immature?" she demanded. She had not wanted to ask, to twist the knife in her own wounds, but she found she was unable to keep the words inside.

Nat laughed, a harsh sound that ripped at her soul. "Where shall I start? You have no interest in anyone or anything beyond your own concerns and opinions. You flaunted yourself brazenly at the assembly on the very day that my engagement to Flora was announced, and that could only have been to take attention away from her. You flirt with anything in

trousers. You have kept both Lowell Lister and John
Jerrold dancing on a string for months when you
have no interest in them other than in the way they
feed your vanity. And if we are talking about serious
lack of consideration for others, you bought some of
Miles Vickery's most valued possessions at the sale
of Drum Castle and never had the generosity to give
them back to him—"

Lizzie covered her ears. Nat caught her wrists and
dragged her hands away.

"You wanted to know," he said. His voice was
hard. "I knew you would not be able to take the truth."

He dropped her wrist as though he could not bear
to touch her, and they fell apart. Both of them were
panting. Lizzie felt as though her skin had been
flayed bare by his words. Her eyes prickled with hot
tears. She forced them back.

After a moment Nat raked his hand through his
hair again and made a visible attempt to keep calm.

"Give me the key and we'll forget this ever happened," he said.

It was too late for that and they both knew it.

"No," Lizzie said. She crossed her arms. "I don't
have it."

*"You are a pampered brat. You need to grow up.
You are spoiled and selfish…"*

She told herself that she did not care what he
thought. She knew she was lying. It hurt horribly.
Something precious, something she had cherished,

had been broken beyond saving. Nat's opinion had always mattered to her. She had respected him. Now she felt as though she hated him.

Nat's gaze stripped her, suddenly shockingly insolent. "I suppose you have hidden it about your person."

"No, I have not!" Lizzie was taken aback both by his tone and the look in his eyes. He had never looked at her like that before, as though she was some Covent Garden whore displaying her wares for the purchase. She felt humiliated; she told herself she was livid. Yet something in her, something shocking and primitive, liked it well enough. The blood warmed beneath her skin, the heat rolling through her body from her cheeks down to her toes and back up again, setting her afire.

Nat grabbed her so quickly she did not even see him move. His hands passed over her body; intimate, knowing hands, seeking and searching. The goose bumps rose all over her skin, following the path of his touch. The heat intensified inside her, burning hotter than a furnace. She squirmed within his grip, protesting against the humiliation of his restraint and her body's response to it.

"Let me go! I don't have it, I tell you!" There was more pleading than she liked in her tone.

"But you know where it is." He let her go, breathing hard. There was some expression in his eyes, something feral, something different. It made her tremble. She remembered for the first time that he was a man who habitually, ruthlessly and coldly hunted down criminals in the course of his duty. She did not think about that often for that was the side of Nat's life that she seldom saw, but she thought about it now because she could sense the rage in him and the desperation. She remembered that he had said he needed Flora Minchin's fifty thousand pounds very badly indeed. She knew that he had wanted to restore Water House and provide for his family—his parents were old and his sister Celeste an invalid—but recently it had seemed there was an added urgency to his actions as though something else had happened to make his pursuit of the money even more pressing. She did not know what it was. She had never asked. Perhaps Nat was right that she was always wrapped up in her own concerns. The thought disturbed her.

She searched his face for the Nat Waterhouse she recognized and saw a stranger.

It chilled her so much that she teetered on the brink of capitulation and Nat saw her hesitate on the very edge of defeat—and he laughed.

"That's right, Lizzie. Act like an adult for once. Go and fetch the key."

It was the contempt in his voice that decided her, that and his laughter ringing in her ears. She could imagine him telling his friends Dexter Anstruther and Miles Vickery all about her plan, how she had thought to put a stop to his marriage because she was so young and immature and spoiled, and because she was harboring a not-so-secret *tendre* for him. She burned with humiliation to think of him ascribing such feelings to her and laughing over them with his friends because, she told herself fiercely, it simply *wasn't true*. She had tried to rescue him and he had scorned her efforts and for that she would make him pay. The need to make him suffer—to make him hurt the way she was hurting—ached in her chest and ran through her blood like poison.

She drew herself up and stared him in the eye.

"No. I am not going anywhere and neither are you." She spun away from him across the tiny chamber.

"You're bloody mad." Nat was furious and had given up any pretence of courtesy now.

"And you are bloody rude." She whirled around to look at him, heady with power now. "And arrogant and conceited to think that I care for you."

"Don't you?" His eyes glittered.

"Of course not. I *detest* you. Especially now, after all those *wicked* things you have said about me. What do you think this is, one of Monty's ridiculous medieval laws?" She flicked him an impertinent smile even though her heart felt, oddly, as though it was breaking. "The *droit de seigneur?* Surely you don't imagine that I kidnapped you in order to have my wicked way with you on the night before your wedding?" She allowed her gaze to slide over him with an attempt at the same insolence with which he had looked at her earlier. It was more difficult than she had thought. She had little experience in eyeing up a man as though he was a commodity for sale.

"You wouldn't have the nerve to carry off something like that." Nat's arrogant assumption twisted the knife. "Come on, Lizzie. You are out of your depth. Admit it. This is one of your childish games that has gone too far."

Don't dare me…

Their eyes met. The air between them seemed hot, heavy and pulsing with tension. Lizzie put a hand on his arm.

"You think I could not seduce you, Nat Waterhouse?"

His hand closed hard about her wrist, holding it still. Beneath his fingers, her pulse jumped. "Don't be absurd." His voice was rough.

Lizzie stood on tiptoe and pressed her lips inexpertly against his. He remained completely unresponsive beneath her touch even though she knew—she *knew*—he was not indifferent to her. She could feel the conflict in him for his body was tense, tight as a whip, but his response was battened down now, held under iron control. She moved her lips against his, willing him to react, to grab her, kiss her back, thus proving that she had won, but he stood completely immobile. Damn him. She was starting to feel foolish, reaching up, kissing him, and he as still as a marble statue. He wanted to embarrass her and he was succeeding. Perhaps she was no good at kissing; she did not really know. Several men had kissed her and it had been a severely disappointing experience each time, though whether that was because her expectations were too high or her suitors too incompetent, she was not sure.

She stood back a little and looked at Nat through half-narrowed eyes. Perhaps he was not as restrained as he wanted her to think. She was inexperienced, but some knowledge, deep and instinctive within her, told her that Nat was closer to the edge than he pretended. He was breathing fast and a pulse beat in his cheek. The knowledge that she was pushing him so hard made Lizzie feel heady, as though she had drunk too much wine. The thrill of danger blotted out the pain of the bitter words they had thrown at one another.

"Have you quite finished?" Nat's politely disdainful voice cut through her thoughts. So he wanted to make her feel naive and humiliated. Anger and desperation surged in her blood. She was not going to let him win; not when he was a great deal less composed than he pretended.

"No," she snapped. "I have not."

She came close to him again, so close she could feel the heat emanating from his body. She looked up into his hard, unyielding face. What would it take to shock him? She did not have to go too far, just far enough to force him to admit he had been wrong in underestimating her. She was no child and she was not going to be dismissed as one. She put her hand on his chest and could feel the thunder of his heart.

"Lady Ainsworth was your mistress, was she not," she whispered in his ear. She skimmed her hand down his shirt, pulling it loose from the band of his pantaloons. "I heard the maids talking about it. They had it from her dresser that you were mightily well endowed. Huge, so they said. They made me very curious about you…."

Nat's whole body shuddered. "Lizzie. Stop this." His tone was violent. "You don't understand what you are doing."

"Oh, but I do," Lizzie said. "I'm no child." She tugged his shirt free and slid her palms over his bare stomach. He felt smooth and shockingly delicious. The exquisite sensation distracted her for a moment. She had had no idea…She heard him gasp and felt the muscles jump and quiver beneath her fingers. A reaction at last…Emboldened, she turned her face into his neck and pressed her lips against the skin of his throat. He tasted of salt and heat and he smelled of bergamot cologne and of leather and of something she recognized as Nat's own scent. It was familiar to her yet intensely exciting.

He turned his head slightly. Their lips were only inches apart now. She could feel how close he was to the edge of the precipice. Her senses spun with triumph and something else so strong it made her tremble. He was not so indifferent to her now. She had won. She slipped her hands around his back, reveling in the hardness of muscle beneath her questing fingers. She dug her nails into him and felt him flinch.

"Lizzie, for Christ's sake—"

She liked the note of desperation in his voice. It soothed her wounded feelings to think she had driven him to this. She knew she should stop now, draw back, but she allowed one hand to drift to the fastening of his pantaloons, then a little lower. She felt light-headed, drunk, and a little mad perhaps. Her hand brushed the front of his trousers, tracing his erection. The hard, huge bulge of his arousal shocked her even through the straining material of his pantaloons. She heard Nat suck in his breath and swear harshly, and she paused for a second and stepped back, heated anger and passion abruptly doused by the cold realization that she had gone far too far. Bravado and fear struggled in her but beneath her apprehension was a fast, wicked current of feminine curiosity that was so powerful that it stole her breath and made her heart race.

They stared at one another for one long, laden moment then Nat grabbed her, moving so fast that Lizzie did not even have time to anticipate the action. His mouth came down hard on hers. Clearly the other men had not known how to kiss and equally clearly, Nat did. It was Lizzie's only coherent thought before she went under and was submerged in a surge of sensation so violent that she almost fell.

As kisses went, it had little in it of love or even liking and a great deal of lust and anger. The pressure of Nat's lips forced hers to open and then his tongue slid across hers, taking ruthlessly, with no consideration or gentleness. Lizzie did not know if he meant it to punish her, but it did not matter because suddenly she wanted whatever he had to give. She felt breathless with excitement, driven far beyond sense or rational thought. She forced a hand into Nat's hair so that she could keep his mouth on hers, and she nipped his lower lip and felt him pull in a breath before he plundered her mouth ruthlessly. Her lips felt swollen and ravished from the assault. The heat pooled low in her belly and she ground her hips against his enormous erection. Nat made a sound in his throat that was half-groan, half-snarl.

He put his hands on her shoulders and pulled apart her riding habit and her chemise, stripping her to the waist. The laces tore and the hooks went flying across the stone floor. His hand was on her bare breast. Her mind reeled. She heard a moan and knew it was hers. Nat pushed her down onto the window seat and then his mouth was at her breast and she felt his teeth and his tongue on her, and she cried out, the sound echoing off the stone of the folly walls. Her body was shuddering with a need that threatened to devour her. She felt simultaneously shocked and excited and so desperately wicked and wanton that she almost screamed with the pleasure of it.

Nat pulled up the velvet skirts of her riding habit. She reached for the fastening of his pantaloons and their hands bumped. They were both shaking. The material gave and then she felt him hot and hard in her hand and she gasped with astonishment and wonder, and Nat covered her mouth roughly with his again. His hand was on her thigh, pushing her legs apart; she felt him at the very core of her and then he was deep inside her with a single thrust. The pain of it was sharp and violent. She gasped but he did not stop.

She was braced against the window embrasure and he pushed her back and back each time he took her. The stone was cold against her bare back but the friction of Nat's body was fierce and heated between her thighs and the sensation of it was too overwhelming and too insistent to escape. The pain faded and blissful tremors rippled through her, gathering pace, building, exquisitely intense. She screamed as her body seemed to come apart with blinding pleasure. She heard Nat call out, felt him hold her even tighter, plunge even deeper and pulse as he emptied himself completely into her.

There was silence, a moment when time seemed suspended, when Lizzie could neither breathe nor think, nor feel anything but the most perfect sense of rightness. It felt heavenly. Her body felt ripe and sated and her mind felt a deep content, as though at last she had come home and was at peace. For Nat had spoken the truth when he had said that she loved him—she could see that with utter clarity now, all pretence and pride torn away in the honesty of their lovemaking. Nat was hers and he always had been, and now she was truly his.

And surely Nat must love her, too, because that was the way it was meant to be.

Lizzie opened her eyes and blinked a little. The candlelight seemed too harsh and bright, stinging her eyes. Nat had withdrawn from her. He had turned away, fumbling with his clothes. His face was in shadow. Lizzie waited for him to speak, to tell her he loved her. And then suddenly he turned to look at her fully and her heart leaped in anticipation of the words she would surely hear and the love she would surely see in his eyes. The moment spun out and she searched his face, and saw bewilderment and disbelief and a dawning horror there.

"Lizzie…" He said. His voice shook. The horror in his expression was raw and painful.

Lizzie felt cold. Something inside her seemed to shrivel and die, shredding like petals falling from a blown flower.

Nat did not love her. He had never loved her.

She could see it in the appalled dismay in his eyes.

She pushed down her skirts, dragged the fragments of her bodice together and tried to stand. Her legs were shaking and she stumbled and almost fell. Her weakness horrified her. Nat was coming toward her now and she felt panic clogging her throat. She could not talk to him now. She could not even look at him. She felt too shamed as though every last defense had been stripped away leaving her emotions as exposed and naked before him as her body had been. She had to get out. She had to get away from him before he guessed the truth of her feelings, before he put it into words and made her humiliation intolerable.

She overturned the table, blocking his path and sending the candle flying, and then she was running down the stone spiral stair, reeling off the wall as she almost fell in the darkness. She heard Nat swear and saw a flare of flame behind her as the wall hangings caught fire from the candle, and then she was in the guardroom, groping for the key on its ledge, and for a split second she could not find it and the panic clawed at her chest. She heard Nat beating the flames out and hoped it would hold him for a precious few seconds. The door… It seemed to take forever for her to open it, whilst her cold and shaking fingers slipped on the key, and then she was out in the night and she could hear Nat's steps on the stair behind her and smell smoke on the air.

Where to run? Where to hide…

The wood closed about her. It was dark, deep and anonymous. That comforted her. She could hear Nat calling her name and there was an edge of fear to his voice as well as anger, but the sound was fading as he moved away from her. The relief washed through her. He would not find her now; would not find her again until she was ready to be found. She did not need anyone to help her. She could put herself back together, good as new. She could pretend that this had never happened.

Nat did not love her. He had never loved her. She had made a terrible, terrible mistake.

The thoughts jostled through Lizzie's head, dark and menacing like monsters in a nightmare. She pushed them away. She had to forget what had happened. And now that Nat was at liberty to attend his wedding, he, too, could join in the pretense. He could marry Flora, just as he had intended, he could gain the fortune he needed, and neither of them would say a word about this night ever again.

Except that Nat had never been very good at pretending. Lizzie had always said it was because he had no imagination, but Nat had always had a nasty habit of facing his demons and of making her face hers as well.

Not this time…

"Nothing happened," Lizzie said aloud. She smoothed the torn remnants of her bodice and wondered why her fingers were still shaking. "Nothing happened at all."

CHAPTER TWO

NAT WATERHOUSE STOOD in front of Fortune Hall, stared up at the darkened window of Lizzie's bedroom and tried to think. What would Lizzie do now? Would she run? Would she hide? Where would she go? He should know the answer to these questions. He had known Lady Elizabeth Scarlet for ten years, since she was eleven years old, and he a youth of eighteen. He had seen her grow from a child into a woman. He had thought he knew everything there was to know about her. How wrong he had been.

Where was she?

His mind did not seem to be functioning as clearly as usual. He could not seem to focus on the practicalities of his situation, what to do, how to put matters right. All he seemed capable of thinking about was Lizzie.

What the hell had he done?

Pointless question. He knew precisely what he had done. He had seduced a woman who was not his fiancée on the night before his wedding.

He had ended over a year's celibacy by making love to the one woman he should never, ever have touched.

He had ravished a virgin.

He had been too weak and too lacking in self-control to resist.

None of the above actually did justice to the heinousness of the situation, though. He faced it squarely.

Lizzie. Hell. He did not love her. He had not even liked her very much for the past few months. Once upon a time they had been friends but she had been getting under his skin recently, trying to persuade him not to marry Flora, provoking him, using him, taking him for granted. He had already been aggravated almost past bearing when he had received her note that night. He had almost ignored the summons and only habit and that damned sense of responsibility he had always felt for her had prompted him to go to meet her. He wished he had not.

Regret speared him, painfully sharp. That was pointless, too. It was done. Lizzie had goaded him, pushed him beyond bearing but he was not going to blame her. The truth was that she could not have provoked him into doing anything unless he wanted it, and he had wanted to make love to her. He had been *desperate* to make love to her. He still was. It shocked him that he could be in such a godforsaken mess and all he could think about was Lizzie's beautiful silken white skin beneath his hands and her body, unbearably hot and tight about him, and the dazzling, blinding pleasure of taking her. He was no saint when it came to women, but nor was he a rake. And Lizzie was the last woman whom he would ever have imagined wanting. How could he when he had always seen her as in need of protection? From the moment he had first known her he had sought to make up for the fact that the two men who should care for her—her half brothers Montague and Tom Fortune—were a feckless idiot and a dangerous wastrel respectively.

He was worse than both of them.

Damn it all to hell and back.

The chimes of the church clock wafted over the fields from Fortune's Folly village. One o'clock. Less than an hour for his whole life to change…

Where was she? He had to know she was all right.

Anxiety ran through his blood. Of course she was not all right. How could she be? He had ravished her, ruthlessly seduced her. He had known that she must be a virgin, still innocent despite her wild, wayward behavior. What gently bred debutante of nearly one and twenty was not? And she had shown her inexperience when her shameless provocation had disintegrated into shock and she had run from him, appalled and fearful in the end. It was true that Lizzie was outrageous. She frequently went too far but this time she had frightened even herself. And she was no longer innocent and it was his fault.

He had to speak to her.

He looked again at the blank, dark windows of Fortune Hall. He could raise the whole house, of course, and wake everyone up looking for her. It would cause outrage, scandal. If she were found to be missing that would cause even more. Lizzie was already known to be wild. If word went around that she was not in her own bed in the middle of the night, gossip would simply speculate on whose bed she *was* in. Her reputation would be in tatters.

He laughed mirthlessly. Reputation? Lizzie was ruined. If there was to be a child…

His blood ran cold. He could not leave her to face that alone. He had never abandoned her before and he would not do so now. For the first time he thought about his rich marriage of convenience. He should have thought about it before since he was so desperately in need of money, but somehow his concern for Lizzie had blotted out all other thoughts. His marriage had been the perfect solution to all his financial problems. And Miss Flora Minchin would have been the perfect refined, biddable wife. She was Lizzie's opposite in almost every way. He had never had the remotest desire to rip Flora's clothes off and make love to her. No doubt she would have been utterly aghast if he had expressed such a desire. But Flora was rich—so very, very rich—and he needed the money so desperately. He was in a trap. People depended on him, his parents, his sister Celeste… The anger and fear tightened within him when he thought what might happen to Celeste if he let her down. He would never in a thousand years have thought himself the kind of man to succumb to blackmail and yet when his sister's life, her future and her good name, were in the balance, he had not even hesitated. He knew he could not. It was his responsibility to protect those who relied on him. So he needed a fortune...

Lizzie was rich, too.

The thought slid into his mind and the relief flooded through him.

He had to marry Lizzie.

It was the perfect solution. It would put matters right. It would save her reputation, solve his need for money...

Lizzie would be the wife from hell.

The thought came swift on the heels of the others. The devil was in Lizzie, always had been, since she was small. Perhaps it was because she had had such a ramshackle childhood with a neglectful mother who had run off with a groom and a father who indulged her like a pet for half the time and forgot she was there the other half. When her father had died and she had come to Fortune Hall at the age of eleven to live with her half brothers, the sons of her mother's first marriage, matters had barely improved for her. Neither of her brothers had any interest in her. Monty Fortune had engaged a governess for her to absolve his conscience. Lizzie had put mice in the woman's bed and the governess had left. None of her successors stayed long, stating that Lizzie was unruly, undisciplined and out of control, a state of affairs that Tom Fortune in particular encouraged. Nat could still remember the first time he had met Lizzie when, as a university contemporary of Tom's, he had come to Fortune's Folly and seen a truculent girl in a grubby white dress, all tangled red hair and huge green eyes, climbing the trees in the home park like a tomboy. She had fallen out of an old oak tree and Tom had laughed and Nat had been the one to offer her a hand to help her get up again. And so it had started, with Nat easing Lizzie out of the scrapes she had got herself into, always there for her because neither Monty nor Tom cared a whit.

But this… This was more than a scrape. This was a full-blown disaster. Yes indeed, Lizzie would be the most difficult, intractable, headstrong wife imaginable, the most unsuitable countess and in the fullness of time the least appropriate duchess in the kingdom. Marriage to her might well be a living hell. But hell was precisely where he was heading. He knew there was no escape.

LIZZIE HAD CLIMBED IN at her bedroom window, scaling the ivy, reaching for the handholds that only she knew were there in the old stone of Fortune Hall. She had climbed in and out of the house this way for as long as she could remember, coming and going as and when she pleased, avoiding the discipline of her chaperones, such as it was, and with her half brothers in blissful ignorance of her behavior. Tonight Monty was still awake—when she had slipped past the window she had seen him drinking on his own in the library. There had been no sign of her other half brother, Tom, although the presence of another glass beside Monty's on the table suggested that someone else had been there earlier that evening. Lizzie's half brothers had patched up their quarrel now that Tom was no longer a wanted man. Monty had conveniently forgotten that he had disowned his brother and Tom had seemed prepared to forgive him. Lizzie thought that their rapprochement was largely convenience, since no one else in the village of Fortune's Folly would give either of them the time of day now. Everyone hated Monty for his unscrupulous greed in applying more and more of his medieval taxes to fleece the populace, but people hated Tom more for his ruthless seduction and abandonment of Lydia Cole. Lizzie would not have set foot back in her brother's house if it had not been for the fact that Monty had threatened legal proceedings against anyone else who gave her shelter. He had then neglected to find a chaperone for her with the result that Lizzie had no one to account to on nights like this. Or alternatively, Lizzie thought, one could say that no one actually cared what she did.

She desperately wanted a bath. She was aching,

her body sore *there,* between her legs, and sore inside. Not so raw as her heart, though. She could smell smoke on her clothes and in her hair. She could also smell Nat's scent on her body like an imprint, but perhaps that was a trick of her imagination. She did not want to remember him holding her close enough to put his mark on her. She did not want to remember him inside her. She shuddered, closing her eyes, closing her mind.

Cold water would have to do. She would have jumped into the moat when she had got back had it not been for the fact that she was terrified Nat would find her. Instead she lit one pale candle, making sure that the curtains were drawn so close that no light would show outside, and then she stripped off her tattered clothes. Usually she dropped her gown and underclothes on the floor for the maid to pick up but these were ruined, the laces torn, the hooks ripped out. That would cause gossip. That would be difficult to explain.

Such passion. Such pleasure…

She had thought that she would die from such pleasure. She had never imagined it, never dreamed it. Such bliss at Nat's hands… She had felt as though her very body would melt, honey-soft, with satisfaction and fulfilment.

She had felt a soul-deep contentment as well, but that had fled fast enough when she had seen the expression on Nat's face. Some pain stirred deep inside her and she soothed it quickly back to sleep. No need to think of that. It was over. It was her secret and it would remain so.

She bundled the clothes up carefully and hid them under a pile of blankets in the chest. She would take them out and burn them when she could, and watch the memories drift away on the smoke and ash. Nat would be married by then and gone from Fortune's Folly with his bride.

Avoiding her reflection in the long mirror, she started to wash herself with the cold water from the ewer and the cloth that was on the dresser. Her hair would have to wait until the morning. There was nothing she could do about that. She started with her face, the ice-cold water from the bowl shocking her a little, wakening her. Neck, shoulders, the curve of her arms... She paused as she raised the cloth to her chest, the irresistible memory intruding of Nat's mouth at her breast, tugging, nipping, licking... Her body tightened, aching inside, wanting him again. It was impossible to erase that knowledge now. The hand holding the cloth fell to her side and she turned slowly to examine her body in the long pier glass.

She did not look the same. There were marks on her body, faint bruises that indicated the intensity of their lovemaking and also showed the loss of her innocence, the extent of her experience now. She stared at them whilst her body resonated with the knowledge of what she had done. She waited for feelings of shame or regret. None came. That must prove she was as wild and brazen as everyone claimed. She had no shame for the act of making love. All her regret was saved for the terrible mistake she had made in loving where her feelings were not returned. *That* humiliated her beyond bearing.

There was a small smear of blood on her inner thigh. She scrubbed it away, vigorous now. Her virginity was lost. This was the proof. Some faceless, unimagined future husband would probably cut up rough about her lack of chastity. Men were so often odiously hypocritical about such matters. She found she did not care. Perhaps she should. But she had never been able to imagine herself married. Marriage required compromise and maturity and she was painfully aware that she was not very good at such things. Truth was, she had never wanted to be. Now the possibility of marriage seemed more remote than the moon.

She put on her nightdress but rather than getting into her bed she sat down on the velvet cushioned window seat. Was Nat out there in the shadows of the darkened garden? She felt an almost irresistible urge to pull the curtain back and look. The thing that stayed her hand was the knowledge that if he were there it would be for all the wrong reasons. He would not have followed her because he loved her. He would have followed her because of a sense of responsibility. He would want to make sure that she was safe home and to put matters to rights.

He could not.

Nat cared about her. She knew that. But caring was so mild an emotion compared to the wild love she had for him. Caring was for infants and the old and the sick. Nat did not share her passion. He had shown her lust and she had confused it with love. It was an easy mistake to make, a naïve mistake, she supposed. She felt a boundless love for him. He cared for her. She had poured out her feelings in their lovemaking. He had met her love with his desire. The disparity between their feelings for one another was enormous.

Her hand had crept up to pull back the curtain, driven by the need she had to see Nat again and the crumb of comfort that his caring would offer her. She deliberately let it fall. For her it was all or nothing. Crumbs were not good enough.

She went to bed. She tried to sleep and tried to ignore the ache within her body and the greed with which it grasped after the pleasure it had experienced just the once. Her body, it seemed, did not care whether she loved Nat or not. It wanted him and it did not like to be denied now that it had been wakened. She tossed and turned and when she did sleep she dreamed about her mother, the notorious Countess of Scarlet, wilful, reckless runaway wife. She could smell her mother's perfume and feel the softness of her arms about her. In her dreams Lizzie grasped after the absentminded affection her mother had shown her on the rare occasions that Lady Scarlet remembered she had a daughter. It comforted her but when she woke in the morning she remembered that Lady Scarlet was long lost and she was alone.

CHAPTER THREE

MISS FLORA MINCHIN stood in the drawing room of her parents' elegant home in the village of Fortune's Folly—new, shiny, spacious, everything that money could buy, no converted medieval building for them—and studied the Earl of Waterhouse, who was standing on the Turkish carpet in front of the fireplace in the exact same spot as when he had proposed marriage to her four months before. Four months had been the engagement period prescribed by Mrs. Minchin as the shortest possible time in which to assemble Flora's perfect trousseau. That self-same trousseau was now packed and ready for the wedding trip—Windermere and the Lake District, so pretty, so fashionable—and for the removal after that to Water House, the Earl's ramshackle family estate near York, which was to be restored with Flora's lovely money.

It was not yet past breakfast and they had in fact been roused from the table by the butler disapprovingly imparting the news of the Earl's arrival. It was a shockingly early hour at which to call. It was also the morning of the wedding and Mrs. Minchin had therefore been even less disposed to let Flora see her betrothed.

"Flora, I forbid it," she had snapped, even as her daughter had put down her napkin and allowed the footman to draw back the chair so that she could rise. "It is quite inappropriate and dreadfully bad luck. Humphrey—" She had appealed to Mr. Minchin, who was reading the *Leeds Courier* at the breakfast table. "Tell Flora that she must not speak to Lord Waterhouse until after the vows are made. Whatever he has to say cannot be so important that it cannot wait."

"I rather think it is, Mama," Flora had said.

She had been surprised to find that her heart was beating quite fast. Sitting there, sipping her hot chocolate and nibbling on her toast, she had had a moment of quite frightening prophecy. She had known that Nat Waterhouse was there to break their engagement. And she had felt nothing but the most enormous relief.

Now she glanced at the clock. At least the wedding was not until two in the afternoon. That should give her enough time to inform everyone that it was not taking place after all. She would have to do so herself, as her mother was likely to fall into the vapors and be of no use to anyone.

She looked at Nat. He was looking exceptionally well dressed that morning, almost as elegant as on the day that he had proposed, almost as elegant as he would have looked in church when they came together for their marriage. She was not sure how she felt about him taking so much trouble with his appearance when his purpose was to break rather than make a commitment to her. His boots had a high polish, his cravat was immaculately tied and he was wearing a jacket of green superfine that fitted without a wrinkle. He was not, Flora thought, a good-looking man in the conventional sense, for his features were too irregular to be considered handsome. His nose was slightly bent as though it had sustained a sporting injury and his chin had a cleft to it that lent his face both authority and obstinacy. But even though he was not classically handsome, he had something else, something about him that many women might consider strikingly attractive. He was taller than average and filled his clothes well without the need to resort to the padding and buckram so many men used. His face was lean and there was a hard, watchful look in his dark eyes that had made more than one young lady of Flora's acquaintance shiver soulfully as she commented that did not Lord Waterhouse appear just a tiny bit *dangerous?* Ruthless perhaps, durable most definitely… Tough in adversity, Flora thought suddenly. That was Nat Waterhouse. He was very strong. She would not care to pit her will against his and she knew of only one woman who ever had done…

She looked at him and her heart did not miss a

single beat. She had once thought it unfortunate that Nat did not move her when she had been going to marry him. She had wondered idly if she was missing out on something important, consigning herself to a passionless life. Now she merely felt thankful that she had never loved him and so was spared the pain of loss. And she felt an extraordinary relief that somehow she was going to escape the dutiful marriage that she had been bred to accept.

"I should have been braver from the start," Flora thought. "I should have acknowledged that I did not want to do as my parents wished. But now I have been given a second chance…"

Suddenly she felt very brave.

"Lord Waterhouse." He had not spoken, so it seemed it was down to her to move matters along and make things easy for him. Flora sighed, wishing she were not quite so generous by nature. If he wanted to end their engagement it seemed only fair he should suffer a little.

"Flora." He took her hands in his and drew her to sit beside him on the love seat. "I have something that I must ask you." He hesitated, frowning. The expression in his eyes was so painful, so at odds with his immaculate outward appearance, that Flora felt quite shaken to see it. She had never, ever seen Nat Waterhouse display strong emotion but now he looked grim and unhappy.

She knew exactly what she had to do.

"You wish me to release you from our engagement," she said.

Shock flared in his eyes. "How did you know?"

She freed herself from his grasp. What was she to say now? It could not be anything that remotely resembled the truth. The truth was too personal and they had never spoken of intimate things. Their relationship had been entirely superficial.

What she wanted to say was:

"I know we cannot marry because I have always been aware that there is something between you and Lady Elizabeth Scarlet that is too powerful to be ignored, and I do not wish to play second fiddle to it for the rest of my life. I am sure she is in love with you and that you desire her in a way you never desired me…"

No indeed, the perfectly judged, beautifully behaved Miss Flora Minchin could never utter such words to her betrothed, no matter how much she knew them to be true.

"I think that we would not suit." She smiled brightly at him. "I have thought it for a little while."

He was looking at her as though she had taken leave of her senses, which in all probability it must seem she had. Not suit? How could they not suit when there was not sufficient emotion in their relationship for them ever to disagree on anything? How could they be anything other than perfectly matched when he had the title and she the money? He was a fortune hunter and she an heiress looking to be a countess. She knew that marriage was a business arrangement, or so her parents had told her, with their banking fortune that had bought everything they had ever wanted except, it seemed, an Earl as a son-in-law and the prospect of a dukedom, almost the highest estate imaginable, once Nat's father died.

Flora got to her feet and moved away from him, smoothing her immaculate skirts as she walked across the room.

"It is fortunate that you called this morning," she said, "and that we have had the opportunity to resolve this before it was too late."

Nat was shaking his head. He raked his hand through his hair. "I ought to explain to you—"

Flora raised a hand to stop him. This would never do. The *last* thing she wanted from him was that he should explain. "Please do not," she said.

"But I cannot let you take the sole responsibility for this." Nat sounded anguished. "It isn't right that you should bear that."

It was Nat Waterhouse's tragedy, Flora thought, that he was too honorable a man to do what many other men would do in his position and cravenly accept the lifeline she was throwing him. Many a man, she was aware, would have crept out by now, abjectly grateful that she had absolved him of all responsibility.

"If you are to be free, my lord," she said gently, "you cannot have it any other way. A lady is allowed to change her mind. A gentleman is not in honor. It is as simple as that."

"I don't deserve for you to make it so easy for me," Nat said. He sounded grim. He came to her and took her hand in his, pressing a kiss on the back. Once again Flora's heart did not flutter, but stayed beating as calmly as it always had.

"You are an exceptional woman, Flora Minchin," he said. "I had no idea."

"Which rather illustrates why we should have been badly suited," Flora countered dryly. "Let us leave it at that."

She could tell he did not want to go and leave her with the unconscionable mess of canceling a marriage on the wedding day itself. She could tell that every muscle in his body was straining to tell her the reason for his defection and to take the blame. She could even tell that he wanted her to lose her temper, to rant at him, scream and cry, because in doing so she would somehow lessen the intolerable guilt he was feeling.

It gave her a small amount of satisfaction to appear totally calm and to deny him that relief. She was human, after all.

She waited until he had gone out and Irwin, the butler, had closed the front door very firmly behind him, and then she went to find her mother and father and to tell them that their most cherished dream of seeing their daughter as a countess was over. And the relief to have been given a second chance at the future swelled in her heart until she felt as though she was going to burst.

"YOU WILL HAVE HEARD the news, of course," Mrs. Morton, the draper, said as she wrapped up a parcel of blue spotted muslin for Lizzie. "Miss Minchin has cried off from her wedding this very morning!" She reached for the string and tied an expert knot. "I feel most distraught—a number of ladies have purchased gowns and bonnets from me for the event and now no one will see them! It is very unfortunate and most inconsiderate of Miss Minchin. And why whistle an Earl down the wind when one is only a banker's daughter? Do you think she has had a better offer? A Duke? Are there any dukes newly arrived in the village? That is thirty-six shillings and sixpence, if you please, Lady Elizabeth. Have you taken up dressmaking? You never buy cloth here."

"Yes," Lizzie said. She fumbled in her purse for some coins. She felt a little strange. I am tired, she thought. I did not sleep well. That is all. She tried to concentrate on finding the money but her head was buzzing.

Flora had cried off from the wedding. That was not meant to happen. Nat was supposed to be getting married in three hours time. He was going to the Lake District and from there to Water House near York, and she was never going to have to see him again, and she could keep on pretending that the events of the previous night had never occurred...

"*Thirty-six* shillings, Lady Elizabeth," Mrs. Morton said, a little sharply. "And in ready money, if you please, rather than notes. I don't trust the banks."

"Of course," Lizzie said numbly. She put some coins randomly on the counter. She was feeling very hot. Perhaps it had been a mistake to come into the village. She had not wanted to sit around at Fortune Hall in case Nat had called to see her, but neither had she wanted company. She was not sure why everything felt so difficult and complicated this morning. Her mind felt weighted with lead.

"I hear that most of the fortune hunters have left the village now that almost all the heiresses are wed," Mrs. Morton said, counting out her change. The soft clink of the coins seemed very loud and made Lizzie's head hurt. "A pity. Your half brother's plan to fleece all the ladies of their money was good for many businesses here because it brought in so much new custom. I suppose it is not worth a gentleman the cost of a journey from London now that there are no more fortunes to be had."

"I imagine not," Lizzie said. "And good riddance to them. I am glad," she added, "that Monty has been thwarted in his plans to use the Dames' Tax to take half of our dowries. His money-grabbing ways are a total disgrace."

"The man's a greedy whoremonger," Mrs. Morton

said, with great relish, "and his brother's no better! The way young Tom treated little Miss Cole… Well, she's never going to be able to make a respectable marriage now, is she?" Mrs. Morton shook her head. "And now Miss Minchin as well—I wonder what the scandal is there? For there has to be some, Lady Elizabeth. No girl calls off her wedding on the very morning of the ceremony unless there's scandal afoot. You mark my words!"

Scandal afoot…

Something sharp and painful twisted inside Lizzie. She thought of Nat and of the previous night and pushed away the memory violently. When she had woken that morning she had resolved never to think on it again. But that had been before she had heard about the canceled wedding. Why had Flora cried off? Surely Nat could not have told her what had happened? It was impossible. Lizzie was desperate to know but in order to find out she would be obliged to face Nat, to talk to him, and nothing could be worse when her emotions were still so raw. Panic rose, suffocating, in her throat.

Nothing happened, she told herself. There is no scandal, for nothing happened at all.

She tried to gather up the change from the counter, but the coins slipped and scattered on the floor. Mrs. Morton was looking at her with curiosity in her darting brown eyes. "Are you quite well, Lady Elizabeth? You seem a little distracted this morning. I wondered—" she gave a little artificial tinkle of laughter "—whether you knew aught of the broken betrothal. After all, you are a *great friend* of Lord Waterhouse, are you not? A very great friend indeed."

Lizzie bent to pick up her money. She did not answer. The shop felt airless. She felt a little dizzy.

"And you are the richest heiress left," Mrs. Morton's voice continued, above her head. "A very rich prize indeed. Will you wed, Lady Elizabeth, before your half brother steals your fortune?"

There was a ping as the door of the shop opened and the bell rang loudly. Lizzie jumped. She stood up abruptly. Nat Waterhouse had come in and was standing only a few feet away. Lizzie's head spun with the sudden shock of his appearance when she had been thinking about him only a moment before. She put a hand out to steady herself and the smooth wood of the counter slipped beneath her fingers. Damn it, if only she did not feel so strange about everything…

Nothing happened…

Nat looked so tired, she thought. There were deep lines about his eyes, as though he had not slept, and a grim set to his mouth, but he still looked fiercely intimidating enough to make her legs feel weak.

"Lady Elizabeth," he said, bowing.

He looked the same, Lizzie thought. He looks exactly the same as he did last week, so why do I see him differently? Why do I see him as my lover and see an answering knowledge in his eyes when I do not want to think of him like that because I still love him and it *hurts*… It hurts as though I am wearing all my feelings on the outside and have no protection against him.

"Lord Waterhouse!" Mrs. Morton was fluttering around. "I was so very sorry to hear about your broken betrothal—"

"Thank you, Mrs. Morton," Nat said. He did not take his eyes from Lizzie. Nor did he offer any explanation whatsoever.

He was standing between Lizzie and the door. She realized that she could not get out—and that he had done it deliberately in order to force her to confront him. Suddenly she felt as though the walls of the shop were closing in on her and all the bolts of cloth Mrs. Morton had swathed so artfully about the place to display her wares were swooping down to smother her.

"Are you quite well, Lady Elizabeth?" Mrs. Morton sounded excited. "You look very pale. Are you going to swoon?"

"Of course not," Lizzie said. "I never faint. It is a hot day. That is all. Thank you, Mrs. Morton. Good day, Lord Waterhouse."

She found she could not look at him. He had moved closer to her and his very proximity seemed to hold her still, unable to speak, unable to move. Her awareness of him was overwhelming. She could sense Mrs.

Morton looking from one of them to the other with an expression of most gleeful curiosity on her face.

"May I escort you somewhere, Lady Elizabeth?" Nat murmured. He put out a hand and took her by the elbow. The shivers skittered along her nerve endings. Her heart raced, bumping painfully against her ribs. Nat's touch had never stirred her before. He must have touched her a thousand times in the past when she dismounted her horse or when he acted her friend and escorted her to a ball or on endless other occasions. Only now did he make her body ripple with responsiveness even as her mind despaired.

"Thank you, but no," Lizzie said rapidly. "I have errands to run."

"Then I will accompany you."

"No, indeed—"

"I would like very much to speak with you," Nat said. There was an undertone of steel in his voice now that brought Lizzie's eyes up sharply to his. His dark gaze was implacable. "I believe we have matters to discuss."

"No—"

"Indeed we do."

Mrs. Morton's gaze was avid. Lizzie felt the panic flare inside her and blossom through her whole body, setting her shaking. Then the door chimed again and two ladies came into the shop, and Lizzie pulled her arm from Nat's grip, diving through the open door and out into the street.

Where to run? Where to hide?

She knew she had only a split second before Nat extricated himself from the shop and came after her.

She could not speak to him. Merely thinking about it turned her so cold that she shivered as though she had the ague. She had made a terrible, terrible mistake and the only way in which she could deal with it was to pretend that it simply had not happened. If she spoke to Nat he would make her confront it and that she could not do.

Run away, Lizzie thought. She had always run, all her life. She had seen her mother do it, too. It was all she knew.

"Lady Elizabeth!"

She spun around. Nat was coming toward her as briskly as the crowded street would allow. Saturday mornings in Fortune's Folly were always busy. The road was crowded with carts and horses, with women carrying marketing baskets, children clinging to their skirts, with gentlemen strolling and ladies browsing the windows. Nat ignored them all, cutting a path toward her with ruthless determination. Lizzie dashed down the first arcade that she came to, past the wigmaker and the perfumery, into the china shop, where her flying skirts caught the edge of a display of fine Wedgwood plates, newly arrived from London, and sent them crashing to the floor. She didn't stop, even at the shopkeeper's cry of outrage, but hurried out of the back door, down a passageway, tripping over a rotten cabbage, sending a chicken running for its life. She imagined Nat stopping to pay the china merchant and knew that would buy her a few minutes. He would have to take responsibility for her breakages. That was the sort of thing that he always did.

She had a stitch. She leaned on the edge of the stone parapet of the bridge over the River Tune and tried to catch her breath. There were cabbage leaves stuck to her skirts. Across the other side of the river she could see her brother's land agent collecting payment from the coachmen who had their carriages drawn up on the green whilst the occupants shopped, visited the spa or walked on Fortune Row. This was Monty's latest money-spinner following the tax on dogs he had instigated the previous month. She saw a carriage with the Vickery arms drawn up outside the circulating library. Perhaps Alice was in town and was intending to call on her after she had been to the shops. For a moment Lizzie longed desperately to see her friend and then she realized that it was not possible. Alice knew her too well. She would know instantly that something was wrong and then Lizzie would tell her the truth and that would be a disaster because she simply had to pretend. If she did not pretend—if she told all, and Alice *sympathized* with her—then all would be lost because she would disintegrate in misery and blurt out her love for Nat and the humiliation and loss would drown her.

"Lady Elizabeth!"

Lizzie straightened abruptly. There was Nat, wending his way between the carriages on the bridge and looking cross and disheveled now—he had cabbage leaves on his jacket, too—but still very, very determined. Oh dear. Time to run.

"I don't want to talk to you!" Lizzie yelled, startling several coach horses. "Go away!" She saw Lady Wheeler's startled face staring out at her from one of the carriages and felt the hysterical laughter bubbling up within her.

"Hoyden!" Lady Wheeler's lips moved. Lizzie did not need to be able to hear her to know the words. "Wild, ungovernable, a disgrace…"

If only they knew just how disgracefully she had behaved.

Would they be kinder to her because her heart was broken?

"Lizzie!" Nat bellowed.

Lizzie took her life in her hands and dived between two carriages, hearing the coachman swear and feeling the heat of the horses' breath against her face. Over the parapet, under the bridge, along the water's edge, up into the village on the other side of the river, into the cabinetmakers where her unkempt reflection stared back at her from an endless line of mirrors for sale, the scent of beeswax in her nostrils, the gleam of the wood dazzling her… Someone caught her as she was about to trip on the pavement outside, but even as the panic grabbed her she realized it was not Nat but another gentleman, raising his hat, an appreciative gleam in his eyes. She could see Nat pushing through the crowd. Would he never give up?

She grabbed a hansom cab. "Fortune Hall, quickly!"

The coachman whipped up the horse and they were away before Nat could haul himself up into the cab beside her. Lizzie saw his furious expression as they pulled away. It was twice as expensive to take a hansom these days because Sir Montague taxed half of the drivers' charges. Well, her brother could pay his own taxes this time, Lizzie thought. Her purse was empty anyway and she had dropped the bolt of blue spotted muslin somewhere in the street. She would not go back for it. She was not really sure why she had bought it in the first place.

The important thing was that she had outrun Nat again. She did not look back.

CHAPTER FOUR

DAMN THE WOMAN! He had chased her through every back street and alley of Fortune's Folly. He had had to pay the china merchant and soothe the outraged coachman and calm some skittish horses, and he was sick and tired of acting as Lizzie's conscience and wallet. She was spoiled and headstrong and she never faced up to her responsibilities. She had been running away for as long as he had known her.

She was running away from him now.

Nat smoothed his hair, calmed his breath and watched the hansom cab disappear over the cobbles with a clatter of wheels and a cloud of summer dust. Lizzie did not look back. The tilt of her head, even the back of her spring straw bonnet, looked defiant. But he had seen her eyes and they had looked terrified.

He bent to retrieve the parcel of blue muslin that was resting in the gutter. Goodness only knew why Lizzie had bought it. She was the least accomplished woman in the world with a needle and had always scorned embroidery and dressmaking.

Nat felt a pang somewhere deep in his chest. He

knew Lizzie so well. They had been friends for years. He *cared* for her. It hurt that she used to run *to* him for help when she was in trouble and now she was running *from* him. He did not even understand *why* she was running though he imagined that it must be because she was so shocked and scared and mortified by what had happened that she simply could not face him. But he could put all to rights if only she would let him. The first step was taken. He was free of the engagement to Flora, free to marry Lizzie instead. He could give her the protection of his name and he could claim her fortune in place of the one he had lost.

If only he could make her stay still long enough to hear his proposal.

If only she accepted it.

With Lizzie one never knew.

He twisted the brown paper parcel in his hands and heard the covering rip. He could deliver it to Fortune Hall in person and demand that Lizzie see him. Except that she would probably climb over the roof and run away into the woods again sooner than speak with him.

For a moment he toyed with the idea of going to one of Lizzie's friends, to Laura Anstruther or Alice Vickery, and asking for their help. He rejected the idea reluctantly, for that would involve some sort of explanation and his friends were already curious about the canceled wedding. He had received notes from both Dexter and Miles, his groomsmen, demanding to know what the hell was going on. If he asked their wives to intercede with Lizzie on his behalf the speculation would explode and although none of them would ever spread gossip or scandal, he could not expose Lizzie to such conjecture. No, he would have to sort this out unaided. That was appropriate since the disaster was of his creation. If only he had been stronger, had more self-control, more restraint. If only he had not found Lizzie so damnably physically attractive, if only he did not *still* ache for her with a devouring carnal need that was as shocking as it was misplaced. But again, if he married her that desire would no longer be inappropriate—or unfulfilled. He could make love to her every night and all day if he wished, as much as he wanted, sating his unexpected lust in the respectable marriage bed.

Fortune Street at midday on a Saturday was an inappropriate place to be sporting a huge erection. Nat moved the muslin parcel to provide strategic cover. He had to stop thinking about bedding Lizzie until he had secured her hand in marriage. He had to do everything properly. Better late than never.

AFTER MRS. MINCHIN HAD finished having hysterics and Mr. Minchin had finished raging, Flora had summoned the hall boy, the footman and as many of the maids as could be spared, and sent them out with notes for all the wedding guests telling them that the nuptials were canceled and she deeply regretted the inconvenience. She then informed her parents that she was going out for a walk, alone, and such was their stupor at what had happened that they did not oppose her. It was the first time in Flora's life that she had made them angry and she could tell that they were baffled as well because until now she had never given them a moment's cause for concern, yet suddenly she had turned into a stranger to them.

She went out of the house and turned away from the village toward the moors. She did not walk with any particular destination in mind, but simply followed where her feet were taking her. She noticed that it was a beautiful early summer day, perfect for a wedding. The skylarks were calling overhead, their song fading as they rose higher and higher into the blue. The wildflowers bobbed on the verge beside the track. Presently she found herself up on the hill, high above the village. Fortune's Folly was spread out beneath her with the church spire piercing the sky and the lazy curl of the river and the old abbey ruins and the bridge, and Fortune Row where people strolled and gossiped in the sun. She was beyond the reach of them all, even if they were all talking scandal about her canceled wedding.

She looked down. Her shoes were ruined. It was so stupid of her to have come out without putting on stout boots for even in summer the tracks were dirty and rutted. She supposed that she could at least afford another pair, or a hundred pairs, since she wasn't giving all her money away to Nat Waterhouse anymore. She tried to examine her feelings. She was not sorry that the wedding was canceled. She would have married Nat, of course, and she would have made him a good wife because that was what she had been brought up to believe in. It was what she had *thought* she was going to do with her life. Yet it was odd, because all along she had known that there had to be if not something more, then something different. A dutiful marriage was one path, true—the path that society in general and her mother in particular had decreed for her and she had not struggled against it. But now... Well, suddenly she felt free and it felt rather strange.

She sat down on the wall. The sharp corners of the stone dug into her bottom and thighs and she wriggled to try to get comfortable. She was out of breath. The morning was hot and the sun was climbing high in the sky and she had come out without a bonnet or parasol as well as in her flimsy shoes.

There were men working the fields away to her right. She recognized one of them as Lowell Lister, Lady Vickery's brother. She had seen him escorting his mother and sister to assemblies in Fortune's Folly before Alice was wed. He had never asked her to dance, of course. He was a farmer and she was a lady and it would not have been suitable, despite the fact that his sister had inherited a fortune and gone on to marry a lord.

Flora watched idly as Lowell and his men worked the field, cutting the hay. Lowell was as fair as Alice, and deeply tanned from so much time spent in the outdoors. There was a fluid strength about the movement of his body, a supple smoothness in the way that he bent and used the scythe. Flora could see the muscles in his arms cording as he worked methodically down the field. He led his farmhands by example, she thought. He was not the sort of employer who sat watching whilst other men toiled.

Lowell straightened and pushed the fair hair back from his brow. He raised a stone flask to his lips and drank deep, his throat moving as he swallowed. Then he let the hand holding the flask drop to his side and looked straight at Flora. His eyes were the same deep blue as the summer sky. Flora's heart skipped a beat. Suddenly she felt very, very hot indeed.

He started to walk slowly toward her. A sort of panic rose in Flora's chest and she scrambled to her feet, catching her skirts on the sharp stone, and hearing something rip. She slid down onto the track and hurried away down the path toward the village without a word. She could sense that Lowell was still watching her—every fiber in her body told her it was so—and after she had gone some twenty paces she turned to look back. He was standing by the wall and in his fingers was a scrap of yellow muslin torn from her gown.

"Wait!" he said.

Flora hesitated. Lowell came down the line of the wall and when he had almost reached her he jumped over in one lithe movement and was standing beside her before she had barely time to draw breath. He seemed so vibrant and alive, so different from any man that she had ever known, that her senses were stunned for a moment. She could smell the grass and the sun on him and when he smiled at her she felt her heart lurch strangely in her chest.

"It's a hot day to be walking up on the hills," he said. He had more than a hint of the local accent in his voice. Unlike his mother and sister he had never erased it. "Would you like a drink?" He held out the flask.

Flora took it from him and looked at it dubiously. After a moment Lowell laughed and unstoppered it for her and passed it back. She placed her lips where his had been and drank deeply. The liquid was cold and deliciously refreshing and tasted of apples. She swallowed some more and saw that he was watching her with the laughter still lurking in his eyes. She felt self-conscious then and passed the bottle back to him, wondering if she should have wiped the neck first.

"Thank you," she said.

"Miss Minchin, isn't it?" Lowell said. "Flora?"

She liked the way that he said her name. It sounded very pretty.

She nodded. "You are Lowell Lister."

He sketched an ironic bow. "What are you doing up here alone, Flora?" he said.

"I wanted to think," Flora said. She was starting to feel rather odd. The sun was filtering through the green leaves of the ash tree beside the wall and dancing in patterns across her eyelids. She wanted to sit down and rest her heavy head against the solid trunk. She looked suspiciously at the flask that was still in Lowell's hand.

"Is… Is that…cider?" She had heard that cider was dangerous.

Lowell smiled. "It is. Would you like some more?"

"No, thank you," Flora said. "You should have stopped me. Cider isn't a suitable beverage for a lady."

Lowell laughed. "Why should I stop you? Can't you decide for yourself what it is that you want?"

Flora looked at him. His eyes were the deepest blue but flecked with specks of green and gold and fringed with the blackest lashes.

"Of course I can decide," she said, offended. She sat down on the bank. "I canceled my wedding today. That was my decision."

Lowell's eyes widened. He nodded slowly and sat down beside her. "Was that what you wanted to think about when you came up here?" he asked.

Flora looked sideways at him. His sleeves were rolled up and his forearm, resting beside hers, was tanned dark brown and sprinkled with hairs that gleamed gold in the sun. Flora's throat felt dry. Perhaps, she thought, I will have some more cider after all.

"Yes," she said. "I wanted to think about my wedding and about…other things, too."

"Do you want to talk about it?" Lowell said.

"Yes," Flora said, looking at him and realizing that she wanted to talk to him very much indeed. "Yes, please."

CHAPTER FIVE

"DEAREST LADY ELIZABETH!" Lady Wheeler gushed. "Such a pleasure to have you with us tonight! So unexpected but so very welcome!" She wafted about Lizzie like an enormous moth, all fluttery arms and flapping draperies. Lizzie hoped that she would not go too near the fire or there might be a disaster.

"You never normally grace our functions," Lady Wheeler continued. "This is *most* magnanimous of you!"

"Not at all," Lizzie murmured. Many of the residents of Fortune's Folly considered her to be a terrible snob who seldom condescended to join in their events because she was an earl's daughter and therefore too good for them, but it was in fact because so many people toadied to her so shamelessly that Lizzie tended to avoid their dinners and balls. That, and the fact that Sir Montague neglected his role of guardian so thoroughly and did not give a damn about what she did or did not do.

Lizzie had not in fact had any intention of accompanying her brothers to Lady Wheeler's dinner that night. She barely spoke to Tom these days, despising him for his treatment of Lydia, and she found Monty little better since all he seemed to do was drink like a fish and plan his next assault on the finances of his villagers. But when Lady Wheeler had called to deliver the invitation in person, her daughter, Mary, had grabbed Lizzie's arm and dragged her into a side room and begged her to attend.

"You know how much Mama and Papa despise me since Lord Armitage jilted me," Mary had said, her brown eyes pleading. "They are ready to countenance any suitor now and I cannot bear it. I am sure they will force me to marry Tom or even Sir Montague himself if he makes an offer. I feel like a prize heifer—or perhaps not even the prize one but the one left over at the end of the market that no one wants to buy."

Lizzie had privately thought that Mary looked rather like a heifer as well, with her big brown cow eyes, but for once she had been kind enough not to make the comparison aloud. "Well, I doubt that you need to worry about Monty," she had said, trying to sound comforting. "He never had much desire to wed once he had realized he could fleece everyone of their fortunes in other ways. Tom, though—" She had sighed, for it was quite true that Tom would probably marry anything rich in a skirt. He had already called on Flora Minchin as soon as he had heard she was free.

"Please come on Tuesday night," Mary had pleaded again. "I need you to protect me, Lizzie!"

Lizzie had grudgingly agreed. She had felt sorry for Mary, who had lost her fiancé somewhat abruptly when he had run off with a courtesan. Mary had been hopelessly in love with the worthless Stephen Armitage and his defection had hit her terribly hard. In Lizzie's opinion Armitage had been a scoundrel and Mary was a fool for languishing with love for him, but that did not make Mary's pain any the less. With the insight that her feelings for Nat had given her Lizzie could see how much Mary was suffering.

At least she was unlikely to meet Nat at the Wheelers's house, she thought, as she followed Lady Wheeler into the salon. The Wheelers did not tend to socialize with her set so neither Nat nor any of her other close friends were likely to be present, which was a blessing because it gave her the breathing space she needed. It enabled her to develop the pretense that she was heart whole, helped her to build a new carapace, little by little, step by step, so that she could forget what had happened with Nat and reinvent Lizzie Scarlet, who looked the same on the outside but felt so vulnerable on the inside because she had made a terrible mistake that had rocked the foundations of her world.

Lizzie had not seen Nat for over a week. After she had run away from him that day in Fortune's Folly, he had called at the Hall every day for five days.

Lizzie had pleaded indisposition twice, lied and said that she was not at home a third time and had hidden on the fourth and fifth occasions. Finally Nat had ceased to call and Lizzie had heard from the servants' gossip that he had been summoned to Water House for a few days because his father was ill. She had felt hugely relieved. She was still quite unable to face him with any composure, her feelings raw, the hurt of loving him and mistaking his feelings for her so painful that it was barely beginning to ease.

She had been less happy to refuse to see her friend Alice Vickery. Alice, too, had called on her several times and Lizzie had wondered if Nat had asked her to visit. She doubted it; Nat would not have told anyone what had happened, of that she was sure. Lizzie missed her friends and hated denying them but all she wanted to do was curl up and hide from anyone who knew her. Alice knew her so well. She would instantly be able to tell that there was something wrong, no matter how much Lizzie pretended. She could not let her friends get close, for it was not in her nature to confide. She had always nursed her grief alone because for most of her life there had been no one to help her bear it. Nat, whom she would once have turned to in her misery and loneliness, was forbidden to her now.

How accommodating Lady Wheeler was, Lizzie thought now, as her hostess led her, along with Monty and Tom, into the salon. Lady Wheeler had disapproved violently of her the week before and called her a hoyden, yet now it seemed she had quite forgotten her censure because Lizzie was still an earl's daughter, very rich, beautiful and a valued addition to any dinner party. The Wheelers had a debauched son—George—who was hanging out for a rich wife. Lizzie knew that such considerations would far outweigh any criticisms of her behavior. Indeed if she decided to bestow her fortune on George Wheeler her conduct would be applauded as spirited rather than condemned as wild. And sure enough Lizzie could see George waiting to greet her, with his friend Stephen Beynon at his side, and there was Mary, looking rabbit-scared, and a few other of Fortune's Folly's gentry and…

Nat Waterhouse.

The Earl of Waterhouse, who, as far as Lizzie knew, had never set foot in Sir James Wheeler's house before, was standing by the long terrace windows. He looked darkly elegant and austere in his evening clothes and the look he turned on her was cool, with a dangerous edge to it. Lizzie realized suddenly that if she had thought everything over between them she had made a very big mistake. Nat's look said that they had unfinished business.

Not, Lizzie thought, that Nat had been eschewing female companionship in the meantime. He was making conversation with a willowy blond woman who looked divinely beautiful in an evening gown of soft turquoise adorned with some truly dazzling sapphires. Jealousy hit Lizzie like a thump in the stomach, driving the breath from her body and leaving her sick and dizzy. She vaguely heard Tom make some lewd and appreciative remark to Monty as his gaze took in the Beauty. Sir Montague's gaze in turn took in the Beauty's sapphire necklace and a small, gratified smile curled his lips, too.

The jealousy churned in Lizzie's stomach like poison. Her love for Nat still felt as raw as it had done the previous week. The edges were not even slightly blunted. And seeing him with another woman felt like running a file over that raw emotion, rubbing it to an excruciating pain.

Once before, she remembered, she had been jealous of a woman who had Nat's attention and she had set herself to eclipse her. That had been poor Flora Minchin, whom she had outshone on the very night Nat and Flora's betrothal had been announced. Nat had accused her of it that night in the folly and it had been true. It had not been difficult to take the attention from Flora. Flora was quiet and quite plain, a couple of years Lizzie's senior but in no way Lizzie's equal except in fortune. But this woman… Fair of hair and brilliant of complexion, with sapphire-blue eyes that perfectly matched her jewels, and a long, sinuous figure swathed in that sensuous, almost transparent fabric, and such town bronze…

If Lizzie had felt jealous of Flora, whom she had

always known was no real threat, the pale moon to her own dazzling sun, it was nothing compared to the vicious flare of fury and resentment she felt now. For this woman was not her equal. She was so far out of reach that Lizzie felt smaller than she had done since she was a child, down from the nursery and paraded before the grown-ups for a few brief moments of approval. Her fingers tightened nervously on her fan. Suddenly she felt as though she was in a complicated game she was too young to play. She felt insignificant and anxious but there was no one to bolster her, for Tom had already drifted away to speak to an unwilling Mary Wheeler and Sir Montague was halfway down his first glass of wine and looking around for more. Lizzie wished, oh *how* she wished, that she had taken out her mother's jewels that night—the famous Scarlet Diamonds—and flaunted them on her own rather less opulent cleavage.

Lady Wheeler was urging her forward. "Might I introduce my cousin, Lady Priscilla Willoughby? She was widowed last year and is staying with us for a space."

Lizzie's feet moved forward automatically. Beneath her jealousy was a cold, empty feeling. She had thought that not having Nat's love was the worst thing in the world. Now she realized that she had got that wrong. Seeing Nat bestow his love on another woman would be a great deal more painful.

She looked at Nat and saw that he was watching

her, his gaze as dark and direct as ever, and she raised her chin and tried to compose her face into a look of perfect indifference rather than one that reflected the rawness she felt inside.

Priscilla Willoughby was still laughing at whatever remark Nat had made to her a moment before and now she turned away from him with obvious reluctance in response to her cousin's words:

"Lady Elizabeth, may I introduce Lady Willoughby? Priscilla, this is Lady Elizabeth Scarlet."

"Oh, yes." The beautiful Priscilla smiled, displaying perfect teeth. Her voice was perfectly modulated, her laugh a perfect little musical tinkle of sound. "How do you do, Lady Elizabeth? Nathaniel—" she turned to smile at Nat "—was telling me that he has known you since you were a child. What a cozy little village you have here!"

Nathaniel, Lizzie thought, not Lord Waterhouse. Informal enough to indicate intimacy but not "Nat", which was what all Nat's platonic friends called him. Oh, no, Lady Willoughby had to be different.

"How do you do, Lady Willoughby," Lizzie said. "Have you known Lord Waterhouse since *he* was a child?"

Lady Willoughby's sapphire gaze hardened slightly and she laid one white hand on Nat's sleeve, squeezing affectionately. "Oh gracious, we are old friends, are we not, Nathaniel? One might almost say old flames!" She gave her little tinkle of laughter again and leaned confidingly toward Lizzie. "Nathaniel and my late husband were great rivals for my hand in marriage."

"How close the three of you must have been," Lizzie said. "I trust you made the right choice." She was aware of Nat's unwavering gaze on her and conscious too, of the fact that she was in danger of behaving very badly indeed. She could feel the wickedness, her hoyden tendencies, as Lady Willoughby would no doubt call them, building up inside her, seeking a release. But then, surely Nat would not care, would he? Not now that he had the lovely Priscilla, someone of his own age, an *old friend,* to play with.

"Who knows," Priscilla said, with a little toss of her perfectly manicured head, "that I may have a second chance anyway?"

"A second chance, or a second choice," Lizzie said sweetly. "Good evening, Lord Waterhouse. How do you do?"

"I am very well, I thank you, Lady Elizabeth," Nat said. He took her hand even though she had not offered it.

"And how are you?" he asked. His gaze swept her face and she felt the hot color sting her cheeks as much from the look he gave her as the incendiary burn of his touch. His eyes held a spark of amusement far in their depths; he understood what she was doing with Priscilla, knew she was jealous just as she had been of Flora. She hated herself for giving so much away and she hated him for knowing. For the first time, she was grateful that he thought her to be no more than a spoiled brat who had never been denied the things she had wanted. It saved the further humiliation of him realizing that actually she was so deep in love with him that it ate at her like a canker to see him with someone else. There was a subtle difference there, but in it lay her salvation.

"You were indisposed when I last called," Nat said. "I trust you are better?"

"Oh, ladies are always suffering from trifling indispositions," Priscilla Willoughby said brightly. "It means nothing, does it, Lady Elizabeth? We only do it to appear more mysterious."

"I never trifle," Lizzie said, removing her hand from Nat's grip. "Excuse me. I will leave you to renew old acquaintance."

"I did not expect to find Lord Waterhouse here tonight," Lizzie said as Lady Wheeler steered her on to greet the next group of friends.

"He came because Priscilla invited him," Lady Wheeler gushed. "They are *such* good friends. Is she not the most charming creature? They called her Perfect Priscilla when she was a debutante, you know, Lady Elizabeth, for she was considered so very beautiful and accomplished."

Perfect Priscilla.

Lizzie ground her teeth. Why did that not surprise her? Perfectly hateful Priscilla.

"Everyone was given a sobriquet like that in those days," Lizzie said, "or so my mother told me."

Even Lady Wheeler was not too slow to take the meaning of that remark. She flushed quite red and excused herself.

"It would be cleverer of you to befriend her, you know," an amused masculine voice said in her ear, and Lizzie turned to see John, Viscount Jerrold, at her elbow, a lopsided smile creasing his good-natured features, his brown eyes bright with mirth. "You have no need to be envious," he added. "You're rich, ten years younger and a peerless beauty. Now—will you marry me?"

Lizzie burst out laughing and her sore heart eased a little. Six months before Jerrold had proposed to her and she had turned him down, but it had not been the end of their flirtation. She had sometimes wondered if she had made a mistake in rejecting him. He made her laugh the way that Nat had once done in the days when their friendship had seemed easy and uncomplicated. But on the other hand she had never longed for John Jerrold's touch the way she ached for Nat in every fiber of her being.

"No, Johnny," she said. "Not even your title can persuade me. You know I like you too well to wed you. I would be the worst wife in the world."

Jerrold's smile widened. "You're right, of course, Lizzie. You aren't cut out to be a wife, mine least of all. But I had to ask."

"Why?" Lizzie sighed. "Are you poor, too? No money with that pretty title you've just inherited?"

"None," Jerrold agreed.

"There's a rich widow," Lizzie said, nodding toward Priscilla Willoughby, whose little white hand seemed to have crept up Nat's arm and was now resting on his lapel in a confiding gesture as she spoke in his ear. "Though she's probably too proper to be good in bed."

"Oh, I don't know," Jerrold said, giving Lady Willoughby a thoughtful look. "Maybe she was called Perfect Priscilla for quite another reason. That gown of hers is not designed for modesty."

Lizzie smothered her laughter in her glass of wine. "Thank goodness you are here, Johnny," she said. "I was blue-deviled tonight but now I can have some fun. I believe that you are just as badly behaved as I am."

"Worse," Jerrold said. "You are only talk, Lizzie, but I...Well, I follow through." His eyes narrowed on her face. "What is it? What have I said?"

"Nothing," Lizzie said hastily. She shivered, rubbing her gloved hands over her bare arms where the goose bumps showed. What was it that Nat had said to her on that secret night in the folly? That she did not have the nerve to carry through the *droit de seigneur* and seduce him? She had proved that false. She, with her bodice ripped apart and her skirts pulled up, spread open and wantonly giving herself to him with all the wildness that was in her nature... Oh, she had followed through, all the way, through and through. She shuddered. "Nothing," she said again.

Jerrold was watching her, a frown between his fair brows, and Lizzie turned away from that observant gaze and pointed rather randomly at Mary Wheeler. Tom had briefly left Mary's side in order to cultivate her parents—clever Tom, Lizzie thought—and Mary was standing looking a little forlorn and gazing into her wineglass. "There is an heiress for you," she said. "You would be doing her a favor if you snatched her from beneath my brother's nose before he ruins her. See how Tom is conversing with Sir James and flattering his opinions? And how he is not neglecting to make discreet eyes at Lady Wheeler, too, so that she forgets she is a faded middle-aged woman and thinks herself beautiful again? That is all so that he may gain Mary's money."

"Your brother," Jerrold agreed, an edge to his voice, "could charm almost anyone into forgetting that he is a cad and a scoundrel and a deceiver."

"He has a talent for it," Lizzie said. "I think he inherited his charm from our mother. She was accounted the most fascinating woman in England."

"What happened to her?" Jerrold asked.

"She drank herself to death," Lizzie said briefly. She did not want to think about Lady Scarlet. Whenever she did those memories of her mother's warm arms about her were tainted by the equally strong memory of the mingled scent of perfume and strong alcohol.

"If Mary does not please you as a future bride," she continued, "and I'll allow she is a little dull, although her money is not, you could make up to Flora Minchin. I hear she is on the market again."

"You have such a vulgar way of expressing yourself," Jerrold said, smiling, "but I like you for it."

The butler announced dinner and Lady Wheeler immediately started fussing around about who should escort whom into the dining room. "Lord Waterhouse!" Her fluting tones were shrill. Matters of precedence always made her nervous. "Should you not escort Lady Elizabeth—"

"Oh, let us not be so formal!" Lizzie interrupted brightly, grabbing Jerrold's arm. She moved toward the doorway, leaving her hostess irresolute. "Come along, Johnny."

"Riding roughshod," Jerrold murmured, but he followed her all the same and Lizzie did not need to linger to see that Nat Waterhouse had offered Priscilla Willoughby his arm.

At dinner Lizzie had Jerrold on one side and George Wheeler on the other. Lizzie suspected that Priscilla had called in a favor from her cousin when it came to the table setting, for she was seated beside Nat and seemed vastly pleased with the arrangement. Nor did Nat seem discontented. Lizzie could not help but notice how engrossed in conversation the old friends seemed to be and the way in which Priscilla's tempting little hands crept to touch Nat's wrist or his arm as though to emphasize the points she was making. It made Lizzie's heart lurch to watch them and yet she did not seem able to pull her gaze away. Time and again she would glance down the table and see Priscilla leaning toward Nat so that her milky-white breasts were bracketed by the tantalizingly ruffled neckline of her gown. Damn her, Lizzie thought. She gave her own discreet debutante bodice a tug downward and saw John Jerrold torn between laughter and appreciation.

She drank some wine and then some more. It was very rough. Sir James Wheeler was known for his parsimony when it came to his wine cellar. The food, in contrast, was rich and fussy. Lizzie picked at it. She flirted with John Jerrold. She felt miserable, but after a few glasses of wine even George Wheeler's gallantries seemed charming enough.

"Lizzie, you have been drinking," Mary Wheeler hissed reproachfully when the ladies were obliged to retire at the end of the meal. "And flirting! I saw George kissing your wrist!"

"Mr. Wheeler was merely acquainting himself with my new perfume," Lizzie said airily. She accepted the cup of tea that Lady Wheeler passed to her. It was very strong. Clearly Lady Wheeler felt that she needed to sober up. Lizzie looked at her and thought what a foolish old buzzard Lady Wheeler was. Like everyone else, she wanted to make Lizzie into a person she was not, a pattern card debutante, perhaps, like Perfect Priscilla. Lizzie felt reckless and angry. She knew this to be a sure sign that she was about to behave very badly. But how was she to misbehave, and with whom? The opportunities were rather limited in Lady Wheeler's staid drawing room.

"Let us have an impromptu dance," Tom suggested when the gentlemen rejoined the ladies. "We could push the carpet back and have a little piano music. Lizzie—" he smiled at his sister, a wheedling smile "—plays very well."

It was true, but Lizzie wanted to dance rather than to play. However, she could see that Lady Wheeler was already seizing upon the plan as a way to confine her and a very naughty idea started to form in her head. She took her place meekly at the pianoforte, waited for the servants to roll back the carpet, and then started on a very sedate minuet. Lady Wheeler's face relaxed into a relieved smile. Nat and Priscilla trod a stately measure. Lizzie could see Tom taking advantage of the slow steps of the dance to woo Mary. He threw Lizzie a grateful, conspiratorial smile and Lizzie smiled grimly back. She moved into a rather livelier country-dance. The mood in the room lifted, the dancers smiled, those who were sitting out started to chat. The wine circulated again and the candles glowed. At the end there was a smattering of applause and the servants brought in more refreshment. Lizzie had managed to slip a glass of wine from under Lady Wheeler's nose. She took a gulp and started to sing, very demurely:

"As Oyster Nan stood by her tub
To show her inclination
She gave her noblest parts a scrub
And sighed for want of copulation—"

"More refreshments!" Lady Wheeler bellowed, clapping her hands. She seized Lizzie by the elbow and almost dragged her from the piano stool.

"Mary, dear!" she caroled. "It is your turn to play now. We really must not trespass too much on Lady Elizabeth's good nature!"

"Splendid singing, Lizzie," John Jerrold said, whisking her into the country-dance as Mary struck the first chord. "I was disappointed not to hear verse two."

"I will give you a private rendition of it one day," Lizzie promised, and he looked at her, brows raised, his brown gaze suddenly speculative.

"Careful, Lizzie. I might hold you to that."

Lizzie was enjoying herself. The room was spinning, the candles dancing in beautiful golden leaps and curves. Mary was a far better musician than she was and was playing very nicely indeed. Lizzie executed a turn, lost her footing and almost tripped. Jerrold grabbed her in his arms to prevent her from falling. It was rather nice to be in his arms. He felt strong. Lizzie could see Nat watching her—he and Priscilla were not dancing such an energetic country-dance, of course—and there was a heavy frown on his forehead now. Priscilla was whispering to him secretively behind her fan. And close by Sir James Wheeler was not even bothering to lower his voice.

"The chit is a hoyden, Vera! How you can possibly consider her suitable for George is quite beyond me."

And Lady Wheeler's reply: "James, when a rich, titled heiress behaves like a hoyden then she is merely displaying high spirits."

"I don't think that they should get their hopes up for George," Lizzie hiccupped in Jerrold's ear. "He has no chance of securing either my fortune or my person."

"Hush," Jerrold said, putting a hand over her mouth. "You do not want to offend Lady Wheeler *too* deeply." He bent closer to her. "Would you like to take some air on the terrace?"

Lizzie looked at him. He was not inviting her outside so that she could sober up. She knew that. They would go out into the dark and he would kiss her and she…Well, she would respond because she was curious to know if he was any good at kissing and after all it did not really matter who she kissed now because Nat did not love her… She might even go further if she liked the way Jerrold kissed, because everyone would know anyway that she was a flirt and a wanton so why not? Perhaps it would make her feel less miserable. She felt the edges of her mind starting to fray with despair and jumped when someone spoke from close by.

"Jerrold." It was Nat's voice, very hard and very cold now. "If I might cut in?"

Lizzie saw the smile wiped from John Jerrold's face

like a candle blown out. The sudden tension in the air made her spine prickle as the little shivers ran down it.

"Of course, Waterhouse." Jerrold conceded gracefully, with a bow. "Lady Elizabeth…"

"Do you *mind?*" Lizzie snapped as Nat's hand closed about her wrist and he drew her inexorably to the side of the room. "I was enjoying myself—"

"That is all too evident," Nat said grimly.

"It is Monty's job to take care of me, not yours," Lizzie said, nodding toward where her elder brother was dozing before the fire, face flushed, the inevitable glass of wine in his hand. He might not have inherited their mother's fabled looks and charm, she thought, but he had certainly inherited her taste for drink. The misery twisted in her again.

"Not that I need anyone to protect me," she finished, and hated the forlorn tone that had somehow crept into her voice.

"Can we talk about that?" Nat asked. His gloved hand still rested gently on her wrist and Lizzie looked from it up into his face and found that she could not seem to look away. Had she ever looked at Nat properly before, she wondered. She knew what he looked like, of course. She had seen him so many times during her childhood and youth that she could describe him with her eyes closed. But had she ever stopped to think about the way in which his features had changed as he, too, had grown older, developing from the youth she had known into the man he was now; how the curves and planes of his face had grown leaner and hardened with experience, how the lines had deepened about his eyes and his hair had darkened to the ebony it was now in the firelight?

Had she noticed when first the stubble had started to shadow his cheeks and chin and when the expression in his eyes had changed from the bright eagerness of youth to this watchful calculation? She did not think that she had detected the precise moment. She did not remember why Nat had changed nor how. He was just Nat and he had been there for her from the moment she had arrived at Fortune Hall, a lonely child who had lost both her parents and had been forced to start a new life in a new place with people she did not know.

But now Nat was no longer simply a youth she had once known or a man who had become her friend. She felt a pang of loss although she was not exactly sure what it was she had misplaced. Perhaps she mourned losing the easy friendship they had once had, for despite the disparity in their ages they *had* been close and their friendship had been warm and valuable and precious to her. Or perhaps what she regretted was that she had not seen until it was too late that her respect for Nat, her need to hold his good opinion, had been so important to her. She wished she had realized sooner how deeply she had fallen in love with him. Instead she had been blinded by her pride; she had been in denial about her feelings, pretending that her jealousy was disinterested friendship and that she was acting from the purest of motives when really she wanted Nat for herself with the fierceness of a tigress.

"Lizzie?" Nat's voice had softened now. Perhaps he had seen the bewilderment in her eyes and heard that unhappy tone in her voice. He wanted to protect her. She knew it. Damn it, protecting her was what he had always done. But now it was only a part of what she wanted from him. If she did not have his love then to offer her his protection out of a sense of duty, was simply not enough. She wanted his passion and his wildness and his primitive anger and possession and all the things she had seen in him that night in the folly. But she wanted his tenderness and his love as well, to meet and match with hers, and that was not what he was offering.

"No," she said, meeting his eyes, "there is nothing to talk about."

She freed herself from his touch and walked quickly toward the door. She was tired now and the reckless edge the wine had given her was ebbing from her blood. She wanted to go home. She would send the carriage back for Tom and Monty, send, too, a gracious note of thanks to Lady Wheeler in the morning to prove that she was not entirely bereft of good manners.

Nat was still standing where she had left him. Even as she thought that he would not make a scene in a public place by demanding to accompany her or to speak further with her she realized that she had made a serious mistake. There was a single-minded resolve in Nat now that would not baulk at causing a scene. She saw him start to move toward her with absolute determination—and then Priscilla Willoughby drifted across to him and claimed his attention with a hand on his arm, and Lizzie whipped though the door as quickly as a cat and slipped away, her heart beating fast.

It was warm in the carriage and she was alone and she felt unhappy so she reached for the hip flask that she knew Monty kept concealed there. Actually it was not very well concealed, merely shoved under a cushion. She took it out and drank from it and the brandy was villainously strong and almost made her choke, but she could feel her body relaxing, too, and her mind turning numb again. It made her happier. For a little while.

CHAPTER SIX

HE WAS SO ANGRY he thought that he would explode. He was angry with a special sort of fury that only Lizzie could arouse in him, a mixture of protectiveness and complete exasperation.

Nat had made his excuses to Lady Wheeler, and given his apologies to Priscilla Willoughby, whom he had shed with a ruthlessness she deserved. When had Priscilla become so shockingly persistent? He did not remember her being so pushy as a debutante, but then he had been fathoms deep in love with her in his salad days and so had probably not minded her draping herself all over him and claiming his attention at every possible opportunity. Now her clinging only served to irritate him when all he wanted was to talk to Lizzie. He had to confront her. The need to do his duty, to offer Lizzie the protection of his name, drove him. So did the need to have her in his bed.

He had followed Lizzie back to Fortune Hall and seen her tumble out of the carriage. He had been prepared to accost her on the doorstep, but then she had bidden the coachman and groom good-night and had started to walk away from the house and toward the woods instead. Nat did not approve of her strolling around in the dark on her own, of course, but it did at least give him the opportunity to speak with her alone and he had been waiting for that for over a week. He had called; he had looked everywhere for her. The servants had told him that she was sick, she was out, no one knew where she was. Nat had not believed a word of it and if he had not been called back so abruptly to visit his family he would have forced Lizzie to see him before now.

"Lizzie!" He caught up with her on the edge of the wood and as soon as she turned toward him he could smell the brandy on her and see the flask dangling from between her fingers, gleaming silver in the moonlight. His heart sank. He knew that Monty Fortune had a problem with alcohol; he knew, too, that Lizzie's mother had died abroad, an old soak, people said, disgraced and abandoned. He could not bear to think of the same thing happening to Lizzie herself if she turned to drink in her unhappiness.

"Nat." He had expected her to run away from him as she had done before, or at least to tell him to leave her alone, but she did neither. She stood blinking at him whilst the light and the shadows played around her and turned the rich auburn of her hair to dark.

"You're drunk," Nat said taking, the flask from her

and throwing it into the bushes. "You took too much wine tonight and now you're on the brandy."

"You are a spoilsport." She pouted. So she was sweet drunk not angry drunk. It did not appease him. Fear for her mingled with his exasperation. It was as though she lived on a high wire. He did not understand what it would take to bring her safely back to earth.

"There wasn't any left in the flask anyway," she said. She turned and walked away from him, into the moonlight. It sculpted her face in silver making her look pale and fey, a fairy from another world. Nat looked at her with her bodice slipping and her shawl sliding off her shoulders. She had pulled the neckline of her gown down too far earlier and the curve of one small breast showed now. He wanted to trace the line of it with his finger. He wanted that quite badly. Lizzie did not have Priscilla's opulent curves. He had noticed them since Priscilla had been thrusting her breasts in his face all night. It had not attracted him. He had wanted Lizzie's delicacy instead. He wanted her so much that he ached.

"John Jerrold wouldn't have thrown the flask away." She was taunting him now. "He would have fetched me more brandy."

"Jerrold is a bad influence on you," Nat said. She was surrounded by bad influences, her dead parents, her drunkard elder brother, her profligate younger one, now John Jerrold. He had wanted to hit Jerrold and it was not solely for his lack of judgment in encouraging Lizzie's drinking. If she had gone outside with Jerrold would he have found them with Jerrold's hand down her bodice or up her skirt?

"I was only flirting with him," Lizzie said. Her smile was sweet, her eyes wide and bright.

"You were playing reckless games." Nat sighed heavily. She looked so young in the moonlight with her gown falling off her like a child let loose in the dressing up box. "You don't know how dangerous it is," he said coldly. "Jerrold wanted to kiss you—"

"I've kissed other people before." Lizzie sounded cross, defiant. "It is not just *you,* Nat. I know how to go about it."

Dear God, he didn't want to think about it. Other men kissing Lizzie, plundering that soft, sweet mouth of hers as he had done... And tonight she had been flirting as though her life depended upon it, tempting them with other liberties far beyond mere kissing. There was knowledge in her eyes and the promise of temptation. How far would she go? As far as she had gone with him? He would kill any man who took her up on that offer because it was his fault that she had the experience to follow through.

"You must marry me," he said, following that train of thought. "It is the only way to put matters right."

"No." She swung away from him. "What you mean is that it is the only way to make *you* feel better."

Devil take it, he thought, she was right. He felt all manner of emotions, of which guilt was only a small part. Self-loathing, disgust at his lack of control, regret at the way in which he had obliged Flora to free him and now an equal regret that he and Lizzie were trapped by their situation… And then there was the almost paralyzing fear over the need to gain a fortune and quickly, for his sister's sake if nothing else, to end the blackmail…

But there was also that deep and undeniable sensual attraction to Lizzie, too, which seemed undiminished by the guilt and reproach, a wicked, dangerous desire that tempted him to take her again *because he wanted her.* He wanted her with a hunger so sharp and so deep that it made his breath catch. Lizzie had made love in the same way that she did everything else in life—with hunger, with recklessness, with an appetite that left no space for caution or care.

"Lizzie," he said, "what if you have a child?"

Her face seemed carved from stone in the moonlight. "I won't."

"Do you know that or are you just being wilfully stubborn?"

She made no reply and suddenly he realized with a pang of the heart that the blank look on her face was not obstinacy but fear, that her persistent refusal to face the truth sprang from terror. Lady Elizabeth Scarlet might be twenty years old yet she was still little more than a child herself in temperament. It was one of the reasons why he had always taken care of her, because she had seemed so dangerously careless of herself.

"I won't," she said again. "There will be no child."

"Do you know that for sure?" Nat pressed, wondering as he did so why he was asking. It made no difference to him or to what he had done. Even if there were to be no obvious consequence of their mad, mindless passion, it had still happened and he still had to put it right.

"I don't feel any different," Lizzie said. She sounded very young. "I am sure that if I were pregnant I would be able to tell."

Nat almost laughed but he had heard the edge of fear in her voice again, the note that betrayed her.

"I do not believe one can always tell at first," he said carefully.

She shot him a look that was full of defiance. "How would you know? You are a man."

She had a point, Nat thought. But even so…

"How long is it until you expect your courses?" he said, very careful again. He saw her blush pink even under the pale gilding of the moonlight. She might be wild but she was not so immodest as to be familiar discussing intimacies with a man.

"I…in about five days time, I think. Perhaps a little less…I never pay much attention to them." She raised her chin. "I think it stupid to let such matters govern one's behavior."

Well, quite. He could imagine that Lizzie would

not let such a trifling matter interfere with her riding or her other activities as many women did. Nevertheless it would have been useful if she had paid more attention to them because by his calculations that put their night of mad passion in exactly the most dangerous time of the month.

"Then I think it essential we wed by special licence as soon as possible," he said.

"And I think it better that we do not wed at all," Lizzie said.

Nat looked at her, wondering if she was trying to deny both what had happened and what the consequences might be. He wondered if she wanted children. They had never talked about it. He had thought that they were friends and yet there were so many things that they had never discussed. He wanted children—with the right mother. He had always imagined that he would marry someone like Flora, or Priscilla Willoughby, who were dutiful and well-bred and would surely give birth to dutiful and well bred offspring. Was it wrong to think that Lizzie could not be a good mother, twenty years old and yet still behaving like a child herself? The only real example of motherhood she had had was the Countess of Scarlet, who had been selfish and neglectful.

Lizzie had walked away from him again, graceful as she dipped in and out of the shadows. The leaves rustled in the night breeze and it spun tendrils of her hair.

"You are free," she said, over her shoulder. "There will be no child. I am sure of it. So no one will know what happened and we can pretend that nothing did."

"We can pretend…"

Nat was shocked to realize just how tempted he was to turn his back on what *had* happened and join in the pretence. A marriage made in hell, not heaven, with the possibility of a child that had never been planned…

How easy it would be to put honor aside and agree with her, play along with the charade.

"No one will know…"

He had thought from the first that Lizzie would make the devil of a wife. They were not well suited. In point of fact they were not suited at all. A marriage between them would probably be a disaster. Yet how could he, in honor, join her in her pretense?

It was not just honor, he acknowledged. It was greed for the money. He *had* to have it. And it was lust. Having once tasted Lizzie's tempting beauty he was tormented by her. It was not a good reason for marriage, in his opinion, but it was better than asking her to be his mistress. He wanted her here, now, against this tree, or on the grass beneath them. He had never felt like this before, had never been possessed by such single-minded desire. It still shocked him because he simply was not a man driven by his lusts. Except that he evidently was.

"No." He caught her arm. She felt warm beneath his touch. "*I* know," he said roughly. "*You* know.

Even if there is no child, even if no one else ever found out, we two would know what happened."

"So?" She raised her chin. "I can forget."

Nat thought about how impossible he found it to erase the memory of how she felt in his arms. He could not forget that. There was a tumult of intense emotion within him, the desire, the need, and the longing. He slid his hands up her arms, drawing her toward him. He moved with unmistakable delibera-tion so that she had time to escape him if she wished, but she stood quite still, watching him with those huge, clear eyes.

"Have you forgotten this?" he asked, in the second before his mouth covered hers. "Do you want to forget it?"

Delicious. Hot. Urgent. She matched his passion effortlessly and for a moment Nat felt the world spin and he was in danger of losing control in the same way that he had done the week before. She tasted so sweet, a mixture of brandy and something that was her own essence, fiery, tempting and yet poignantly innocent. She held nothing back and that was almost his undoing. With a fierce effort he reined himself in and kissed her more gently, teasing her tongue with his, courting her response rather than demanding it. Her tongue slid against his, seeking, a little hesitant in her inexperience and all the more seductive for it. And suddenly, helplessly, they were sliding toward heated passion once again and reality splintered around him and he was aware of nothing but his driving need for her as he gathered her closer and the feelings consumed him alive.

It was Lizzie who drew back this time. She was panting for breath. For a brief moment the moonlight shimmered on some expression in her eyes that he did not recognize and could not read and then she moved away from him and the shadows fell across her face and swallowed her up.

"No," she said. "I have not forgotten it."

He came after her, still driven by need, and caught her hand. "Then marry me, Lizzie."

"So that we can make love again?" Her tone was light, unrevealing. "It isn't a good enough reason, Nat."

In that moment it felt like the best reason in the world to him. Devoured by his lust for her, single-minded in his desire, he could think of none better. But Lizzie had freed herself. Her hand slid from his and once again she slipped away.

"I do not wish to marry you," she said. "You know we would not be suited. Even as friends we fight like cat and dog. It would be willfully foolish to make matters worse by marrying each other." She sighed. "This isn't like the time I fell from my horse when we were out riding together and you carried me home, Nat. This time you cannot rescue me. We made a mistake, I provoked you and you were angry with me and it should never have happened."

Nat could not dispute a single thing that she said,

except that he knew that mistakes of that magnitude could not simply be brushed aside.

"You *must* marry me," he said. "It will put matters right."

"So now you give me a different reason," Lizzie said. "First the possibility of a child, then lust, now reputation." She looked at him, a mocking half smile tilting her lips. "And you have not even mentioned my money yet."

She was so cynical, Nat thought. It was experience of life that had made Lizzie such a skeptic for she had seen from an early age the things men—and women— did for money. And the hell of it was that she was absolutely right. He had not mentioned the money because out of all of his motives it seemed the least honorable, yet to him it was becoming the most pressing need. He simply had to pay off his blackmailer before the truth of his sister's disgrace was spilled before the world like an ugly stain.

"There are lots of reasons why we should wed," he argued.

"I do not see it like that," Lizzie said. "I see lots of reasons why we should not."

She was so stubborn that Nat wanted to shake her. "Lizzie," he said. "It will give you the protection of my name. Someone might know what happened. They might have known you were out that night…the servants… You know how they gossip. You would be ruined if it came out, even if you are not pregnant."

She looked up. Her eyes were bright, vivid in the moonlight. Her words were an echo of his thoughts a moment before. "You are always seeking to protect me, Nat Waterhouse."

"And never has there been greater need."

Lizzie stood looking at him thoughtfully, head on one side as though he were a specimen for examination. Nat was not sure he liked it.

"Always you seek to care for people," she said. "Your family, me, even the work that you do for the Home Secretary to keep the country safe..." She left a question hanging in the air. *Why?*

Nat knew full well what it was the drove him, but he did not want to discuss it. Once, years before, he had failed to protect those who depended on him and he had resolved that it would never happen again. Which was why he needed not only to keep Lizzie safe from the consequences of their reckless passion but also to gain her fortune so that his family and Celeste were secure, too. It was his absolute duty and he would not fail in it.

"It is what I do," he said stubbornly.

Lizzie shook her head, disappearing between the trees, almost as though she were slipping through his fingers like water. He followed her, realizing even as he did so that it was always like this. She always ran away; he always followed. The knowledge irritated him. Was he so predictable, so reliable? It seemed so. And yet he could not simply let her go to face the consequences of their actions alone.

"Lizzie." He caught her and held her. She did not pull away from him and yet she did not feel willing in his arms, either. It was as though she was enduring his embrace and waiting for it to pass. He wanted to force a response from her to prove that the desire had not only been on his side that night. A moment ago, when they had kissed, he had been sure that she had been as eager for him as he was for her. Yet there was nothing in her now to indicate that she wanted him. He looked down into her face, so beautifully etched in black and white in the moonlight, and felt again the need that he had for her slam through his body with each beat of his heart.

"No," she said again. She smiled at him. "Marriage should be about the future, Nat, not just the past." She stood up on tiptoe and pressed her lips to his. It was a wistful kiss. He could taste the brandy on her lips again and beneath its smell catch an elusive hint of Lizzie's own scent. It went straight to his head—and his groin. "But I do thank you," she whispered as she slipped from his arms. "You are a good man, Nat Waterhouse. You try to do the right thing."

It sounded, Nat thought with grim amusement, like an epitaph. And it was far more than he deserved. Not all his motives were pure. Most of them were not.

He watched as she crossed the meadow toward the house. The carriage was returning from the Wheelers now and Sir Montague was being helped down by one of the footmen. He seemed too drunk to stand.

Nat watched as Lizzie called for Sir Monty's valet, Spencer, to assist them and calmly organized the removal of her half brother from the gravel sweep into the house. Of Tom Fortune there was no sign. The one brother was insensible with drink, Nat thought, and the other was probably in bed with the serving wench from the Morris Clown Inn. Of the three of them, Lizzie was by far the strongest, most courageous, and most admirable.

He wondered how he was going to persuade her to marry him. She might think that she had a choice. She might even be more mature, more sensible than he, in seeing that to marry would be to condemn them both to a life of misery. Unfortunately he could not let that weigh with him. The letter he had received that morning, reminding him of his financial obligations, threatening his sister Celeste, had helped to seal Lizzie's fate. She would be his bride. He had no other alternative.

"DID YOU ENJOY THAT?" Tom Fortune asked. He propped himself on one elbow and trailed a lazy finger down the bare back of the woman who was lying next to him. She gave a sleepy purr of total satiation and rolled onto her side. The bed sheet lay tangled about her thighs, revealing the dark triangle of hair at the juncture of her legs, and she made absolutely no effort to cover herself. Tom liked that. He liked a woman who was shameless in her sexual needs. This woman, he thought, might hold his interest for several weeks. He suspected she knew all the whore's tricks and would not be slow to use them.

He reached out and started to toy with her breast. She was extremely well endowed, her flesh curving into his hand as he played with her. He liked that as well. He wanted her again already, even though they had only just finished making love. He corrected himself. They had not made love. There had been nothing of love or tenderness in their coupling, nothing but a raw greed and sensuality. Which suited Tom fine. At last he had found someone to play with who matched him perfectly in terms of her lack of moral scruple.

"I hear," he said, touching a finger to the sapphires that were still about her neck, "that you are very rich."

She laughed. "And I hear that you are a fortune hunter." She trailed her hand down his chest. "Tom Fortune," she said. "How inappropriate when you are penniless."

He kissed her, hard and deep, one hand covering her breast the other tangled in her long blond hair. "Perhaps we could share your money?" he suggested when they broke apart.

"Are you proposing to me?" Her sapphire eyes mocked him. "Here, now? How romantic." Her languid gesture swept over the tumbled sheets and the frowsty little tavern room. "No, dear Tom—" she took his erection in her hand, stroked, rubbed, fondled him with such ruthless efficiency that he struggled not to come there and then "—you are good for one thing—" She squeezed his cock to make her point. "and at that you are *very* good indeed, my dear—but not to marry. I have other plans. Don't come," she added sweetly as he struggled with both his anger and his arousal, and the fusion of both of them into a mad desire, "I need you."

With a swift, voracious movement she straddled him and took him inside her. He gasped aloud.

"Your plans—" he said, grabbing her hips to control the tantalizing pace she set. "Do they involve Nat Waterhouse? Do you want to be a countess?"

She checked for a second and her eyes narrowed. He felt a flash of triumph and a return of a modicum of control. With this woman, he suspected, it would always be a battle.

"They might," she said, punishing him with the most shallow of movements atop him. "I might. Why do you ask?"

"Because—" Tom was struggling to keep his mind clear against the onslaught of sensation. "Because if so you should know that your gallant earl is not as honorable as you might think."

She was so surprised that she stopped moving altogether. Her palms rested on his chest. Her thighs pressed closely against his. He was captured, encased, held still.

"Whatever can you mean?" she said.

"I can't tell you that," Tom said, savagely pleased to be able to thwart her. "Trust me, though—he is not as worthy as you think."

She squeezed him tight and he writhed beneath her, groaning. "Do you have some sort of hold over him?" she asked. "Are you extorting money from him?"

"I wouldn't tell you if I was," Tom panted.

"I suppose not." She started to move again and Tom felt relief and a renewed hunger. "Perhaps it just makes him more exciting," she whispered. "Perhaps he would not be as boring in bed as I suspected—"

Tom rolled over suddenly, impaling her beneath him. "Are you thinking about him now?" he demanded, his mouth hot against her breast, biting hard, wanting to mark her white skin.

She gasped, but not with displeasure, and arched upward to his mouth.

"I might be," she whispered.

Tom pulled on her nipples until she screamed.

"You think about your plans," he taunted, "and I will think about mine."

"Not my frumpish little cousin Mary," she gasped as he started to drive into her with ferocious strokes. "She's so dull."

"But her money is lovely," Tom said. He forced her legs further apart. "I worship it. Lovely," he repeated as the violence of his thrusts almost lifted her from the bed. "Lovely."

LATER, MUCH LATER, Sir Montague Fortune awoke in his bedroom at Fortune Hall. Lizzie had instructed the servants to put him to bed but Spencer, his valet, had done the bare minimum of work and merely removed his jacket and cravat, not even bothering to take off his boots. Nor had the man closed the curtains and it was the moonlight, falling across his face, which woke Sir Monty up. For a moment he lay quite still, for his head hurt vilely and there was an unaccustomed sickly sweet taste in his mouth. Then he realized that he needed both the jakes and a drink of water, and he groaned. His whole body felt soft and leaden at the same time, too heavy to move. He knew he should not have had that last glass of claret, but he had been celebrating the advent of yet more money into his coffers. He had never planned to wed, but now he could see what a splendid and enriching idea it was…

The moonlight flickered as a shadow crossed the room and Sir Monty turned his head. His heart jumped. Just for a moment he thought that he had seen the figure of a woman there; a woman in a cloak with her hood up carrying, most bizarrely, what looked like an umbrella in her hand. But there was no one there. The moonlight rippled across the room and Sir Monty groaned again and closed his eyes.

He did not see the blade and only opened his eyes a second before the knife slid silently between his ribs and by then it was too late to do anything at all.

CHAPTER SEVEN

LIZZIE WOKE with a headache from the brandy and a bad taste in her mouth. The house was silent. Monty, she knew from past experience, had taken so much drink that he would not wake until past noon. Tom was probably not even home yet though the bright yellow of the sun cutting through the gap between the curtains told her that it must be late morning.

What had happened the night before? Her evening gown and shawl were lying in a puddle on the floor. Her evening slippers, resting in a patch of sunlight, looked discolored and spoiled. She stared at them and the memory flooded in, pushing back the tide of brandy-induced forgetfulness. Of course—she had walked into the wood, amongst the dew-stained grass. That was why the hem of her gown and slippers were ruined.

Other memories were impossible to ignore. Nat had followed her and had proposed marriage to her and she had turned him down. He had kissed her and it had been as deliciously seductive as before. The temptation to melt into his embrace and promise to wed him had been so strong. But instead she had found the strength to reject him. She loved him too much to condemn them both to half a marriage. She knew that he did not love her, and marriage, to her mind, should be about the building of a future relationship, not about regrets over a past one. Love should be overwhelming and all consuming, the type of love she felt for Nat and that he so manifestly did not feel for her. Otherwise there was too much inequality in it.

Nat had kissed her with lust and this time she had not confused it with love. Desire was delicious, hot, strong, seductive, but she had been burned so badly that night in the folly, confusing lust with love in her naïveté, that she was never going to make the same mistake again.

She thought of her mother then, as she so often did when she was unhappy. The Countess of Scarlet had been reviled for her unfaithfulness, but the truth, as Lizzie well knew, was that her mother had been a victim of love not a heartless wanton. She had run away from a husband who gave her everything in a material sense and nothing in an emotional one. Lizzie had only been young when her mother had fled but she had sensed Lady Scarlet's unhappiness with the acute sensitivity that children can possess. She had known that her mother wanted nothing other than her husband's love and had been driven to despair by the lack of it. People thought that her mother's bad example should be a warning to Lizzie and it was, but not in the way they imagined. All it had taught Lizzie was not to give her heart when there was no prospect of seeing her love returned. She had forgotten that, briefly, that night in the folly. She had loved Nat and thought she was loved in return. She had been wrong and now she was never going to forget that painful reminder.

So it was over. She felt miserable. Nat had proposed and she had refused and that was an end to it. Now she really was free to forge that pretence, to remake her memories, wiping out that night in the folly whilst the days, weeks, months passed and after a while the new memory became the truth.

Nothing happened...

She sat up and hunted about for her underclothes. There was no point in calling for a maid. Tom had tried to seduce her most recent lady's maid and the girl had left in high dudgeon a week ago. There was only Bridie, the housemaid, left to do everything. Besides, she could manage perfectly well on her own. She always had done.

What if there was a child...

Nat's words echoed unbidden through her head and she froze for a second, her blood feeling stone-cold despite the warmth of the summer morning. That was one aspect of her situation she had blindly refused even to consider until Nat had put it into words the previous night.

She allowed her hand to slide down over her night rail, following the flat planes of her stomach. She looked the same. She felt the same. In fact she felt sick, but that was the brandy rather than anything else. She could not be pregnant. That truly would be a disaster. The thought of it terrified her. It was all very well for Laura Anstruther, for example, to have a child. Laura was old—at least thirty—and already had a daughter and anyway, she was a grown-up. And Lydia Cole—well, Lydia's pregnancy had caused a most terrible scandal but Lydia herself would be a wonderful mother because she was so sane and so calm and so loving that she could surely look on her baby and feel all the right emotions rather than the sheer terror that Lizzie would feel if only she permitted herself to think about it for a second…Her thoughts ran wild like rats in a trap until she took a deep breath and calmed herself.

Nothing happened…

Her heart steadied. She would carry on as before. What to do today? Life felt strangely empty. All her tomorrows stretched out before her now and it was odd that she could think of nothing that she wanted to do with them. She realized that so many of her activities had been shared with Nat in the past. They had particularly enjoyed riding out together. A summer morning like this was made for a gallop on the Yorkshire fells. Except that she would be going out on her own in future.

She found a clean gown folded in the wardrobe and struggled to put it on, bundling her hair up with a ribbon. When she threw back the curtains the sunshine was bright and hot, pouring into the room and showing up the dust and cobwebs. Something had to be done about Fortune Hall, Lizzie thought. It was going to rack and ruin whilst Monty grasped after people's money and spent it all on drink. Soon—in two months time, in fact—he would be entitled to enforce the Dames' Tax and to take half the dowry of any heiress left in the village who had not wed. That included her, of course. She was the only heiress left, apart from Flora Minchin and Mary Wheeler. Monty's money-grubbing ways really had to be stopped once and for all, Lizzie thought. She knew that Laura Anstruther had instructed her lawyers to start working on the case the previous year. She needed to talk to Laura and see what they could do about Monty. She would go to the Old Palace after she had scraped together some breakfast. She could see Laura and Lydia, too, and inquire after their health, for both were advanced in their pregnancy now. And she need have no fear that her friends would suspect that anything was wrong with her because all was settled.

Nothing happened... Lizzie remembered her childish nightmares, and how she would pretend that if she did not look at the monsters that would mean that they really weren't there at all.

She went out onto the landing. The door of Monty's bedroom was closed whilst that of Tom's stood ajar with the light streaming out into the corridor. Dust motes jumped and danced in the sunlight. The plaster was peeling from the walls and the floorboards creaked beneath Lizzie's feet. At times like this Fortune Hall seemed every one of its three hundred and more years old. It feels like I do, Lizzie thought, old and worn. She had come to Fortune Hall to live with her half brothers after her father had died. She had been eleven years old and to be plunged from the warmth, laughter and hedonism of Scarlet Park into the peeling and decrepit existence of Fortune Hall had been a terrible shock. Scarlet Park had been a bright, shining world. Fortune Hall was its opposite in every way.

Shivering, Lizzie hastened down the wide wooden stairs and into the kitchen, where a sullen youth was listlessly sweeping the flagged floor and the kitchen maid was peeling a pile of rotting vegetables and grumbling to the Cook at the same time. They all smiled as Lizzie came in though, and Cook pushed a plate of eggs and gammon toward her along the trencher table.

"There you are, pet," she said. "Thought you might need something solid after last night. You should keep off the brandy," she added, "or your head will be as addled as your brother's."

"God forbid," Lizzie said, shuddering. She looked

at the plate of congealing food and felt her stomach lurch. How on earth did the servants know of her drinking habits? Nat was right when he said they knew everything. She felt a little shiver of apprehension.

"Get it down you," Cook said, slapping a beaker of strong tea down beside her. "Nothing's so sovereign for the headache, in my experience."

Lizzie managed to force some of the gammon down and drank the tea, then clapped a bonnet haphazardly over her head before setting off down the drive toward the village. None of the gardeners were about. The weeds grew plentifully through the gravel and even Sir Monty's flower garden, for many years his pride and joy, was a tangle of nettles and dock now that he had abandoned gardening as a pursuit in favor of stealing people's money.

Lizzie walked along the river to Laura's house, The Old Palace. The day was hot and the water glinted appealingly in the sun. Lizzie's spirits lifted as she contemplated a swim later on. As a child she had swum in the lake at Scarlet Park and then the moat at the Hall and she had no time for the shrinking of those who considered bathing to be unhealthy and unladylike.

She could hear voices on the terrace as she approached The Old Palace and coming up through the meadow gate she found not only Laura Anstruther and Lydia Cole but Alice Vickery as well. They were sitting beneath the shade of an enormous striped umbrella and taking tea. Laura and Lydia looked hugely pregnant for they were both near their time now and as Lizzie stood unnoticed in the shadow of the gate, she felt another pang of emotion like the one that had struck her earlier as she was dressing. The mysteries of motherhood were utterly unfamiliar to her and she was not sure that she could even begin to comprehend them, yet there was something about having a child that felt infinitely precious to her even as it terrified her. She took a deep breath. It would not happen to her. She was sure of it. It was better simply not to think about it at all and pretend once more that nothing had happened. She pushed open the gate and went forward onto the terrace, a smile firmly fixed on her face.

"Laura, you are blossoming!" she said. "I am so glad to see you well!"

"Lizzie!" Laura's face broke into a warm smile and she grasped Lizzie's hands and drew her forward to kiss her cheek. She had been sick for most of her pregnancy but now she was indeed looking extremely well, her skin glowing and a very warm and contented smile in her eyes. "We were worried about you," she added. "Alice said that she had called several times but that you were either indisposed or from home. I would have come myself but it takes me a good half hour to move five paces!"

"I'm sorry," Lizzie said contritely, going across to kiss Lydia and Alice before taking a seat back beside

Laura on a long, cushioned bench in the shade of the parasol. "It was only a trifling chill and I am quite well now." She did not miss the look that flashed between Alice and Lydia. She knew what it meant. They were her best friends and they knew her so well and they did not believe her. They knew she had never had a day's illness in her life.

"Lemonade or tea, Lizzie?" Laura asked, breaking the rather odd moment. "And would you like some plum cake?"

"If Alice has made it then yes please," Lizzie said, smiling at Alice. "And I shall have lemonade please, Laura."

"We heard that you were at Lady Wheeler's dinner last night," Alice said, her blue eyes bright as they rested on Lizzie's face. "Mary called this morning. She said that Viscount Jerrold was paying you a great deal of attention."

"Oh, Johnny is an old friend of mine, as you know," Lizzie said lightly. She noticed that Lydia had blushed a little at the mention of John Jerrold's name and she wondered at it. Lydia had been completely ruined by not one but two love affairs with Lizzie's half brother Tom and had sworn off men forever as a result, but Lizzie remembered that John Jerrold had paid Lydia considerable attention before Tom had trampled all over her heart and her reputation. Lydia had also lost her fortune and her parents had been arrested for murder and her life was utterly in tatters. Lizzie knew that no man of consequence was ever likely to pay Lydia any honorable attention in future yet she could not but hope that one day her friend would find happiness. She wondered how Jerrold felt about Lydia now.

"There is nothing going on between Johnny and me," she said. "It was a dull evening and I drank more than I ought and now I have the headache, which I suppose serves me right."

"Mary said that Nat Waterhouse was also there," Laura said, passing Lizzie her glass of lemonade and cutting a slice of the cake for her. "I was surprised to hear it—I did not know that he was a friend of the Wheeler family."

Lizzie felt the jealous bile rise in her chest as it had done the previous night. The others were all looking at her and she tried to keep her face blank. She had never been particularly good at hiding her feelings although she suspected she was getting better at it lately. She had certainly managed to deceive Nat as to how she felt about him. But she wished she could stop thinking about him. That would be a step forward.

"I believe that Nat was there at Lady Willoughby's invitation," she said. She stumbled a little over Nat's name, which was odd. She could not call him Lord Waterhouse, of course, for they had been friends for years and everyone would think it odd. But nor could she apparently talk of him with the same casual carelessness she had always used. She felt very self-conscious, all the more so as Lydia's steady gaze was on her and was making Lizzie feel horribly vulnerable.

"Lady Willoughby is Lady Wheeler's cousin and I understand she is also an old flame of Nat's," she added hurriedly.

"I wonder then if Lady Willoughby had anything to do with Flora jilting Lord Waterhouse?" Lydia said. "Perhaps if he met her again before the wedding and they rekindled their romance—" she broke off. "That would not be like Lord Waterhouse, though. He is far too honorable to trifle with a lady's feelings like that." She turned her inquiring gaze back to Lizzie. "Has he confided in you, Lizzie? We are all quite puzzled as to why the wedding was called off."

"He has said nothing to me," Lizzie said. She stared hard into the depths of her lemonade glass. "I have no notion."

"He won't tell Miles or Dexter, either," Alice said. "It is very odd."

"Perhaps," Laura said, "it is Flora who has another beau. I hear she has been walking up near High Top Farm lately, Alice."

Alice laughed. "I have heard that, too. There is not a secret to be kept in this village! Lowell will not talk to me about it, though." She turned to Lydia. "You do not mind, Lydia? I thought at one time that you and Lowell might make a match of it."

Lydia laughed. "You must know that I will not

make a match of it with anyone, Alice! Lowell is a dear friend to me and I value him enormously, but there is nothing more to it, I assure you."

"Well, if Flora is the jilt here at least Lord Waterhouse is not lacking consolation," Alice said, with a sideways glance at Lizzie. "What is Lady Willoughby like, Lizzie?"

"She is rich, widowed, spiteful and *frightfully* beautiful," Lizzie said sharply. "May we talk of something else?" She realized from the arrested look on Alice's face that she had sounded as irritable as she felt and tried to moderate her tone. "I am sorry. I feel preoccupied today. There are only two months left before Monty can take half of the fortunes of any ladies who are still unmarried." She nibbled some of the plum cake and realized with surprise that it was so good that her appetite was coming back. "In addition to the Dames' Tax, Monty is planning to extort ever more greedy and pernicious fees," she added with her mouth full. "I heard him talking to Tom about a tax on chickens. People will have to pay or he will eat their livestock! His avarice is insatiable. We have to do something."

Laura sighed. "I asked Mr. Churchward, my lawyer, to look into this months ago, but he tells me that unfortunately Sir Montague is within his rights. These taxes existed in Fortune's Folly in medieval times and they were never repealed. The only way we could get them annulled is to go to parliament and that would take years."

"He will pocket a cool seventy-five thousand pounds if neither Flora nor Mary nor I marry before the time is up," Lizzie said. "That is bad enough, but it is the other taxes that are more burdensome where people have so little to start with. Mrs. Broad now has to pay a tax on her three chickens or see them in the cooking pot. Monty has already eaten her sheep! She has little income and can barely survive. When I see cases like hers it makes my blood boil!"

"I agree," Alice said. "We must find a medieval law that frees us from the tyranny of Sir Montague! Either that or murder him!"

"I would do it myself, but it would not do any good," Lizzie said, "for Tom would inherit both the baronetcy and the right to inflict his will on us and he is even worse than Monty. I would rather marry ten times over than give half my fortune to Tom!"

They were still laughing when there was the sudden sound of masculine voices and the quick rap of footsteps on the terrace and then Dexter Anstruther, Miles Vickery and Nat Waterhouse came around the side of the house and up the steps to join them. Lizzie's breath caught and her heart did a ridiculous somersault. She realized that Lydia had noticed her reaction, and she looked away hastily, affecting indifference. Except that it was impossible to be indifferent to Nat. He looked so virile and alive, and in his casual sporting attire so dark and handsome. The jacket accentuated the broadness of his shoulders and his trousers clung to his muscular thighs. Lizzie found she was staring—staring at Nat Waterhouse whom she had seen a thousand times before. Her heart somersaulted again and she tried and failed to calm her fluttering pulse.

Nat's gaze sought her out at once. Lizzie could feel him watching her with that long, intense scrutiny that was so disconcerting. She tried very hard to avoid his gaze but the harder she tried the more she found herself drawn back to him.

"Every chaperone's nightmare," Lydia was saying mischievously. "Aren't they handsome, Lizzie, and almost too overwhelming to be allowed out together? Though it is touching to see how devoted Miles and Dexter are to their wives." Lizzie caught the undertone of wistfulness in her voice and for a moment she was distracted from her own feelings. Her heart bled for Lydia, for Tom had never been devoted to anything other than money and his own pleasure and now it was Lydia who was paying the price for that.

"Dexter!" Laura was smiling as she beckoned to the footman to fetch some more chairs. "How charming that you could all join us. Will you take tea—" Her voice dwindled away and in the same instant Lizzie became aware of the curious tension surrounding the men. Alice caught Miles's hand and gave him a questioning look, but Miles shook his head and turned toward Nat. As Nat started to move toward Lizzie she had the terrible conviction that something dreadful had happened. A feeling that was icy-cold and hard formed in her heart. Nat dropped to his haunches beside her and took her hand in his. Lizzie could feel the tension coiled within his powerful frame.

"What is it?" she said, her voice coming out as a whisper from between dry lips.

"It's Sir Montague," Nat said. His tone was very steady and there was tenderness in his eyes and gentleness in his voice that made Lizzie's heart falter. "Lizzie, I am very sorry. He was found murdered this morning. He had been stabbed to death."

There was absolute silence for a moment and then Alice gave a gasp and clapped her hand to her mouth. "We were talking of murdering him just now," she said, "but only in jest!"

Lizzie shook her head. It felt muzzy, as though she was still suffering the effects of too much wine. "Monty dead? Murdered? But who—" She stopped, for even in her shock and horror she could see that it was more a question of who did *not* want Sir Montague dead rather than who did.

Alice came across to her in a rustle of silk and put her arms about her. "Lizzie," she said, "I am so sorry. I know he was a difficult man—"

"He was loathsome and unpleasant and greedy and rude," Lizzie said, her voice a little choked, "but I do not have many relatives and I did not wish to lose him." Her eyes felt hot and hard with unshed tears.

"Damn Monty for getting himself murdered like this!" she said unsteadily. "I would kill him for it if it were not already too late."

Laura pressed a cup of tea into her hands and she gulped it down, feeling the hot strength of it steady her a little. Both her brothers were despicable men, she thought despairingly, but they were all that she had. She might have wanted them to be different, but she had not wanted to be without them. She had lost too much of her family ever to desire it.

"When did it happen?" she asked, looking up at Nat. His dark eyes looked tired, she thought. The lines she had noticed on his face the previous night seemed deeper still, grim and harsh.

"We do not know for sure yet," he said. "Sometime in the night, we think."

"But you will be investigating?" Laura looked at her husband. "Or is it a case for the constable?"

"We're taking it on," Dexter said. He looked at Lizzie. "The Home Secretary has been taking an interest in what has been happening in Fortune's Folly and—" he paused "—forgive me, Lady Elizabeth, but we had already had reason to warn Sir Montague that he might be in danger. A great many people have taken against him as a result of the punitive taxes he has been inflicting."

"He had received letters," Miles put in. "Death threats." His hazel eyes were grave. "Were you aware of this, Lady Elizabeth?"

"No!" Lizzie was shocked. "He said nothing to me," she said. "But then, we did not talk much. He was usually either drunk or asleep."

"We need to ask you some questions, Lizzie," Nat said gently. He released her hand and straightened up and Lizzie felt shockingly bereft. She desperately wanted him to hold her so that she could take comfort from him but knew she could not without showing how much she needed him.

"Of course," she said. "Here? Now?"

"That is up to you," Nat said. "If you were rather it was in private—"

Lizzie looked at Laura and Alice and Lydia. "I would rather have the support of my friends about me," she said, and saw Lydia and Laura smile. Alice squeezed her hand and sat down beside her.

"Tell us what happened last night," Miles said. He glanced at Nat. "We know that you were at the dinner held by Sir James and Lady Wheeler."

"We all were," Lizzie said. "Monty, Tom and I." She glanced unconsciously at Nat, wondering how much he had already told Dexter and Miles.

"Monty was drunk when he came back from dinner last night," she said. "I asked Spencer, his valet, to make him comfortable and then to leave him to sleep it off."

Dexter nodded. "Spencer told us the same. He said that he and the footman between them managed to get Sir Montague up the stairs and onto his bed. They did not attempt to undress him but left him to sleep."

"Did you retire yourself after that?" Miles questioned.

"I did," Lizzie said. She looked at him. "I'm sorry, Miles. I heard nothing. I can't believe—" She stopped. "My room is at the end of the corridor," she said, "so an intruder would not need to pass it to reach Monty's chamber. That is probably why I knew nothing of it." It almost beggared belief, though, that someone had crept along those uneven treads of the landing on their way to stab Sir Montague to death. Lizzie shuddered and felt Nat shift beside her. He was standing by her chair, one hand resting protectively on the back of it. Lizzie wanted to touch him in order to draw strength from him but once again she denied herself the comfort. She knew she could not do it, not without giving her feelings away not only to Nat himself but also to all her friends.

"You did not go to Sir Montague's room this morning?" Miles continued.

"No," Lizzie said. "The door was closed. I did not want to disturb him. It was not unusual for him to sleep until noon or beyond if he had had too much wine the previous night."

Miles nodded. "And Tom?" He asked. "Did he come back with Sir Montague?"

"No," Lizzie said. She flicked a look at Lydia. She did not want to add to her friend's bitterness or misery if she could help it. Although Lydia had no illusions about Tom now, it was quite another thing to talk of his conquests in front of her.

"I do not think Tom came back last night," she said quickly. "I do not know where he was or with whom."

Dexter and Miles exchanged a look. Miles got up and walked across the terrace before turning back. Lizzie felt her nerves tighten further. She could feel the tension in Nat, too, wound tight as a spring.

"The servants," Miles said slowly, "tell us that ten days ago, on the Friday, someone called on Sir Montague late in the evening. They could not tell us who it was but they heard raised voices in the library and thought Sir Montague might be quarreling with someone. Were you present, Lizzie?"

Lizzie closed her eyes for a moment.

Ten days ago, on the Friday night...

She felt Nat shift again and fiercely resisted the urge to look at him. On that Friday night she had been locked in the folly with him, lost to everything but the touch of his hands on her naked skin, the taste of him and the absolute searing need to make love with him...She swallowed hard.

"I know nothing of any visitors," she said carefully. "I am sorry, I cannot help you."

Miles's hazel gaze was very keen on her face and Lizzie could feel herself blushing as though she was guilty of the murder herself.

"But you were at Fortune Hall that night?" Miles said.

"I…" Lizzie hesitated, unwilling to lie. "I was…I saw that Monty had had a visitor because there were two wineglasses on the library table, but…" Again she hesitated, seeing that the more she tried to help the deeper she was digging herself into trouble.

"Lizzie was with me that night," Nat said. He took a deep breath. "She was with me last night as well, before Sir Montague returned home. I can vouch for the fact that after we talked she helped her brother inside the house."

There was a very long silence. Miles looked at Dexter and raised his brows. Laura and Lydia and Alice also looked at each other and then, simultaneously, looked at Lizzie. The atmosphere was suddenly alive with speculation though no one said a single word.

Lizzie bit her lip hard. A wash of panic took her, depriving her of breath, followed by a second wash of fury. She looked at Nat. His expression was dark and unyielding.

"For pity's sake, Nat," she snapped, "there was no necessity for you to say that."

"Did you want me to lie?" Nat snapped back. There was tension in the line of his shoulders and his expression was hard. He met Lizzie's furious gaze with a fierce one of his own. "I don't think you understand, Lizzie," he said. "This isn't a parlor game, it is a murder inquiry. Miles's next question was going to be whether or not you killed your brother."

"Well, not quite," Miles said ruefully. He rubbed a hand over his hair. "May I clarify? Lady Elizabeth—" Suddenly he sounded extremely formal, "I apologize for the necessity of asking you this, but it is very important. Is it correct that you spent these two nights with Lord Waterhouse or is he merely trying to protect you?"

"Damn you, Miles—" Nat sounded absolutely livid. He took a step forward, but Dexter caught his arm.

"Nat," Dexter said, "it seems that you are scarcely objective in this. Keep out of it."

Nat set his jaw. He looked ready to explode, but he kept quiet. He was looking at Lizzie and his expression was dark and hooded, challenging her to deny the truth. Lizzie trembled beneath his gaze.

"To clarify," she said. She cleared her throat. "I was with Lord Waterhouse on both occasions, although not all night."

Miles inclined his head. "Thank you. The two of you were, I take it, alone?"

"We were," Lizzie said. Her gaze slid to Nat's furious face. He had himself under tight control now, but there was a pulse pounding in his cheek. He shook Dexter's hand from his arm. "Lady Elizabeth is going to marry me," he said.

"To clarify," Lizzie said again, angrily, "I am *not*." She looked at Nat. "We have had this conversation, Nat. You proposed. I refused."

Nat swore under his breath. Lizzie sensed rather

than saw the look that flashed between Alice and Laura. She knew that all her friends were absolutely desperate to brush the men aside and to ask her what on earth was going on. Alice knew—and no doubt Laura did, too—that she was in love with Nat. Alice had realized it before Lizzie had herself, and had challenged her about it months before. In fact everyone except Nat himself must know and she could only pray that he remained in ignorance, for she was not sure that her pride could take the blow.

"I am relieving you of your part in this investigation, Nathaniel," Dexter said courteously. "You must see you have a major conflict of interest."

Nat said something very sharp and to the point that made the ladies wince again and stalked over to the edge of the terrace.

"Lady Elizabeth," Dexter said, turning to her, "I don't think we need trouble you any further at the moment. Thank you for being so honest with us."

"I don't think Lord Waterhouse gave me much option," Lizzie said bitterly.

"I will escort you back to Fortune Hall to start making the arrangements for Sir Montague's funeral," Nat said, coming forward.

"No," Lizzie said. The panic clutched at her again. She did not want to be alone with Nat, not now that he had made their association public and would surely use it to press her to marry him. "No, thank you. I would rather do things alone."

This time Nat swore aloud. "For God's sake, Lizzie, must you always reject my help?"

They stood staring at one another as though the others were simply not there.

I cannot, Lizzie thought. I cannot take your help, Nat, I cannot rely on you as I want to, draw comfort from you, trust in you, *love you* as I want to do because it hurts too much. I will always want more than you can give.

She stood looking at him, seeing the puzzlement and the frustration in his face, seeing how much he cared for her and how that very deep concern and protectiveness only served to emphasize that he did not love her as she loved him. The pain of it felt like a red-hot coal against her heart. She had to send him away before he hurt her all the more, unknowing but none the less painful for that.

"Thank you," Lizzie said again, wrenching her gaze from the burning demand of his, "but I would rather be alone."

Nat swore again and walked off and Laura got ponderously to her feet and put a hand on Lizzie's arm. Lizzie knew Laura must be able to feel her shaking.

"Lizzie," Laura said gently, "would you like to come inside out of the sun for a little? You may lie down if you wish, or have a cool drink, perhaps…"

Miles kissed Alice's cheek. "I will see you later, sweetheart," he said. "We must try to find Fortune now."

Lizzie realized with a shock to the heart that he

meant Tom. Now that Monty was dead Tom would be Sir Thomas Fortune. She could think of no one less appropriate to be the squire of Fortune's Folly. Worse, she would not even put it past Tom to have murdered his brother for the title and the potential riches that the Dames' Tax and the other medieval laws would afford him. She shuddered at the thought. Then she saw Lydia's face. It was a tight, white mask of misery. Lizzie felt dreadful. Lydia had been betrayed twice over by Tom. Bad enough for her that Tom had returned to Fortune's Folly and was lording it about the place with his whoring and his gambling and drinking. Now he was Sir Thomas he would be intolerable.

She went across to Lydia and put her arms about her friend. "It will be all right," she whispered, though she hardly believed it herself.

They went into the cool darkness of The Old Palace and Lizzie sank gratefully into one of the chairs in the drawing room. Alice poured her a glass of brandy and brought it over to her, pressing it into her hand.

"I know it is probably the last thing you want," she said with a smile, "particularly if you took too much wine last night, but you probably need it."

Lizzie forced some of the spirit down, recognizing as it bloomed inside her, hot and strong, that she *had* needed it. She shivered and Alice grasped her cold hands in her own.

"Lizzie," she said. "Why do you not want to marry Lord Waterhouse?"

"You don't have to tell us," Lydia hurried to add. "We only want to help you and to be here if you want to talk…"

"And none of us will moralize," Laura said. She looked down ruefully at her hugely swollen belly. "Goodness knows, I shall be producing what the matrons euphemistically call a seven-month baby which we all know was conceived before Dexter and I wed, and Alice was the talk of Fortune's Folly when Miles seduced her—"

"And I am ruined twice over," Lydia finished, "so who are we to criticize? We are the most scandalous ladies in the village."

Lizzie tried to smile. It came out very lopsided. "Nat wants to marry me because he…because we…"

"We guessed that bit," Laura said dryly. "You made love on the night before his wedding to Flora."

"Yes," Lizzie said dully. "We made love."

Except that they had not made love. She knew that now. Oh, she had slept with Nat, had sexual intercourse with him; she had *fornicated* with him, as her old nurse, Mrs. Batty, would probably have put it, in her deeply disapproving way. But she had not made love with him because although she had loved him— and all the terrible hurtful things that he had said to her about wanting him for herself had been so shamefully true—he had not loved her in return.

"I asked Nat to come to me that night because I wanted to talk to him," Lizzie said. "I told myself that I wanted to save him from making a huge mistake in marrying Flora, but the truth was that it was because I loved him and could not bear for him to marry someone else."

"I remember that you were quite vehement on the subject of Lord Waterhouse's betrothal when we discussed it a few months ago at the spa rooms," Alice murmured.

"Then you will also remember that when we spoke of it you told me that if I had feelings for him I should do something about them before it was too late," Lizzie said.

"I scarcely meant that you should seduce him," Alice said wryly. "Perhaps you took me a little too literally."

"Oh, I am not blaming you," Lizzie said hastily. She knitted her fingers together, pressing hard. "I know that this whole affair is no one's fault but my own. Not even Nat's, for I goaded him beyond endurance and provoked him and made him exceptionally angry with my interference and all the time I was pretending that it was for his own good." She sighed. "Anyway, it was a disastrous mistake, for he does not love me." She looked up and saw Alice watching her with nothing but gentleness in her blue eyes, and saw Laura's sympathy and Lydia's kindness and wanted suddenly to cry.

"I am not naive," she said. "I understand that men and women come together for a number of reasons that have nothing to do with love and in our case it was frustration and fury and lust—" She stopped and shrugged a little hopelessly.

"But you do love him," Laura said softly.

"Yes," Lizzie admitted. "I do. I love him so much…" She hesitated. "If you had asked me even two weeks ago I think that I would have denied I loved Nat," she said. "I was trying to fool myself as well as everyone else." She made a brief, impatient gesture. "Oh, it does not matter how I feel! What matters is that for one stupid, deluded moment I thought that Nat might love me, too, but the truth is that he does not, and that is what hurts." She pressed her hand to her heart in an unconscious gesture. "I have been so foolish," she said starkly, "but I will not compound my stupidity by marrying Nat when he does not love me."

"But he cares deeply for you—" Alice began.

"Would you want to be married to Miles if he merely cared for you?" Lizzie said bitterly. "If you loved Miles, adored him as you do, with every fiber of your being, and in return he *cared* for you?" She saw Alice's stricken look and felt terrible. "I'm sorry, Alice," she said remorsefully. "But it would be such an unequal match. It would break my heart each and every day."

"But love can grow," Alice argued.

"And if it does not?" Lizzie said. She thought of her mother again. "What if you wait and wait and that never happens? What then?" She shook her head. "It would be the worst match in the world," she said. "You all know that Nat and I simply would not suit."

No one contradicted her and that, Lizzie thought, rather proved her point.

"So you are saying that Nat has proposed simply out of a sense of honor," Laura said slowly, "and because he cares for you and wants to protect you? That sounds good enough to me."

"I do not deny he is a good man," Lizzie said.

"But you want more than that," Lydia said.

"I do when the whole of the rest of my life is at stake." Lizzie shrugged, uncomfortably aware that Lydia, betrayed by her parents and her lover, would probably feel she had nothing to complain about. "I could not bear it if Nat fell in love with someone else after we wed," she said honestly, "someone like Priscilla Willoughby. Better to lose him now, when he is not truly mine, than to another woman after our marriage."

"But if you were to have a child," Lydia began hesitatingly, her hand resting protectively on her own stomach, "then surely it would be better for it to have a loving father?"

Lizzie felt humbled. There was a huge lump in her throat and a raging anger inside her for her feckless, libertine brother and what he had done to Lydia.

"There won't be a child," she said. "It was only once and anyway I do not feel in the least bit pregnant—" Her voice broke a little.

"Oh, Lizzie," Lydia said, reaching out to her. Lizzie could see pity in her eyes. "Don't be afraid. Everything will be well—"

The fear and the misery fused in Lizzie's chest in one tight, hot ball. She wanted to take comfort from her friends but she did not want them to see her cry. She had always preferred to be alone with her misery, ever since she had been a child.

"Please excuse me," she said. "I must go back to Fortune Hall now. There is so much to be done."

Alice put out a hand. "Would you like me to come with you, Lizzie?"

Lizzie shook her head. "Thank you, but no. I will manage quite well on my own."

As she walked down the path to the water meadows she reflected that she knew what her friends would be thinking. Because Laura and Alice and Lydia knew her well, they would not ascribe her damned independence, as her brother Monty had called it, to snobbery, which many people did. They knew she often chose to be alone because she had been accustomed to solitude since childhood. It had become a habit for her. She preferred it.

She skimmed a stone across the swift flowing waters of the River Tune and thought about Monty's death. He had been the second worst brother in the world, after Tom, but she still wanted to cry for him because she had lost him; lost both the real Monty, weak and worthless, and the brother she had desperately wanted him to be.

She thought of Nat Waterhouse, too, as good a man as Monty Fortune had been a bad one. Many women would settle for what Nat was offering her. She knew that. Many would think her mad, bad and foolish to refuse him simply because the one thing that he could not offer, his love, was the one thing that she wanted most in all the world. Yet when she thought of marrying Nat and the possibility of losing him to another woman, to someone he could love, like Priscilla Willoughby, her blood ran cold. She could not bear the thought. She had seen her mother run mad because her father had withheld his love from her. Society had called Lady Scarlet a bolter, because she had run away from her marriage, disappearing in a perfumed rustle of taffeta and lace to Ireland with her horse-master. She had been condemned as a faithless wife but Lizzie knew it was not love but a lack of it that had caused her mother's downfall. She had seen her mother, day after day, neglected and alone whilst the Earl had pursued his mistresses and his Town entertainments. Lady Scarlet had waited and waited for the Earl to love her and when he had not she had taken second best and run and been damned forever for it, lurching from affair to affair, from men to the brandy bottle, until she died.

So she, Lizzie Scarlet, would not make the mistakes her mother had made. She had sent Nat away now, before it was too late. It hurt to love him and to make herself give him up but that was nothing to how much it would pain her to lose him if they were wed. She would not make Lady Scarlet's mistakes. Not now. Not ever.

CHAPTER EIGHT

DESPITE DEXTER relieving him of any responsibilities in the investigation into Monty Fortune's death, it was Nat who found Tom Fortune that afternoon in an advanced state of inebriation at the Half Moon Inn, some ten miles distant from Fortune's Folly. Nat had not been able to sit idly by whilst his colleagues hunted Monty Fortune's murderer. For Lizzie's sake, if nothing else, he wanted to do whatever he could to help. He had seen her face, stricken and pale, when she had heard the news of Monty's death. He knew how much she was hurting over the loss of her brother, even a brother as feckless as Monty had been. The scoundrel had not deserved a loving sister. It pained Nat that Lizzie would not turn to him in her misery and loss, but he knew that she had always been one to deal with her unhappiness in private. A girl who could also be spectacularly, publicly outrageous, Lizzie was nevertheless one of the most contained people he knew.

The landlady of Half Moon Inn, Josie Simmons, had just thrown Tom bodily into the courtyard when

Nat arrived and Tom was shouting and swearing most horribly as the tapster, Lenny, poured barrels of cold water all over him in an attempt to sober him up. Nat looked down on Tom's drunken and unkempt state and his heart sank. He would as lief leave Lizzie in Tom's care as he would abandon her with a pack of wolves. Yet Tom was her guardian in law now—Sir Thomas Fortune, the squire of Fortune's Folly.

"Take him away and good riddance to him," Josie said as Nat hauled Tom to his feet and told him sharply that they wanted to question him over his brother's death. "He's been bragging all afternoon long about being Sir Thomas now and not a word of sympathy for his dead brother." She rested her huge fists on her hips. "Not that Sir Montague deserves any sympathy, mind," she added. "One's as bad as the other, if truth be told. There's terrible bad blood in that family. Makes me fair grateful we're outside the parish here."

Tom's face had set in a mask of malevolence when he saw Nat. "Well, if it isn't that worthy citizen the Earl of Waterhouse!" he taunted. He grabbed Nat's lapels, almost lurching off his feet in the process, and stuck his face close to Nat's own. His breath reeked of ale and smoke. "Don't forget my money," he slurred, turning Nat's blood cold. "Did you get my letter? I'll broadcast the truth about your sister, Waterhouse, unless you give me the twenty-five grand. I'll go to your father. She's a strumpet, Lady Celeste, and the world deserves to know her perversions."

"I'll get your money," Nat said, through his teeth. He kept a tight grip on his temper. He had hated Tom Fortune long before the man had started to blackmail him over Celeste's indiscretions. He hated Tom for the utter lack of care he had for Lizzie, for his dishonorable treatment of Lydia Cole and the fact that he was an all-round cad. He looked around to see if anyone had overheard Tom's mocking words. He knew Lizzie's brother could hardly be relied on for his discretion. If he spoke out, Celeste would be completely ruined.

"Don't see how you'll get my money now that Flora Minchin has thrown you over," Tom sneered. "Keep away from Mary Wheeler. I have a fancy to wed there myself, though she is probably as frigid as a corpse. But you—" He prodded Nat's chest, "You come up with the goods or Lady Celeste's name will be bandied around through all the coffee shops in England. Men would pay good money to see what I saw. Perhaps they would offer her a job in a whorehouse if your father threw her out—"

Nat repressed a furious urge to hit him. He knew that Tom cared for nothing beyond money and now that he was squire of Fortune's Folly he would be bound to extort all the taxes Sir Montague had charged and more. He would need it, Nat thought, to pay his drinking and gambling bills. And a little extra blackmail, holding the honor of the Dukes of Waterhouse in his hands, was an absolute gift to him.

"Give me one more month," he said. He abhorred giving in to extortion, but with Celeste's reputation at stake and no way out he knew he was trapped.

Tom laughed. "Two weeks," he said. "I'll give you two weeks, seeing as you are begging me. And then—" He laughed again. "I'll go to your father and tell him all about his precious daughter and her sexual proclivities." He put his head on one side. "That could be to your advantage, now I come to think of it. The news might kill the old man and then you'd be Duke of Waterhouse—"

Whatever else he had been about to say was lost as Nat's fist made contact with his jaw and he fell over backward into the ordure from the stables. Josie and Lenny and half the occupants of the taproom, whom Nat was appalled to see had come out into the yard to watch the altercation, burst into a spontaneous round of applause.

"Nice one, Lord W," Josie said. She lowered her voice. "Can't pretend I didn't hear about your sister, though. I'd kill him, if I was you. Never give in to blackmailers. That's my motto. Kill 'em instead." She slapped him on the shoulder in a blow Nat assumed was intended as encouragement and helped Lenny haul Tom back to his feet.

"You're barred from Half Moon House," she hissed to Tom. "I hope they convict you of your brother's murder. I don't care if you did it or not."

Nat was of a similar mind himself. He was so

blinded with impotent fury that it seemed the greatest pity to him in that moment that they had not been able to pin a single crime on Tom Fortune and rid the world of him, justice or no justice.

"Present yourself to the magistrate tomorrow morning or we'll come looking for you," he said to Tom, who now smelled of dung along with the drink and smoke. He ducked out of the way just in time as Tom tried to spit in his face.

From the Half Moon Inn Nat went to seek out Miles Vickery to report Tom's whereabouts. As he rode he thought about what Tom had said.

"I'll go to your father. She's a strumpet, Lady Celeste, and the world deserves to know her perversions…"

Celeste had always been so gentle and frail. Nat still did not know what terrible error of judgment had put his younger sister in Tom Fortune's power, for when he had tried to ask her about it she had broken down and he had feared for her sanity. He had known then that he had no choice other than to agree to Tom's extortion, for it was unthinkable for the truth about Celeste to be revealed. Not only would it ruin her, but the scandal would almost certainly kill his father, who was old and infirm, and would devastate his mother. His entire family would be destroyed because of Tom Fortune's greed. The only other alternative was to kill the man and Nat was very, very tempted. Tom Fortune was vermin, a blight on mankind. If it were not for Lizzie, Nat would have been even closer to murdering him, but he knew that for Lizzie's sake he could never do it. She had the same desperate regard for Tom as she had had for Monty, an affection that was immune to sense or reason, a desperate need for family. Nat's heart ached for Lizzie that she so longed to have about her a family she could love when all she was left with was Tom, who was an utter bastard, and a distant cousin who did not give a rush for her. It seemed monstrous unfair.

As it was, Lizzie was the one who would rescue them all. She did not know it, but she would save him and Celeste and his family. Nat's only hope now was to marry her. Lizzie's money would buy Tom's silence. There was some irony in that, Nat thought. But Lizzie must never, ever know about Tom's blackmail. Nat knew he had to protect her from this latest proof of Tom's villainy. Monty's death had hurt her profoundly. To show that her other brother was even more of a criminal than she suspected would devastate and disillusion her.

Nat rode into the stable yard of Drum Castle, left his horse with the groom and sought Miles out in his study. Although Miles was no longer Marquis of Drummond now that his errant cousin had been found still to be alive, he and Alice had taken a lease on the castle in order to stay in Yorkshire.

When Nat went into the study, Miles and Alice were standing in the window together and talking, their heads bent close, their voices low and intimate. Nat hesitated a moment on the threshold, because they looked so loving that he felt like an interloper and did not wish to interrupt them. But then Miles looked up and invited him in. Nat stepped forward into the room and noted wryly that Alice's blue gaze was flinty and less than welcoming as it rested on him. He knew she was thinking of Lizzie.

"Lord Waterhouse." Alice's tone was almost as cold as the look in her eyes. She looked from Nat to Miles. "I will leave you to talk business," she said.

"Lady Vickery," Nat said. "Please…" Alice paused and Nat pressed his advantage. "You know that I wish to marry Lady Elizabeth," he said. "If you have any influence with her…"

He thought Alice almost smiled. "You know as well as I do that no one can influence Lizzie once she has set her mind to a thing," Alice said. Her voice softened. "I wish you good luck, though."

She went out and Miles gestured Nat to a seat beside the fireplace. There was a fine carved wooden chess set on the games table between the two fireside chairs. The room was warm and smelled of beeswax and flowers. It felt like a home, Nat thought, remembering the cold emptiness of Drum before Alice had married Miles. Alice had wrought that change in the castle, and an enormous change in Miles, too. Marriage, Nat supposed, could be like that but it was a far cry from both the cold distance of the arrangement he had contemplated with Flora and the fiery quarreling he was already anticipating with Lizzie.

"I found Tom," Nat said, without preamble. "I've told him to report to the magistrate and to you and Dexter in the morning. He's too drunk to talk sensibly now." He sighed. "Not that he is likely to be much more sober on the morrow."

"Do you think he murdered his brother?" Miles asked.

"No," Nat said. "Unfortunately not."

"He had a strong motive," Miles pointed out. "The baronetcy, the prospect of wealth under the Dames' Tax. Everyone knows that Monty kept Tom on a tight allowance and Tom hated him for it."

"Too many people had a motive to kill Sir Montague," Nat said, shrugging, "though I will allow that Tom's is one of the best. I imagine," he added, "that he will be able to claim he was with someone last night."

"A woman," Miles said, nodding.

"Or several," Nat said, ironically. He sighed. "Lady Elizabeth's motive is less strong."

"I don't need you to tell me that," Miles said, laughing. "In point of fact she was better off with Sir Montague alive."

"Quite." Nat shifted. " Miles, I have a problem. You know that Lizzie is only twenty and therefore requires her guardian's permission to wed?"

Miles nodded. "And her legal guardian is now Tom Fortune."

"Precisely," Nat said. "Tom will never give his consent, because he would thereby lose out on claiming half of Lizzie's fortune under the Dames' Tax. In two months' time he can take her twenty-five thousand pounds."

Miles grimaced. "I see your problem."

"What can be done?"

"You could elope with her to Gretna," Miles said, "or apply for a special licence and swear on oath that the guardian had given his consent, knowing full well that he had not."

"I would have to perjure myself," Nat said, nodding.

"Effectively, yes." Miles moved a chess piece idly. "Or, if the guardian was clearly a man—or woman— of dubious moral stature, you might find another reputable family member who could give their consent." He shot his friend a look. "In Lizzie's case we know that her guardian is a blackguard, but she also has an irreproachably respectable third cousin in the current Earl of Scarlet."

"A man who has taken not the slightest interest in her welfare since he inherited from her father," Nat said a little grimly.

"He would take an interest soon enough if he heard his cousin would one day be Duchess of Waterhouse," Miles said, "and he would, I am sure, do all in his power to assist the match."

Nat smiled reluctantly. "You are so cynical, old chap."

"But also so very correct," Miles drawled. "Scarlet Park is less than a half day's ride to the west of here," he added. "It would be a simple matter to sound Gregory Scarlet out."

Nat shifted. "One further complicating factor…If I cannot persuade Lizzie to accept me…"

Miles laughed. "I suspect I should be offended that you think me the expert, albeit theoretically, on the carrying off of unwilling brides."

"I remember you once contemplated carrying Alice off," Nat murmured, "before you resorted to blackmailing her into marriage, of course."

"Touché," Miles said. "Abduction is the answer. You would also need to bribe a crooked clergyman. Not ideal, especially for one of your rarefied moral principles," he added sardonically, "but it depends on how much you want the prize."

There was a short silence. "I want the money," Nat said, after a moment. "I need it very urgently." He had toyed on more than one occasion with the idea of telling Miles and Dexter of his predicament, but in the end he had kept silent because he knew that both of them would advise him to tell Tom to go to hell and take his blackmail with him. They could not approve—how could they when they all worked for the Home Secretary to protect against criminal activity and he was contradicting every principle that they held sacred? Yet moral dilemmas were seldom so easy to resolve, Nat thought bitterly. He appreciated that now.

"You want the money but not the bride who goes with it?" Miles's expression was suddenly sober. "My advice? Don't do it, old fellow. A lifetime is a hell of a long time to be tied to a woman whom you don't love."

"The ultimate irony," Nat said, "is that you, the most cynical amongst us, are always preaching to marry for love, Miles."

Miles shrugged elegantly. "What can I say? I am a convert."

"I care for Lizzie," Nat said slowly. "I may not love her the way that you love Alice, but I care a damn sight more than Tom Fortune does for her as a sister. Is that so bad?"

He saw some expression change in Miles's face. "I cannot answer that, Nathaniel," Miles said slowly. "Only you and Lady Elizabeth can resolve that between you and I think you have already made up your mind." He stood up and Nat had the strangest feeling that Miles not only knew something that he did not but also that he had, in some way, disappointed his oldest friend. He struggled with the thought. In his day Miles had been the most ruthless of fortune hunters, prepared to take risks that Nat would never contemplate. Miles was no hypocrite, so why would he disapprove of Nat marrying for money?

Miles held out his hand to shake in an oddly formal gesture. "Good luck, old fellow."

"Thank you," Nat said, taking his hand and wishing he did not have a strange and superstitious belief that Miles thought he would need all the luck in the world—and more—to get him through.

IT WAS VERY LATE the following day that Nat rode up to Fortune Hall. He had been to Lancashire and spent some time with the Earl of Scarlet, a meeting that had been congenial and had ended in a most satisfactory outcome as far as Nat was concerned. He did not like the man particularly—Gregory Scarlet was selfish and lazy and self-interested—but the Earl had agreed that Tom Fortune was not fit to be any young lady's guardian and had been pleased to give his consent to a match between Nat and Lizzie. Now all Nat had to do was obtain Lizzie's consent, a task he was all too aware was of far greater difficulty and complexity.

As Nat approached Fortune Hall he wished that he had not been away for quite so long. He had felt uncomfortable leaving Lizzie to make the arrangements for Sir Montague's funeral on her own—for Tom would hardly have put himself out to help—and he felt even less happy at leaving her at Tom's mercy. As he rode up to the house his fear for Lizzie increased, for he could see the main door flung wide and the candles blazing in every room. Something was clearly afoot. Shadowy figures moved behind the windows. Nat wondered for a moment whether Tom's finances were so parlous that the bailiffs had already moved in to take everything, and then he heard the music and voices and laughter and realized that this was no house clearance and nor was it a wake for Sir Montague, either. It was a party. Tom was celebrating his brother's death and his inheritance of the baronetcy and the estate. Tom, the ultimate hedonist, was dancing on his brother's grave.

Lizzie. Nat's heart contracted. He could hardly bear to think how Lizzie would fare alone and unprotected whilst her brother caroused with his drinking cronies. God knew, Tom Fortune was capable of any degraded and degrading thing imaginable, but would he involve his own sister in his amoral games? Perhaps he would if the price was right…

Nat dug his heels into the horse's side and galloped the remainder of the way up the drive. He swung down out of the saddle and strode into the hallway, almost stumbling over one drunkard who lay insensible and muttering to himself in a heap at the bottom of the stairs. There was a goblet lying near him on the flagstones and red wine spilling out of it across the floor. Remembering Sir Montague's attachment to his wine cellars, Nat wondered whether there was anything left or if it was all gone already.

Where was Lizzie?

The anxiety tightened within him.

In the great hall he found even more bacchanalian

pleasures and the remains of a feast scattered over both the table and the floor, empty bottles rolling, and one of Lizzie's dogs in a corner gnawing on a chicken carcass. A couple were fornicating noisily on the shiny surface of the long dinner table, the man's boots gouging deep scratches into the wood, and in front of the window a rowdy group of men were enthusiastically taking turns with a woman who was spread-eagled over the back of a sofa. Her breasts had escaped from her loose bodice; her skirts and petticoats were hitched up to reveal a pink garter, rounded thighs and plump buttocks. Nat paused, recognizing Ethel, the barmaid at the Morris Clown Inn, though he had never seen her in quite this position before. No, he thought, after a moment as he took in her dizzily blissful expression, Ethel did not require his aid in any shape or form. She was having as good a time as her partners.

Another man took his turn with Ethel, tumbling her over so that he could take her a different way and the girl screamed in pleasure. Nat moved on, stepping over the prone bodies of yet more drunks, avoiding a man who was being sick in the fireplace, looking for Tom, *looking for Lizzie…*

The fear he felt for her transcended every other emotion. This was like a scene from hell, so much worse than anything he had imagined. How could he have left her with this?

He went out into the hall again and caught a

glimpse of a blond woman whisking through a doorway and out of sight. She was patting into place a sky-blue gown and the back of her head looked vaguely familiar. Dismissing the thought, Nat opened the door of the room she had vacated and found Tom Fortune in his brother's study, lying back in a chair, booted feet up on the desk, pantaloons unfastened, a wine bottle in one hand, papers and books scattered about him. He had evidently been enjoying both the attentions of the woman and the contents of the bottle very recently. He raised the wine to his lips, took a long swallow and then wiped his mouth carelessly on his sleeve. His gaze was both inebriated and insolent as it rested on Nat.

"Delicious," he drawled. There was humor deep in his eyes. "You have no idea, Waterhouse…"

"Where's Lizzie?" Nat demanded, grabbing Tom by his cravat and pulling him up out of the chair. "Where is she?"

"What do you want with her?" Tom slurred. "My property, my business."

"I've come to take her away," Nat said. "I'm going to marry her." He watched Tom's face crumple with shock and anger.

"You?" Tom said. "Damned if you will. You won't cheat me out of her money." His eyes narrowed. "Lizzie is not yet one and twenty and I'm her guardian. Rich, isn't it?" Suddenly he laughed uproariously. "She cannot wed without my permission and I refuse it."

"I thought of that," Nat said steadily. He patted his pocket. "Gregory Scarlet supersedes you. I have his written agreement. No one will quarrel with that, I think."

Tom's face twisted into a mask of malice and hatred. "Bastard!" he hissed. "I'll see you damned. If you don't pay me—"

"You'll get your blackmail money," Nat said, "as soon as I can borrow on the promise of Lizzie's fortune."

For a moment he thought Tom was going to hit him, but then Tom shrugged, reaching for the bottle again. "Take her, then," he said indifferently. "What's left of her." He glanced at the clock. "Thought I'd let some of my friends have a turn with her. They were hot to bed her and I thought it was a good idea. Thought that no one was likely to want to wed her after they had all ploughed her, so I'd get to keep all her money. Even you might think twice, Waterhouse." Once again his gaze was a narrow, malicious gleam. "Other men's leavings… How much do you want that money?"

Nat threw him violently back into his chair but Tom's laughter followed him out of the room. Terror gripped Nat's heart. He took the stairs two at a time, slipping on the uneven oak treads, praying that he was not too late. He turned a dark corner and tripped over an entwined pair of lovers on the floor. Another blond woman… Not Lizzie, thank God.

"Lizzie!" he yelled. Someone swore at him.

"Lizzie!" He could hear the ragged fear in his own voice.

He tried a door. It was locked. He hammered on it. Several voices howled at him to go away. He steadied himself to break it down and then—

"Nat." Lizzie's voice, behind him. He turned and saw her standing in the pool of light from her bedroom. She was in her nightgown and the light shone through the transparent lawn of the material and illuminated her, hollows, curves and shadows, in a gentle glow. Her auburn hair was down and flamed in the candlelight. Nat's mouth dried at the sight. He thought that if any of those jaded libertines even caught a glimpse of her they would die to have her.

"Tally ho!" Sir Wilfred Hooper, the magistrate from the next parish, was galloping down the landing brandishing a hunting crop as he chased a couple of squealing women. He paused when he saw Lizzie and his mouth dropped open. "I say!" he spluttered.

Nat grabbed Lizzie's arm and bundled her into her bedroom, locking the door behind them.

"I say, Waterhouse," Sir Wilfred said plaintively, banging on the other side of the thick oak panels, "share and share alike!"

"I'm sorry," Lizzie was saying, grabbing a robe from the bed and flinging it about her shoulders, "I did not hear you calling me, Nat. If I had known you were here I would have let you in sooner."

She scrambled back onto the bed and tucked her feet under the covers. Perched there in her swansdown-trimmed robe, with her hair falling loose about her shoulders she looked young, like a child in a fairy tale. Nat started to wonder if he was in a dream rather than an orgy. Everything that was happening seemed so unreal. Then he saw the pistol on Lizzie's nightstand and saw that she was shivering and shaking like a dog left out in the rain. It was real enough; hateful, intolerable for her to be subjected to Tom's loathsome whims like this.

Lizzie followed his gaze. "I judged it better to be safe than sorry," she said. "I thought that if anyone tried to break in and rape me—" For a moment she looked so lost that Nat's heart seemed to skip a beat. She turned her head and in the candlelight he saw the marks of tears on her cheeks.

"Lizzie," he said. He sat down on the end of the bed. "What happened?"

She shrugged her slight shoulders under the robe. "Tonight? Just one of Tom's orgies." She met his gaze and sighed. "He did not come back until an hour ago. I had already retired." She gestured to her nightclothes. "As you see."

"Have you been locked in here all the time?" Nat asked. He tried to keep a grip on his temper. Every primitive impulse he had was directed on going back downstairs and tearing Tom Fortune apart, but every protective one he possessed forced him to stay with Lizzie.

"I went down to speak to Tom when he first returned," Lizzie said. Her head was bent, her hair falling forward in a thick curtain to hide her face. "So stupid of me, but he was alone at first and I was tired and not thinking straight and I wanted to consult him about Monty's burial. I did not realize he had invited all his cronies to join him—" She stopped, shuddering a little. "When I saw that he was drunk I asked him to show a little respect with Monty's body still lying next door." She shuddered again. "He said that Monty could rot in there for all he cared and then he—" She gulped. "He…"

Nat grabbed her hand. "What, Lizzie?"

"He killed Mrs. Broad's chicken and threw it on the fire!" Lizzie wailed. "He said he had brought it in lieu of payment of tax and it was just the first of many fines he was going to inflict now he was squire and he might as well cook and eat it there and then!" She gulped in a breath, the tears shining on her cheeks again. "I hate him!" she said vehemently.

Nat drew her into his arms and stroked her back as she cried against his coat.

"Then he said he was going to hire me out—whore me out was the phrase he used—to his friends," Lizzie finished, muffled. "He said he wanted all my money, so he had to be sure no one wished to marry me so they might as well make use of me. I ran up here and grabbed my pistol and barricaded the door. They came for me," she added, "but they couldn't get in and soon they got bored and turned to easier game."

"Christ, Lizzie…" Nat pressed his lips to her hair. He was shaking with rage and with despair that she had had to suffer this. "He's mad," he said. "He has lost his mind."

"Tom always was unstable," Lizzie said. She was shaking, too. Nat could feel it as she lay in the curve of his arms.

"But this…" Nat soothed her, stroking his hands up over her gently. "He needs to be locked up."

"He has not done anything illegal," Lizzie said. "Not yet."

Nat shifted. "You said that this was just one of Tom's orgies," he said. "Those were the words you used. Has he then done this before?"

"Not like this," Lizzie said. She fidgeted, playing with the buttons on his jacket. "We all know Tom's proclivities," she said. "We all know he ruined Lydia twice over and she was hardly the first. Oh, he would bring women back here sometimes. So would Monty. I saw things…heard things. But not like this. It was never as blatant as this before."

"You never said." Nat was appalled. He had known Montague and Tom Fortune for years because his family lands had run with theirs, but he had never realized the scandalous truth of what went on at

Fortune Hall. He felt obscurely ashamed now that he had not known about it or prevented it from touching Lizzie's life.

"It must have been shocking for you," he said.

Lizzie shrugged again. Her face was averted from his. "I was not naive, Nat. Not in that sense. When Mama ran away I knew exactly what she had done to earn her disgrace. People made sure that I knew all about her trysts in the stables. They told me so that I could be ashamed of her. And Papa…" Her mouth drooped, a beautiful curve. "Well, he was the most loving papa to me, but I understood about his mistresses. I heard things and saw things at Scarlet Park, you know."

Nat stared at her wordlessly. His own introduction to the world of physical pleasure had been the straightforward one that, he imagined, was the experience of many youths of his class and generation. A willing courtesan or two, then various eager widows of whom Lady Ainsworth, the mistress Lizzie had mentioned that night in the folly, had been the most prominent. It was a world away from Lizzie's vicarious, furtive and confusing experience of sex. Her true innocence had been stolen years before their night in the folly.

"I am so sorry it was like that for you," he said.

She shrugged again. "I loved living at Scarlet Park," she said. "It was warm and opulent and as I said, Papa doted on me. Until I was older I did not realize that not all men keep their mistresses accommodated openly in their homes. It seemed quite natural to me. Although sometimes I think Papa forgot I was there so I did see more than I ought..." She sighed. "And whilst Monty was alive I could bear living here. At least he had some sense of common decency—until recently. Tom has none."

"No," Nat said. The whooping outside the door grew louder, accompanied by the sound of the riding crop raining down on some eager person's bare rump. "I have to get you out of here," he added, "but I doubt we can go now or we shall probably both be overpowered and ravished indiscriminately, even with your pistol to protect us. We will have to wait until they drink and fornicate themselves into a stupor and then we shall be able to slip away."

Lizzie looked at him. "You want me to leave with you?"

Nat held her gaze. "You cannot stay here, Lizzie," he said. "Not now. It is impossible for you to live at Fortune Hall whilst Tom is here behaving like this."

Lizzie's shoulders slumped. "I suppose so," she said. "Damn him." She looked up, an angry spark in her eyes. "I will go and stay with Alice and Miles until Tom drinks himself to death."

"A charming solution," Nat said, "but sadly, one that might take some time." He shook his head. "Alice and Miles are too much in love to wish for a permanent houseguest. You would be better off married to me."

Lizzie was silent for a moment, but when she looked at him there was a spark of amusement in her green eyes that reminded him of the way things had once been between them before it all became so intolerably complicated.

"How neatly you have maneuvered me," she said lightly, "until I can see I have no choice." She sat up, out of his arms. "I don't have a choice, do I, Nat?"

"No," Nat said. "Not anymore. You owe me fifty thousand pounds," he added, "and I know you always pay your debts."

He saw her fingers pause in their fidgety pleating of the bedspread. She looked at him, head on one side. There was a different glint in her eyes now. She was surprised and a little taken aback. She had not been expecting this. Lizzie was accustomed to seeing the gentler side of him. Normally he kept the iron fist for his work and she saw the velvet glove. Not anymore.

"How so?" she said.

"I called off my marriage to Flora because of what happened between us," Nat said. "I lost her fortune. So now I am claiming yours in its place."

She chewed her lip. "I see. And what is in this arrangement for me?"

"You escape your brother," Nat said, "and thwart his plans to steal your money."

"So that you can steal it in his place?" She was cool, noncommittal.

"It's the best offer you'll get," Nat said. "I'm tired of being nice about this, Lizzie."

She gave him another sideways look from those slanted green eyes. He could see that his determination had intrigued her rather than repelled her. It excited her and appealed to the wilder side of her nature. Suddenly, violently, he wanted to kiss her. Tom's orgy, whilst repellent in some respects, had, inevitably, aroused him and he did not resist the impulse. He took her by the shoulders, feeling the slippery slide of the swansdown wrap beneath his fingers and beneath that the slenderness of her. He laid his mouth against hers. She felt cool and sweet and her skin smelled of roses. Nat took a gentle handful of her hair and buried his face in it, inhaling the scent. It was soft, slipping in sleek threads through his fingers, catching against his lips like silken bonds. He raised his head and kissed her again and this time her lips parted against his and the hunger roared through him and he kissed her deeply, searchingly, desire leaping to further desire, and she reached for him and drew him down onto the bed beside her, her hands moving over him, encouraging him out of his clothes even as she kissed him with a feverish need.

"I want you," she whispered and the robe slipped from her and Nat pressed his lips to the hollow at her throat and to the freckles that dusted her shoulders. He pushed down her nightgown and saw that she had freckles scattered across the swell of her breasts as well and for some reason that excited him beyond measure as he lowered his head to lick and kiss them and she writhed beneath the caress of his mouth and tongue.

He had shed his jacket and now she was tugging at his shirt so that she could slide her hands beneath it and touch his naked skin. She was wild, insatiable, nipping and kissing him, running her fingers over him in blatant curiosity, her nightgown long gone, her alabaster-white skin stung pink with passion and the effect of his kisses. He was enormously aroused, even more so as Lizzie's hand closed about his erection, as curious and questing as she had been in her exploration of the rest of his body.

"Not now. Not this time…" He knew if she touched him he would explode and he did not want that. Not this time. Later there would be time for her to learn and discover and for him to study every inch of her.

When they were married he would keep her in his bed until they were both sated.

The thought almost sent him straight over the edge.

He eased back a little and ran his hands down the length of her naked body, over the curve of her breasts and the gentle swell of her stomach and the glorious arch of her hips. She felt soft beneath his hands, delicate and yet with a core of strength that he knew would never break. He cupped her small breasts, holding them up so that his lips and tongue could plunder and ravish them, and he heard her moan. His hands slid to her waist, then down again in greedy demand over her hips and thighs and he pushed her legs apart, readying her.

And then he felt her pause and go very still.

The hesitation in her, the fear he suddenly sensed, cut through his arousal like a knife. He drew back. She lay spread beneath him, tumbled and abandoned, her body utterly open to him in the pale flare of the candlelight. Her limbs were pale golden in the light except for where the touch of his mouth had nipped her skin to pink. The soft hair at the juncture of her thighs was even more defiantly red than the cloud of auburn that swathed her shoulders. She lay completely, strikingly still, not even pressing her thighs together to hide the petals of her sex that were so blatantly, temptingly exposed to him. Nat swallowed hard and forced his gaze to her face. The dizzy, unfocused, sensual look had fled from her eyes leaving something that looked like apprehension and alarm.

Understanding swept through him and with it a deep tenderness. The last time—*her first time*—had been fierce and mindless and intense. They had both been lost in the experience at the time but now, perhaps, Lizzie was afraid remembering the mutual violence and greed of their encounter. She had no comparisons to make, no experience on which to

draw. He had to make it good for her and show her
that making love was not always like that.

"Lizzie." He gathered her to him, feeling the slick
heat and the smoothness of her body, trying to ignore
the arousing effect of her nipples pressing against his
chest and the hot, sweet nakedness of her in his arms.
He stroked her hair. "Don't be afraid," he whispered.
"I didn't think last time, but now I will be gentle, I
swear it. I won't hurt you."

He felt her shiver a little but he kept up the
rhythmic, soothing stroke of her hair and after a few
moments he felt her body shift a little and relax
against his; a change came over her, the tension
seemed to flow out of her leaving her feeling warm
and soft and acquiescent. He drew back to look at her
face and saw that her eyes were closed now. Her
head rested against his shoulder and her hair spilled
over his chest. Her lips were parted and her breath
was coming a little more quickly now. Nat kissed her
gently and felt her response with a kick through the
blood that rearoused him in one second flat. He laid
her back against the pillows and feathered kisses
over her face and neck, working his way down her
body with a light, teasing touch that soon had her
squirming restlessly on the covers and reaching for
him again. He evaded her. He wanted her to be so
dazed with desire this time that she was aware of
nothing but their mutual need. He swirled his tongue
in her belly button and pressed a stealthy kiss in the

sweet curve of her hip and another against her inner thigh. Her legs fell apart again irresistibly to the slide of his fingers and the glide of his lips. He could smell her scent and it almost drove him wild with longing but he held himself back, using his tongue on her very core, stroking, caressing, thrusting, blowing softly on her damp flesh, teasing her with tantalizing promise as he led her to the very edge of pleasure and then drew back. He watched her reactions, saw her entire body start to glow and burn up with sensual heat as he drove her closer and closer, then he sucked on her, gentle, harder, alternating the sensations as she hung helplessly at his mercy, as her hips twitched and she desperately searched for the surcease he kept just beyond her grasp. Her hands came down to pull his hair and force his tongue deep inside her and her hips arched and she gave a scream of pure, keening pleasure and fell sharp and fast into her climax.

After that there was no restraining her. She grabbed his shoulders, scored his back with her fingernails and dug her fingers into his buttocks as she pulled him inside her. He could feel the pulse of her climax still shaking her body and it almost destroyed his resolve but still he fought for control. He obliged her with a couple of inches and no more, and she swore at him in so unmaidenly a fashion that he would have laughed had he not been so desperate himself. He moved into her with infinite slowness and unhurried strokes until her silken walls gripped him even tighter and he knew that she was going to climax again and then he, too, was lost in a maelstrom of sensation as the pleasure crashed through him and everything was swept away.

LIZZIE LAY AWAKE IN Nat's arms, her eyes open wide, her gaze following the shift and dance of the shadows on the wall. The house was silent. Tom's cronies must finally have drunk themselves into oblivion.

Nat was asleep. Lizzie turned slightly in order to look at him and felt him shift and draw her closer against his body. The sight of him defenseless in sleep made her heart feel hollow with love and tenderness. He held her gently and the solid warmth of his body against hers should have comforted her but oddly it only made her feel more alone. The tears pricked her eyes.

Once could have been considered a mistake, Lizzie thought. Twice was not so easy to explain away. She must at least be honest with herself and admit that she had made love with Nat because she had wanted him. In her grief over Sir Montague's death and all the memories it had unlocked for her, she had turned to Nat utterly as a means to block out the pain of the present and the uncertainty of the future. But then, in the moment when he had been about to take her, she had not been able to deceive herself any longer. She had remembered that Nat did not love her and she had drawn back, suddenly acutely aware that if she gave herself to him again, with all the love that was in her, it would only make her feel more cheated and hollow that he did not love her in return.

Nat had misunderstood, of course. He had assumed that she was nervous because the only previous time that they had made love it had been wild and elemental and violent in its feral intensity. He had thought that she was fearful of being hurt. It was an understandable mistake to make—it was gentle and generous of him—and she had not corrected him, for what could she say?

I am fearful because I know you do not love me as I love you and I am afraid that if I respond to you with everything in my heart you will see my love and see me in all my terrifying vulnerability....

She could not bear to expose that to him. Far easier to expose her body physically than to strip her feelings naked and tell Nat the truth. So she had pretended that she was scared and she had allowed him to lull her with his kisses and caresses, she had closed her mind and simply allowed her body to feel, and it had been magical and deeply pleasurable and yet at the end, even as her body ached with satisfaction, she was left feeling empty and wanting to cry. She did not want to feel so sad, so distant from Nat, but even as she sought the warmth of his body she felt her soul move further from him.

She would marry Nat now, of course. He had

spelled the matter out to her in brutal detail. He needed her money and in return he would give her protection against Tom's vicious, dangerous ways, the threat that Tom had demonstrated so clearly tonight. Oddly this bargain, with no emotion on either side, was more comfortable to her than any arguments about pregnancy or honor or reputation. It was a business arrangement now, pure and simple. Or—Lizzie looked down at their naked, entwined bodies—not so pure, perhaps. It was a business arrangement with insatiable lust as the sweetener, if only until they tired of one another.

Just for a moment she panicked because she knew in her heart of hearts that this was not what she wanted from Nat. She thought about escaping, about running away from Nat and the agreement they had tacitly made. She eased a little way out of his grip, putting her thoughts into action before they were even properly formed. Running away was a habit with her, after all. But then Nat's hand snaked out and clamped about her wrist and she saw in the moonlight that his eyes were wide and steady and fixed on her face.

"Running from me again?" His tone was pleasant but brooked no argument. "You have made your bed, Lizzie, and now you must lie in it with me."

As he spoke he was drawing her beneath him, pinning her with his body above and against hers, and Lizzie felt her bewitched and traitorous senses start to spin even before his lips came down on hers with renewed need and painful desire. He was hard for her again and the knowledge filled her with a wicked sense of power. She did not need to think about the things Nat could *not* give her. She knew now how much he wanted her and how much it tormented him. That would have to be enough. She could feel the edge of desperation in his touch—it seemed that as such a restrained and controlled man he could not quite believe what she could do to him. When he slid into her he groaned aloud and devoured her as though his very life was in her hands. Lizzie let the delicious sensations of mutual ravishment fill her and take her but as Nat came, racked by spasm after spasm, she held him and thought again, *It is enough.*

It would have to be enough.

PART TWO

CHAPTER NINE

July—2 weeks later

FLORA WAS OUT OF BREATH as she approached High Top Farm. She was nervous and she also felt hot and flustered, for the night was humid and the air itself seemed too thick to breathe. The last shreds of twilight were fading from the night sky and no moon or stars showed. Away on the horizon there was a flicker of lightning.

Flora shivered. Only the direst necessity could have prompted her to come out alone at night, especially on a night like this when there was something strange and elemental in the air. She had been to High Top three times since the day of her canceled wedding a month ago. On the first occasion she had hidden from sight and had watched Lowell working in the fields. He had glanced in her direction on more than one occasion and she had had a lowering feeling that he knew she was there, but he had not broken off his work to come over and speak with her. On the second occasion they had had a short conversation and she had pretended that she was passing during a walk on the hills. She had known that Lowell had not believed her even though he had not challenged her and she had blushed extremely red.

On the third occasion he had told her bluntly not to call again.

Flora paused by the five-barred gate that led into the farmyard. Lights showed in the kitchen. She had seen the interior of the farmhouse on her last visit, when Lowell had drawn her aside from the curious eyes of his farmhands and had then proceeded to tell her in no uncertain terms that she was not welcome at High Top. The kitchen had been exactly as she would have imagined it; neat, clean, functional and lacking the feminine touch. She had longed to pick a posy of summer wildflowers to soften the bare acreage of the wooden table. She had felt strange when she had realized that she had never been in a kitchen before. At home it was the realm of the servants and her mother had never permitted her to visit there.

The gate opened silently to her touch for it was well oiled. She would expect that from Lowell Lister for he kept his farm running smoothly and efficiently. Flora found that she was tiptoeing toward the door, trying to avoid making any sound, and that struck her as amusing for in a moment she would knock—assuming that her hands did not shake too much—and would alert Lowell to the fact that she was there, and then she would have to explain… The nervousness pressed on her chest again, making her catch her breath.

He would think her mad.

He would think her desperate, which she was.

Several dogs barked loudly inside the house and suddenly the door was thrown wide and they streaked out into the yard, circling and barking aggressively. Flora gave a little scream. She did not like dogs. They frightened her.

"Meg, Rowan, here to me!" Lowell's sharp command subdued them and they slunk back to his side with a wary eye still on the interloper. For that was what she was, Flora thought. She did not belong here.

"Miss Minchin?" There was incredulity in Lowell's voice as he held up the lantern and the light fell on her face and pooled around her. "What the devil are you doing here at this hour?" His tone quickened. "Has there been an accident? Is something wrong?"

"No," Flora's teeth were chattering. "I needed to see you."

Lowell looked exasperated. "Miss Minchin… Flora, this is ridiculous. I told you last time. You must not come here."

"Well, I *am* here," Flora said, with more bravado than she was feeling, "and I am not going until you hear me out."

They stared at one another for a long moment whilst the dogs circled and growled and then Lowell gave a frustrated sigh and stood aside to permit her to precede him into the house. He did not invite her to sit down. The dogs slunk off back to their box.

Flora wrapped her arms about her as she stood in the neat little kitchen. There were the remnants of a meal of bread and cheese on the table and a pitcher of ale. She wondered how much Lowell had drunk. Not enough to make him receptive to her suggestions, she thought. He looked all too sober, standing there with a mixture of anger and resignation in his eyes, running one hand impatiently over his tawny fair hair as he waited for her to speak.

"I know what you are thinking," she said suddenly. "You think that I am here because I have developed a *tendre* for you and now I am following you around in a most embarrassing way."

"Haven't you?" Lowell said abruptly. "Aren't you? Just because I was foolish enough to take pity on you that morning of your wedding." He sounded savagely annoyed with himself.

Pity. Flora felt shaken, naive, but she was not going to waver now.

"That is neither here nor there," she said. "What I am here for is to make you a proposal. I need someone to marry me and I want it to be you."

She was aware that the words had come out all wrong, but it was difficult for her to keep calm under the scrutiny of Lowell's cool blue gaze. He is going to refuse me, she thought, and the panic welled up in her throat.

"Why?" Lowell said after a moment. He paced across the kitchen, his boots sounding loud on the red tiled floor. He shot her a look. "Are you pregnant?"

"No, of course not." Flora could feel her whole body blushing. She knew perfectly well how such a situation might occur; she had simply not done it herself. "I haven't…I don't…I've never…"

"I didn't think so," Lowell said. There was a half smile on his lips that made Flora think that he, on the other hand might have a great deal of experience.

"Then why suggest it?" she snapped, pride overcoming her embarrassment. She turned away from him. This was all going wrong already. She might have known it would never work. She did not even know why she had thought to propose marriage to him. She barely knew Lowell Lister and now it seemed that pity had been his overriding emotion toward her. She clenched her fists tightly at her side, wanting to leave—preferably through a large hole in the floor that could just open up and swallow her— but Lowell was between her and the door.

"So if you are not pregnant, Flora—" Lowell's drawl seemed to have become even more pronounced, sending hot shivers along her skin "—then why would you urgently require a husband?"

"Because in six weeks' time I will lose half of my dowry to Tom Fortune," Flora said, glaring at him, "and since I am to lose control of my money one way or the other I would rather it be to a man I chose rather than to a blackguard like that."

Lowell inclined his head. "Sound logic."

"Thank you," Flora said huffily.

"So any man would do?" Lowell pursued.

Flora could see another trap yawning. Her temper tightened. "No, of course not! I chose you." She shot him another look. "Do you need me to flatter you and say why?"

Again that half smile twitched at Lowell's lips. "I think I do," he said, "for believe me, you would make the worst farmer's wife in the world, Flora." He looked at her and under his appraising glance Flora felt her body prickle with mortification.

"How do you know I would be bad at it?" she challenged. "I haven't tried yet."

"You are completely unaccustomed to living under straitened circumstances," Lowell said. "You have no idea how to work."

"Circumstances would not be straitened if we had my fifty thousand pounds," Flora said. "Neither of us would need to work."

"I don't want to play at farming like a gentleman," Lowell said, the contempt dripping from his voice. "I need to work hard, Flora. I want to." He came close to her and she could smell the summer scent of cut grass on him, mingled with something else more primal that seemed to cause a hollow ache in her stomach.

"You're a lady," Lowell went on. "You know

nothing of rising at five in the morning, winter as well as summer, to light the fires and clean the house and milk the cows and make the cheese. You know *nothing* of working in the fields until your bones ache or riding to market to sell the fresh produce or of plucking a chicken for the pot." He turned away. "You are no use to me as a wife, Flora."

"Very well, then," Flora said. "I am not going to beg." She certainly was not going to stay to hear any more. She had evidently made a grave miscalculation in thinking that Lowell would want to marry her for her money if for nothing else. No one she knew had ever turned down a fortune of fifty thousand pounds. It was extraordinary.

She walked toward the door, but when she got there she stopped and turned back. Lowell was watching her, his face quite expressionless, his jaw set hard.

"You asked why I chose you," Flora said. "I chose you because I thought you were lonely." She gestured toward the box where the dogs lay curled around each other now, snoring peacefully. "What self-respecting farmer allows his working dogs to sleep in the house?" she said. "You must need the company." She put her hand on the latch, preparing to leave.

"They are a damn sight less trouble than taking a lady to wife," Lowell said.

Flora turned back and looked at him. He sighed, and ran a hand over his hair again, then pushed a chair out from the table with his foot. Flora accepted the unspoken invitation to sit and Lowell poured her a beaker of ale, taking the seat next to her. After a moment she tried the ale. It tasted vile. She almost spat it out.

"I don't make fruit juices," Lowell said, "elder-flower and blackcurrant and the like. My mother did." He looked at Flora. "Perhaps she could give you some hints. Or perhaps not." He sighed. "She has just taken the journey you want to do in reverse. She's a lady now, thanks to my sister's money and her grand marriage. She would never in a thousand years under-stand why a lady would want to be a farmer's wife."

"I'm not a lady," Flora said. "My father made his money in trade and my grandfather was a walking-stick maker. Ladies look down on me."

Lowell laughed. "Now that I do understand." He sobered. "Even so, you have never had to work for a living."

"It's true that I have never had to work," Flora said, "but I am willing to try." Her heart was pounding, absolutely thundering in her ears, at the thought that Lowell might even be considering her proposition. It made her wonder whether she had assumed he would reject her and so she had never really been prepared for the shock of his acceptance.

Lowell took her hand and turned it over, his work-roughened fingers abrasive against the softness of her palm. "I can see that you've never worked," he said as his fingers traced gentle circles over her skin.

Flora had a sudden overwhelming image of what his hands would feel like on the rest of her soft, pampered body and almost fainted. She took a gulp of ale to steady herself. It tasted slightly less vile this time.

"Is there someone else that you would rather wed?" she blurted out. "Lizzie Scarlet used to flirt with you, though she is married now. Today," she added, in some surprise, for she had only just remembered that Lady Elizabeth and Nat Waterhouse had wed that very morning in the private chapel at Scarlet Park.

"Lizzie flirted with everyone," Lowell said. "It meant nothing." His tight expression eased a little. "I thought that might have been why you came to find me tonight," he added. He glanced at her with his blue, blue eyes and Flora felt the cool shivers ripple over her skin again. Outside there was a sudden flash of lightning, livid against the hills. The crockery on the dresser rattled at the crash of thunder and the dogs woke up and barked until Lowell hushed them.

"Why…? What?" Flora had jumped, too, at the cacophony of noise. She felt confused. "What did you think I came here for?"

"For consolation," Lowell said. He was still holding her hand. "Because Nat Waterhouse is married."

"Oh," Flora said, looking at their linked hands. "No."

"Just no?" Lowell sounded amused. His thumb was rubbing gently over Flora's palm in distracting strokes.

"I…um…" Flora blinked. A hot, heavy feeling

was beating through her blood. "I like Lord Water-house," she said, "but I didn't choose to marry him the way I chose you."

There was a moment's stillness broken by another huge crash of thunder and a sudden engulfing downpour of rain, hammering on the roof of the farmhouse. Flora met Lowell's eyes and saw that the amusement was still there, but behind it was something bright and intense and breathtaking. Flora found she was shaking. She withdrew her hand from Lowell's rather quickly and took refuge in the beaker of ale.

"I am glad," Lowell said. "It made me angry to think that you only sought me out for comfort."

"I told you," Flora said, "I want to marry you so that I don't have to give Tom Fortune half my fifty thousand pounds."

"Oh, yes." Lowell was smiling. He stretched, muscles rippling, hands behind his head. "I remember."

For some reason the panic that had filled Flora earlier now came back with a vengeance and she jumped to her feet. "I must go," she said. "It is late and my parents think me abed and I cannot afford to be seen out alone at night."

"You cannot go yet," Lowell said. "You will be soaked before you go five paces. Wait until the rain stops," he added, "and I will escort you back."

"You can't," Flora said. "If someone saw us together—"

Lowell stood up. He was so close to her, his

presence so strong and powerful, that Flora tried to take a step back and bumped into the dresser.

"You are not walking back on your own at night," he said. He cupped her face between his hands. There was an expression in his eyes of tenderness and exasperation and it made Flora go weak at the knees.

"You could marry anyone you wanted," Lowell whispered. "You are beautiful and rich and sweet and brave…" He closed his eyes for a moment. "Why me, Flora?"

Flora braced herself against the dresser and looked up into his face. No more prevarication, she thought, no more pride, no more excuses.

"When you found me that day," she said, "the day I canceled my wedding, I felt as though I had been given a second chance. Up until then I had not really lived. Oh, I had gone to balls and parties and gone shopping and paid visits and given the servants orders and done a hundred and one things that *ladies*—" she emphasized the word "—of my age and class have done before me, but I had not done a single thing that had made me glad to be alive." She swallowed hard. "I do not wish to sound ungrateful," she said. "The possession of money is an enormous blessing, but I do not wish to live off my fortune forever, doing something and nothing, sitting in my drawing room, entertaining my friends and wondering when my life is going to start until I have the vapors out of sheer frustration." She looked at

Lowell. His eyes were moving over her face as though he was committing her to heart.

"And then I saw you," she said. "The day that I was given a second chance." She cleared her throat. "I had seen you before, of course, at the assemblies and in the village, but I thought…" She paused. She could hear her voice trembling and she knew she had humbled her pride and the rest of her words came out in a rush before she lost her nerve. "I thought you had so much life and vitality and passion and I wanted that. I wanted that passion so much I was prepared to come here today to pretend to buy you with my fifty thousand pounds—" She stopped. One look at Lowell's face told her there was no point in continuing. And the strange thing was that she knew it was not because he pitied her, as he had claimed when she had first arrived. He wanted her. She could see it in his face and feel it, even though he was not touching her. But…

"I'm sorry, Flora," he said, and his eyes were full of pain. "I cannot marry you. You think that you would be able to adapt to life as a farmer's wife but you have no real idea of what that means. I know you would not be happy. It would be too different and in the end it would tear you—and us—apart."

Flora drew back. She felt sick and tired to have tried and failed, but more than anything, she felt disappointed.

I will not cry, she thought. *He does not deserve me.*

"At least I was willing to try," she said huskily. "I

was wrong about you, Lowell Lister. I thought that you had courage as well as passion, but in the end you were not even prepared to take a risk."

And she turned away and walked out of the house and into the storm without a backward glance.

LIZZIE SAT BY THE WINDOW and looked out at the rain-swept street. It was late and the village was deserted, as silent as the grave. Lizzie had never lived in Fortune's Folly itself and she had thought at first that she might enjoy having the bustle and activity of the village all around her but this silent night seemed dark and quelling. Nat had taken a short-term lease on a town house called Chevrons that was let by a lawyer who had gone to Bath for the winter and had decided to remain there. The Duke and Duchess of Cole had rented the property when they had been trying to find a suitor for Lydia the previous year. That had ended badly, Lizzie thought, and now *her* marriage had barely got off on a better footing.

Lizzie had no idea how long Nat planned to stay in Fortune's Folly, because he had not discussed it with her. As she had sat alone that evening she had come to realize, slowly and a little painfully, that she and Nat had talked about nothing of significance at all and she had no idea about any of his thoughts and plans. In fact, Lizzie thought bitterly, they had barely seen each other during the two weeks of their formal betrothal. The morning after Tom's orgy, Nat had taken her to Drum Castle to stay, most respectably, with Miles and Alice. Nat had also arranged Sir Montague's funeral, which had been a miserable affair with very few mourners. Tom had failed to turn up and even the servants had had to be bribed.

And then Nat had left Fortune's Folly for London, to make whatever arrangements were required for the wedding. Lizzie, left behind and fretting over all the uncertainties in her future, had spent the time exactly as she had spent the rest of her life up until that point: riding out on the hills, visiting her friends, shopping in Fortune's Folly and avoiding Alice's perceptive questions on how she felt about her impending nuptials. In some ways it had felt as though nothing had changed at all but in other ways it was a terrifying time as she had waited, her life seemingly suspended, for Nat to return.

She and Nat had married that morning in the chapel at Scarlet Park with her cousin Gregory, the Earl of Scarlet, as one witness and some official from the Chancery as the other. The match had been rushed through as a favor to Nat and to her cousin, who had considerable political influence, and Lizzie had felt completely ignored in the process. None of her friends had been invited to attend and when Lizzie had protested about this Nat had told her that her cousin the Earl had requested a private ceremony and, as they were trespassing on his hospitality, she could have no say in the arrangements. Lizzie had felt as though Gregory Scarlet had hushed the whole thing up because he was ashamed of her—as indeed he might well be.

After the ceremony there had been a cursory wedding breakfast hosted by the Countess of Scarlet, a bossy, sharp-natured woman who had given the impression that Lizzie was creating a vast amount of trouble for her long-suffering relatives. The countess's gaze had repeatedly flickered over Lizzie's stomach as though she was trying to assess whether she was *enceinte* or not. Lizzie had lost her temper and had said sweetly that dear Charlotte should not concern herself because she was sure she was not pregnant, and was that not a mercy since she had only been married for two hours? The countess had hustled her two young daughters away at that point, covering their ears and looking at Lizzie as though she was the source of a major contagion.

Lizzie had found it odd and nostalgic to be back in her old home and yet to feel it was no longer familiar to her, her father's somewhat risqué paintings and sculptures gone from the walls and everything stifled in dark and somber colors. Nothing could have spelled out more clearly for her how her old life was closed to her once and for all. She had no place at Scarlet Park and now she no longer had a place at Fortune Hall, either, so where did she belong? She was not sure; nor did she know what sort of life she and Nat could forge together.

They had returned to Fortune's Folly in the afternoon of the wedding and Nat had promptly disappeared without telling Lizzie where he was going. Lizzie had sat alone in the unwelcoming surroundings of the Chevrons drawing room and had wondered what on earth to do with herself now. She had been on the point of going out for a walk simply to banish the blue devils when Nat had returned, carried her up to bed and made love to her, and then equally promptly had informed her that he was spending the evening with Dexter, discussing the latest developments in Sir Montague's murder case. Apparently he was going to rejoin Miles and Dexter on the investigation. He had been brusque and impersonal and Lizzie's pleasant feelings of sensual languor had fled and she had sat in the big bed and watched him dress speedily and efficiently. She had felt bewildered and lost. For a moment, lying there with Nat, she had been able to pretend that they were like any other newlywed couple. Nat's departure with no more than a hurried kiss ripped that illusion apart and left a hole within her for the despair to flood in. Leaving her alone on their wedding night spelled out more clearly than any words the fact that he had married her to fulfil his responsibility and protect her reputation. Now his duty was done.

Was this what marriage was about? Lizzie wondered. Did Dexter habitually leave Laura sitting around on her own whilst he went out to do whatever

it was that gentlemen did? Would Miles have abandoned Alice on their wedding day to go out to his
Club? She thought not but she was not sure. And
what was she supposed to do in the meantime? The
house required no running because Nat had hired the
servants along with the property and it already func-
tioned like well-regulated clockwork. Was she
supposed to sit in the drawing room and read, or, God
forbid, *embroider* something? Suddenly she did not
seem to know anything, nor did she have anyone to
ask. Laura, Alice and Lydia had all sent messages of
congratulation on her marriage and Lizzie fully
intended to call on them in the morning, when, no
doubt, the rest of Fortune's Folly society would also
call to hear about her wedding to Nat. They would
all be expiring with gossip and curiosity. Tonight,
though, she was alone and she was bored and she felt
neglected and not a little afraid.

I don't like being married, Lizzie thought,
drumming her fingers irritably on the windowsill. I
knew it would not work and I was right. My husband
is already ignoring me after only twelve hours of
married life. He behaves as though he were still a
single man. I have no notion what he plans for our
future, when we will go to Water House to meet his
family, where we will live, what shape my life will
take. I should have thought about this before; I should
have talked to him.

I should not have married him.

The thoughts, so jumbled and painful, made her realize how distant she was from Nat and how, in the aftermath of Monty's death and in her desperation to escape Tom, she had allowed Nat to take all the decisions almost unchallenged.

She looked outside at the puddles of water lying on the cobbled street and the sky lightening in the west as the thunderstorm receded. A solitary carriage rumbled past, breaking the silence. A shadowy figure in a black cloak slipped by so quickly that Lizzie wondered if she had imagined seeing it. Who could be out on a night like this?

"I wish mama were here to advise me," she thought. There was a hot lump in her throat and suddenly she felt very young and very small. "No, perhaps I don't, because she was not very reliable. But I wish she were here simply to reassure me."

She sat very still. The ticking of the clock was the only sound in the entire house, the only indication that anything was alive beneath the stifling weight of soft furnishings. Perhaps when we have a house of our own I might decorate it, Lizzie thought. She could not touch Chevrons, despite finding the decoration fussy and ugly, because it was let with the furnishings. The frustration and the fear gripped her again. What was she supposed to *do* with herself? And why had she not thought about this before? She was trapped, and this time she could not run because she was married and she would *not* repeat her mother's pattern. That was the one thing on which she was determined.

She had been married for less than a day and her husband was out carousing with his cronies. It simply was not appropriate for Nat to marry her and then go out and leave her behind as though she was a part of the furniture, just another commodity that he had acquired, a little wife waiting patiently at home for him when he deigned to return.

The anger flamed through Lizzie, hot and reassuring. She preferred it to the cold grip of the fear and panic. This is my wedding day, she thought, fanning the flames of her own indignation. I will *not* sit at home, alone and disregarded. If Nat wishes to go out that is his affair but I shall do likewise.

She went over to the drawing room door and flung it open. Immediately the door to the servants' quarters opened, too, and Mrs. Alibone, the housekeeper, emerged, moving smoothly and silently as though she had oiled wheels beneath her prim black gown. There was something a little sinister about Mrs. Alibone, Lizzie thought. For all her apple-pink cheeks and neat white hair and kindly expression she was so efficient she seemed almost mechanical.

"Good evening, madam," she said. "Can I help you?"

"Thank you, Mrs. Alibone," Lizzie said. "Please ask the coachman to have the carriage ready. And please send my maid to me. I am going out."

Mrs. Alibone's eyebrows rose smoothly into a gray fringe of hair. "Out?" she said. "But madam, you are in deep mourning! It is not appropriate for you to go out in the evening, least of all without your husband."

"It is my brother who has lost his life," Lizzie said sharply. "I don't see why I should lose mine, as well. And why should I cease to be a person in my own right when I wed?"

"Then I will have your black crepe gown laid out if you insist, madam," Mrs. Alibone said, her nose twitching with disapproval.

"No, thank you," Lizzie said. "I require my silver silk evening dress—and the Scarlet Diamonds. I intend to make an impression."

"I DIDN'T EXPECT YOU TO be free on your wedding night, old chap," Dexter commented as Nat joined him in a quiet corner of the Granby's taproom. "How is Lady Waterhouse?" he added. "I am surprised that you were able to tear yourself away from her."

"Lizzie is fine," Nat said. He took a long, appreciative mouthful of ale and settled back on the bench. "She is very tired," he added. "It has been a long day for her. I left her reading quietly at home." By the time that he had left the house, Lizzie had been dressed and sitting in the drawing room at Chevrons, flicking through the *Lady's Magazine*. It had been a sight that had pleased Nat and had made him feel very content—his demure wife rising from the bed where she had just pleasured him most satisfactorily and then taking up her books or her sewing to sit quietly at home. It seemed that he had tamed his vixen and she would be the perfect wanton in the bedroom but a paragon of wifely virtues out of it. Indeed, Nat had begun to think that perhaps Lizzie had it in her to be the calm, decorous wife that he had desired all along. Perhaps she would surprise him. Maybe their marriage would not be the disaster he had predicted.

Perhaps all Lizzie had needed was a settled home and a secure background. Nat was proud that he had been able to give that to her. She had certainly been a great deal quieter and more malleable in the weeks preceding their wedding. She had accepted his proposal without further argument, she had agreed to all the arrangements he had made and she had been remarkably reserved and quiet.

Dexter was looking at him a little quizzically. "If you say so, old chap," he said. "It doesn't sound much like the Lady Elizabeth Scarlet we all knew before, but you must know her best. She is your wife, after all."

Nat nodded. He reflected that the past couple of weeks had gone exceptionally well. From the moment he had rescued Lizzie from Fortune Hall on the night of Tom's orgy he had been completely focused on doing what he had to do to protect her, to secure her fortune and to pay off Tom's blackmail.

Today had been the culmination of all his work. He had married Lizzie, thereby saving her reputation, gaining her dowry and in some indefinable but deeply satisfying way, *putting matters right*. He had paid off her brother with a draft advanced by his bankers. He had been able to keep safe the secret of his sister Celeste's sexual indiscretions. He had shielded his family from harm, which had been his prime concern from the very first. He was entitled to feel satisfied with his efforts. Everything was safe, everything was ordered again. He had done his duty.

Nat took another mouthful of ale as he silently congratulated himself. Once Sir Montague's murder case had been successfully resolved, he thought that he would take Lizzie to Water House to meet his family again. She had known his parents when she was younger and had even been a friend to Celeste during his sister's first London season, for Celeste and Lizzie were of an age. Perhaps Lizzie would be pregnant by the time they went to Water House. Perhaps she already was. She had not mentioned that she had had her courses in the six weeks since they had first made love. A beautiful, *dutiful* wife and an heir…Nat felt remarkably expansive. He gestured to one of the inn servants to refill his glass and the conversation turned to the murder case.

Nat's good humor lasted for precisely two hours.

"Excuse me, my lord." By the time one hundred and twenty minutes had passed Nat had consumed several pints of the excellent local ale and was feeling very mellow. Then one of The Granby servants approached discreetly and slipped a note into his hand. It was short and to the point, clearly written in haste.

"Please come to the card room as quickly as possible. Lizzie is here and there is a problem. Alice Vickery."

Nat frowned. He had been aware that The Granby was hosting one of its fortnightly assembly balls that night. When Sir Montague had died it had been suggested that the program of entertainment in the village should be canceled for the summer as a mark of respect, but Tom had promptly vetoed the idea because he wanted the income that the balls and other social events brought. Nat knew he was traditional in such matters but he realized that he was shocked to think that Lizzie would attend a ball only three weeks after her brother's death. Disquiet stirred inside him. He knew that Lizzie frequently behaved unconventionally and chose to do precisely as she pleased, but surely that should all have changed now that she was his wife? He had thought that she had understood that and had settled down in her new role. Perhaps his earlier optimism had been premature. The mellowness that had possessed him was draining away now and he felt exasperated with himself for his complacence. Evidently he had imagined matters to be how he wanted them rather than seeing them as they really were. How foolish he had been to picture Lizzie sitting quietly at home when she had never done such a thing in her life.

"Is something wrong?" Dexter asked, brows raised.

Nat crumpled the note fiercely in his hand. He looked at his friend's face and then sighed. "Lizzie is apparently here at the assembly, in the card room, and Alice has asked me to join them. There appears to be some sort of problem, so I can only imagine that she is gambling." He got to his feet.

"If Miles and Alice are present they will be keeping an eye on Lizzie," Dexter said reassuringly, getting up, too.

Nat knew that Dexter was right but he admitted to himself that the last thing he wanted was for their friends to witness any discord between him and Lizzie. They were all so happy in their own marriages that he felt hopelessly lacking. Dexter and Laura had practically fallen in love at first sight, years before, and although the road to marriage had proved decidedly bumpy for them they were now incandescent with bliss. Miles was even more irritating because he had been the sternest opponent of marriage imaginable, had cynically denounced love as nothing more than a fig leaf to make lust appear more acceptable, and had even tried to blackmail Alice into marrying him so he could have her fortune to save him from debtors' prison. Yet here he was now, the most sickeningly uxorious of husbands and desperately in love with his wife. It made Nat feel ill with envy because he had a depressing feeling that he and Lizzie would never achieve the sort of deep understanding that was blossoming between Miles and Alice. True, he had married Lizzie under different circumstances, primarily those of finance—his—and reputation— hers—and as such they could not really expect to experience the dizzy heights of love. He had run through that sort of emotion in his salad days anyway, with Priscilla Willoughby, and had no inclination to suffer it again. No, he had wed Lizzie out of duty and desire. Yet despite telling himself that his reasons for the match was perfectly adequate, somehow he felt perfectly *in*adequate in the face of his friends' wedded happiness.

And now it seemed that his wilful wife was already behaving very badly indeed, just as he had feared she would...

Nat quickened his pace from the taproom down the stone corridor, round a corner, through a doorway and into the Granby ballroom, his temper rising at each step as he wondered what on earth he would find when he caught up with Lizzie. A country-dance was taking place in the main assembly room. It was very calm and decorous. Nat looked around but he could see neither Lizzie nor Alice nor Miles. Alice's note had mentioned the card room. Nat skirted the dancers and strode through the doorway, past the long table that groaned under the weight of refreshments. He could already see a crowd in the card room. They were pressing close around one of the tables and a feverish atmosphere was in the air. As Nat and Dexter entered, Miles Vickery pushed through the throng toward them. Nat grabbed his arm.

"What's happening?"

"Lizzie is playing Three Card Monte with Tom," Miles said tersely. "He challenged her for the Scarlet Diamonds."

"What?" Nat froze.

"Tom challenged her," Miles repeated. "He said the diamonds should have been his because he was the elder. Lizzie said their mother had expressly left them to her but she would play him for them, the best of three games. So far they have won one each."

Stifling a curse, Nat cut his way through the crowd about the table. Lizzie looked up as he pushed his way to the front. She was wearing a concoction of silver net, scandalously low cut, and her auburn hair was piled up in a diamond clasp on the top of her head. She looked ethereal and fey. Her green eyes were smoky and slanted and when she saw Nat her mouth curled in the smile that always did strange things to Nat's insides, turning them molten with lust. There was a champagne glass by her elbow and she looked more than a little cast away for her cheeks were flushed pink and her eyes glittered. The Scarlet Diamonds, a necklace that the late Earl had given to his wife when first they were wed, lay sinuous and gleaming on the table between her and Tom.

"Good evening, my love," Lizzie said brightly. "I hope you are enjoying your wedding night."

"I've come to take you home," Nat said. He clamped down on his anger. He was very conscious of the silence in the room, of everyone watching them, but more than anything else, he was aware of Tom Fortune's triumphant, mocking gaze. So Tom had not been content with relieving him of a draft for twenty-five thousand pounds earlier in the day, Nat thought savagely. Tom's greed was uncontrollable. He always wanted more.

Lizzie's eyes had narrowed at his words. "But Nat, darling," she said, "I am having *such* a lovely time! You cannot make me go home now!"

"Don't spoil sport, Waterhouse," Tom drawled. "Can you not afford a trifling twenty grand for a necklace now that you have Lizzie's money—and more besides?" His dark, insolent gaze told Nat exactly how much he would disclose if he was pushed and Nat felt a bolt of fear. He had thought the matter of the blackmail settled, but now he realized just what a fool he had been; blackmailers were never satisfied and if Tom breathed a word of Celeste's disgrace... Suddenly Nat's ordered world lay teetering on the brink of disaster again.

"I don't see why you assume I will lose, Tom." Lizzie pouted. She shuffled three cards with expert precision, two black and a red queen, and laid them facedown on the table. "You know I have the luck of the devil."

"When it comes to cards, perhaps," Tom said, smiling at her, his eyes empty of affection, "though not, I think, in your choice of men."

Nat made an uncontrollable movement of anger and Lizzie's bright green gaze rested thoughtfully on him for a moment before it flickered back to her brother.

"Find the lady, Tom," she goaded, "and the diamonds are yours."

Nat's body was tight with tension. Tom looked up at him again, malice in his eyes. "Find the lady indeed," he murmured. "A relative of yours is she, Waterhouse?"

Nat felt Miles shift beside him and felt rather than saw the quizzical look his friend bent on him but he kept his eyes fixed on Lizzie now. Her face was pale, her eyes narrowed on the cards as she waited for Tom to choose. Her fingers tapped her half-empty champagne glass.

Tom put out his hand and turned a card. It was the seven of spades. Lizzie gave a delighted little squeal and clapped her hands. "I win!"

There was a smattering of applause from their audience.

"You're worse than a card sharp," her brother said sourly, vacating the table. "How the hell do you do these tricks?"

Lizzie picked up the necklace and fastened it around her neck. It rested on the upper curve of her breasts, where it flashed fire and ice with each breath she took. Nat dragged his gaze away with difficulty and caught the look of challenge in Lizzie's eyes.

"Who'll play me next?" she demanded, looking around. Once again the smile curved her lips and the lust kicked Nat hard in the groin. How could Lizzie make him so angry and yet so hot to have her? It was not a comfortable feeling and yet he could not resist it. It was as though she infected him with her own madness, driving him far beyond the rationality that normally governed his life. Well, if he had to play by her rules this time then so be it.

He grabbed a chair.

"I'll play," he said.

A ripple of shock ran around the group of onlookers and Lizzie's eyes widened in surprise.

"I did not think you approved of gaming," she said.

"I don't," Nat said. He sat back, undid his jacket and loosened his cravat.

Lizzie took a long gulp of the champagne. Nat watched her throat move as she swallowed. The diamonds danced and glittered about her neck. She picked up the pack of cards and started to shuffle it again.

"Basset?" she said.

"Piquet."

Lizzie shrugged one white shoulder. "Whichever you prefer. The stake?"

"You," Nat said. "You coming home with me. To our bed."

Again the group of onlookers rippled with scandalized shock and some moved away, Dexter, Miles and Alice amongst them. Lizzie looked up at Nat, her eyes wide and very bright with the excitement and wildness he had come to recognize. "You'll lose," she warned.

"No, I won't," Nat said.

Out of the corner of his eye Nat could see that Alice was clasping Miles's sleeve and speaking to him urgently. Miles's face was grim, but after a moment he shook his head and they left the card room, Alice throwing one troubled, backward glance at Lizzie. Nat felt the tension tighten within him, straining the muscles across his shoulders, drawing the material of his evening jacket taut. His entire attention was riveted on Lizzie, on the way the silk and net of her gown clung to each line and curve of her body, on the provocative rise and fall of the diamonds at her breast, the slender flick of her fingers as she dealt the cards. Their gazes locked. Hers was vivid and excited and challenged him so that the blood burned fierce within him.

"You have always been a poor card player," she taunted.

"I have been an indifferent one," Nat said. He held her gaze with his, intense, direct. "Perhaps I will surprise you."

"You frequently do." Lizzie bent her head over her cards and promptly won the first two *parties*. Nat won the third, then the fourth and the fifth. He could see that after a lapse in concentration Lizzie was trying very hard now, her lower lip pressed between her teeth. Most of their audience had wandered away now in search of fresh entertainment. There was only Lizzie and him left, swept up in their tight little circle of mutual tension and desire. The longer the game ran the more his lust drove him. He was determined to win, and to have her.

"You should not have drunk all that champagne," he said. "It undermines the concentration."

Lizzie shot him an irritated look. "You should drink more and then perhaps you would not be such a stuffed shirt."

"Why the necklace?" Nat said. "Why gamble something that is so important to you?"

She flicked him another look over her hand and put a card down. "Why not? What does it matter?"

"It's worth twenty thousand pounds."

Her head was bent, the candlelight playing on the golden, bronze and red strands in her hair.

"It isn't always about the money," she said.

"No," Nat said. "It's about the fact that your mother gave it to you and that you value inordinately anything that connects you to her."

She shot him a very sharp look at that. For a moment she looked afraid. Her hand stilled on the cards. "How do you know that?"

"Because no matter what everyone else says of her, you have always idolized her."

He saw Lizzie swallow hard. Her lashes hid her expression from him. "I miss her."

"So why gamble away something of value that she left to you?" Nat persisted. "It makes no sense."

Lizzie slapped a card down onto the pile and leaned forward, her green eyes pinning him with their anger. "Sense! What sense is there in loss? I lost my mother—am I supposed to value a necklace in her place?" She sat back, the anger leaving her as swiftly as it had poured out. "I lost both my parents," she said. "I lost Monty. None of them were perfect, but they were more valuable than this." She touched the necklace with her fingertips and it caught the light and blazed with rainbow colors.

"Is that why you came out tonight?" Nat asked. "Because you felt lonely and you wanted to gamble to pass the time?" He could not understand her and with a moment's surprise and pain he realized that he never had. He had never really tried; she had just been Lizzie and he had indulged her moods and had laughed at her wildness, but now everything seemed different because she was his wife, and he was baffled as well as dazzled by her. Everything that should have been simple—their marriage, his life— suddenly seemed intolerably complicated.

"I was bored." She played her hand faster now, throwing the cards down as though she did not really care. "It was my wedding night and I was lonely. What about you?"

"I had business—"

"Oh, well." Lizzie smiled at him, mocking, the smile not reaching her eyes. Her words stung him like tiny thorns. "That makes it all right, then. When men say they *have to deal with business* it is so important that it excuses all, does it not?"

"You're angry," Nat said.

"You're perceptive." Her expression was contemptuous. "It is our *wedding night,* Nat Waterhouse. You gain fifty thousand pounds from me, you have me in your bed—" her gaze, burning and intense, reminded him of how that had been "—you take the things you want," she continued, "and then you go out *on business* and leave me alone. You treat me like a possession and then you behave like a single man." She threw her cards down in a gesture of disgust. "I have *carte blanche* and no picture cards. I suspect you win."

"Four games to your two." Nat looked at her. "You should have declared earlier. You're reckless."

"Clearly," Lizzie said. "How exciting for you to be proved right." She stood up and the silver net dress rustled softly as it slid over the lines and curves of her body. She looked ice-cool and composed whilst Nat felt so hot he was burning up. It maddened him that she could provoke him and his body would respond to her so violently even when his mind rebelled against the hold she had over him.

"Come with me," he said roughly. He stood up. "We are going home."

She looked him up and down slowly like a queen appraising a peasant. Even the tilt of her chin was haughty. Her gaze rested disdainfully on the bulge of his enormous erection. "Home?" she said. "You'll never last that long. You want me too much."

Nat was afraid that she was right. He wanted to make love to her here on the card room table or against the wall or anywhere that would soothe this unbearable ache in his body. His desperate arousal was all he could think of. He grabbed Lizzie's wrist, careless of who was watching.

"I won, so…"

"So you claim your prize." Lizzie was smiling though her eyes were still cold. He wanted to kindle a matching heat in her, to master her and force a response. He pulled her to him and kissed her. He was not the sort of man to kiss a woman in the very public surroundings of the Fortune's Folly assembly rooms but one touch of her lips, cool and firm, and he forgot where they were. He almost forgot *who* he was. He kissed her hard, tasting the champagne on her tongue and the sweet taste that was Lizzie herself and he did not stop kissing her until the Master of Ceremonies approached them to say that their carriage was waiting and if they could leave at once it would be much appreciated because they were creating a public disturbance.

Lizzie was proved right. In the carriage Nat stripped the silver dress off her, leaving her in nothing but the diamond necklace, and took her there and then on the seat, whilst the coach drove around the village in circles until they had finished. Lizzie smiled her cool smile in the summer darkness and her naked body glistened equally as cool and pale and the sight of it just seemed to fire Nat's lust all the more. He lost himself in her whilst deploring his lack of control. Afterward he felt sated but not happy and Lizzie was silent and withdrawn from him, and the doubts that had shadowed his mind earlier in the evening came back and would not be banished. He had feared that marriage to Lizzie would be a disaster and whilst their lovemaking might be spectacular he was starting to see that his misgivings might be justified. There was some devil of unhappiness that drove Lizzie and he did not understand why, and whilst he wanted to help her he did not know how.

When they finally reached Chevrons he took Lizzie to bed and made love to her again, trying to banish the demons, and then he fell into an uneasy sleep, waking only when his valet brought in the hot water and threw the curtains wide. The bed was empty and Lizzie had gone. Nat felt a strange pang of loss.

Lizzie was already in the breakfast parlor when he went downstairs. She was wearing a dress of pale green trimmed with black lace—her concession to mourning, Nat presumed—and she looked exceedingly pretty except that there were dark circles beneath her eyes. Her hair was ruthlessly restrained in a matching green bandeau and she was picking at a piece of toast and honey as though she detested the sight of it.

Nat took a cup of coffee, dismissed the footman and went to sit across from her. He knew he had to speak to her but there was such a strong reserve about her that it seemed to make it impossible to find the right words.

"I trust that you are well this morning?" he said, knowing even as he spoke that he sounded stilted. Lizzie raised her blank, green gaze to his and he had the oddest sensation that there was nothing behind her eyes at all, no thought, no feeling.

"I am quite well." She sounded as distant as the slightest acquaintance.

Nat cleared his throat. "About last night—"

"I suppose I should apologize for embarrassing you," Lizzie said. She did not look up from her plate. "I apologize."

"No," Nat found himself saying. "No, I don't want an apology." He ran a hand over his hair in an agitated gesture. "I just want to know why you did it, why you went out, why you felt you needed to gamble with Tom?"

Her gaze flickered to his face and then she looked away again. "Because I am wild and ungovernable," she said ironically. "Have you not always said so?"

"Yes, but—" Nat struggled. This, he knew, was not the real answer. There had to be more to her behavior than a simple impulse to be scandalous, yet she offered no explanation. He shook his head, baffled.

"I do not understand why you do these outrageous things," he said. His mind went back to the previous night. What was it that she had said?

"It is our wedding day. You gain fifty thousand pounds from me, you have me in your bed, you take the things you want and then you go out on business."

"I am sorry I left you alone last night," he said. "I should have thought that it was our wedding night and—" He stopped as she turned her face away.

"It does not matter," she said. She spoke very quietly.

He had the impression that it mattered a great deal but she was refusing to acknowledge it.

"I should apologize for the way that I treated you, too," he said. "I wanted you and I was not gentle. I had forgotten you have little experience—"

Lizzie shrugged a shoulder with what seemed to be indifference. "You did not hurt me or shock me," she said. "I am more shocked to discover that we have such a physical affinity when there is nothing else…" She stopped, biting her lip. "Excuse me," she said, rising to her feet.

Nat put out a hand. He knew that this unsatisfactory conversation should not—could not—end here. There was something very wrong and too many things unsaid to let it go. He could feel his marriage slipping, sliding, down a slope toward the inevitable disaster he had predicted for it. He did not know how to stop it even though he desperately wanted to do something.

"Lizzie," he said.

She paused and looked at him and once again her gaze was totally blank and Nat felt frustrated and confused as though he had somehow lost her even though she was standing right in front of him.

"I know there is something wrong," he said. "Lizzie, talk to me."

Her eyelashes flicked down and a hint of color stole into her cheek. "There is nothing wrong," she said. "I am perfectly fine."

"Are you?"

For a moment he caught a flash of the most abject misery in her face and then she raised her chin. "I am going into town," she said. "I wish to visit the circulating library. I hope that meets with your approval?"

"Perfectly. Of course." Nat shook his head slightly at the abrupt change of subject. "I shall be working today," he added. "Dexter has asked me to rejoin him and Miles in the investigation into your brother's death and there is much to do."

Lizzie nodded and went out and a moment later Nat heard her speaking to Mrs. Alibone and the sound of her step on the stairs and then all was quiet. Nat finished his breakfast in silence, trying to distract himself with the morning copy of the *Leeds Intelligencer,* and wondered why he felt worse than before.

CHAPTER TEN

THEY WERE THE TALK of the town. Nat Waterhouse and his blazing, unconcealed lust for his wife—and hers for him—were the *on dit* of Fortune's Folly. Lizzie felt wretched.

She had been the center of gossip many times before and it had never troubled her and if she and Nat had been happy and scandalous together, then the salacious chatter of the village would have meant nothing to her. But they were not. She could not deceive herself. She and Nat were not happy because they wanted different things. He was quite content to use physical passion as a substitute for real intimacy. He wanted nothing more than a dutiful wife in the house and a wanton bride in his bed, whereas she wanted everything: his desire, his love, his very self. In a very short space of time she had learned that the extremes of sensual delight had nothing to do with true love. It was a hard lesson for such a hopeless romantic as she had turned out to be and it made her miserable for with Nat's lust she also wanted his love and he could not even begin to understand that. When he had apologized for leaving her alone on their wedding night and had asked her what was wrong she had felt helpless, for if he could not *see* how could he ever understand? She did not want to have to explain to him that it hurt her feelings to be left alone on a night that should have been special and wonderful and just for them. She did not want to have to explain the gap between her romantic imaginings and the reality, and to see his look of incomprehension and feel his pity. She did not want to have to tell him that she loved him heart and soul, and that she now realized she should never have married him because to him she was no more than another responsibility. Certainly she could not tell him that when they made love it broke her heart because it was so passionate, so exciting and yet ultimately so shallow without love.

Lizzie had a cup of chocolate at the Pump Rooms, bought some red ribbons and a new pair of fine kid gloves at Mrs. Morton's shop and then went to Mr. Tarleton's circulating library just as she had said she would. The day was fine and bright and the village was busy and she was aware of—but felt strangely isolated from—the stares and whispered asides of those she passed. It was evident that her escapade at the card tables the previous night was already common knowledge, as was Nat's ravishing of her in the carriage. There were sly winks and smiles that made Lizzie feel all the more miserable.

She felt exhausted, sore from the demands of Nat's lovemaking but unhappy more from the emotional distress of suppressing her love for him. Her body ached and her mind felt cloudy and dull. She wondered if a hot spa bath would ease her but the thought of taking one seemed too much work. It had been difficult enough to dress that morning.

She looked along the row of books and tried to decide which one to choose. Reading would be good. It would soothe her troubled mind and give her something to do all day. Only she could not seem to decide on a title. All she could see was Nat's face before her that morning. She knew he had tried to reach out to her, to bridge the gap that was widening between them all the time despite the intimacy of their physical relationship. She had not been able to respond to his attempt. She was too tired now and she felt too battered and bruised emotionally to make further effort. It was as though she had encased her feelings in ice now and could feel nothing anymore.

She sat down on one of the comfortable armchairs that Mr. Tarleton had placed in an alcove for the benefit of the library's clientele and stared blankly into space. Last night had been frightening. She had been so unhappy, racked with unexpected grief for Monty and haunted by her memories of the loss of her family. She knew that she had deliberately allowed that misery to turn to anger against Nat because anger and wildness were more familiar to her and more easy to deal with than the deep dark well of grief that reminded her of the last time she had lost all that was dear to her. So she had gone out and behaved badly, drinking too much again and allowing Tom to provoke her into gambling the necklace and then she had taunted Nat and vented her anger and resentment on him. She had welcomed his desperate lust for her because she wanted whatever he could give. And yet somehow what he could give simply was not enough. What she wanted was his love—but that was not on offer.

The murmur of voices roused her. Priscilla Willoughby was on the other side of the bookcase. Lizzie recognized her light, drawling voice and also Lady Wheeler's fluting tones; Lady Wheeler who not so long ago had flattered her and fawned on her and was now busy ripping her character to shreds.

"Did you hear the *on dit?* Yes…totally shameless…drinking gallons of champagne and gambling her jewelry, and her brother only dead a few weeks, though no one really mourns him…"

I do, Lizzie thought. Perhaps I am a fool but for all his faults, I miss Monty. I must be the only one who does.

"It amazes me that Nathaniel married that little hoyden." There was a spiky edge to Priscilla's dulcet voice. "Though it is no surprise to me that *she* behaves so badly. Her mother was nothing but a high-class whore. In fact, I wouldn't be surprised if Lady

Waterhouse herself had had several men before she wed—John Jerrold for one…"

"*Poor* Lord Waterhouse," Lady Wheeler said again, sounding excited at the thought of Lizzie's supposed indiscretions. "Yet he seems to desire her for I heard…" Further furtive whispers ensued, "Yes… In the carriage… Absolutely scandalous… And to think I always imagined that he would much prefer a well-bred wife like Flora Minchin, or you, Priscilla."

"Nathaniel is not thinking with his head at the moment," Priscilla snapped. "All men are the same, led by what is in their breeches."

"Priscilla!" Lady Wheeler sounded faint with outrage. Priscilla Willoughby moderated her tone.

"Lord Waterhouse will regain his senses soon enough once his lust has worn thin. Then he'll see that little wanton for what she really is." She laughed. "He certainly cannot love her. He was hopelessly in love with *me* back in his salad days. He told me I am his perfect woman." She sounded very smug. Lizzie could see her now through the gap between the bookcases. She was dressed in pale lilac with a huge straw hat with lilac ribbons framing her face. She looked cool and glacially composed. "He wrote me endless love letters, you know, Margaret, pouring out his feelings for me." She gave her little tinkle of laughter. "I think he is still more than a little in love with me now, to tell the truth!"

Lizzie stood up abruptly, catching her sleeve on the shelf and sending a stack of books tumbling to the floor. Both Lady Willoughby and Lady Wheeler turned, as did all the other occupants of the library. Lady Wheeler flushed an embarrassed puce but Lady Willoughby stood quite still, a little, triumphant smile on her lips.

"Lady Waterhouse! I did not see you there."

"Indeed?" Lizzie said. She met Priscilla Willoughby's scornful gaze and tried not to feel young and vulnerable. "I was interested in your reflections upon the male of the species, Lady Willoughby," she continued. "Clearly you have had sufficient of them to make a study." She nodded abruptly to them and walked out of the door into the hot street. The sun beat down on her head and the light was so bright it almost blinded her. She had forgotten a bonnet or a parasol. She felt hot and dizzy.

Love letters, Priscilla Willoughby had said. Nat, that most practical and unsentimental of men, had written Priscilla Willoughby *love letters*. She was his perfect woman, well-bred, refined and a lady to the bone. What had the letters said? Had they contained all the words that Lizzie herself wanted to say to Nat and had to keep penned up inside.

I have loved you always…
I will love you to the end of time…

Had Priscilla kept them tied up with ribbon, hidden in a box? Or had she valued Nat's love so little that she threw them away or burned them or simply left them to flake into dust?

Perfect Priscilla, Nat's ideal woman…Lizzie could discount some of Lady Willoughby's words for the jealous spite they most certainly were, but in one case she was horribly afraid that Priscilla might be right. The deep feelings and emotions—the love— that Nat would have for a woman like that would endure far longer than the lust he had for Lizzie. One day his desire for Lizzie would burn itself out, for it was too intense to last and had no deep foundation. And then there would be nothing left at all…

Lizzie found that she was shivering despite the heat of the day. She walked slowly along Fortune Row, largely oblivious to the crowds of people out enjoying the summer sunshine. She sat down on one of the benches in the gardens and stared blankly into space. She had no idea how long she was sitting there for until a shadow fell across her and a voice said, "My lady asked me to deliver this to you, ma'am."

Someone dropped a letter into her hand and Lizzie looked up to see the retreating figure of a maid dressed in a neat uniform. The girl did not look back. Lizzie looked down, puzzled, at the paper in her hand. It looked old and worn and it was not addressed to her—it was addressed to Priscilla Willoughby.

Understanding broke on her then, and with it a

sharp barb of pain. Perfect Priscilla had not wanted her to be in any doubt that Nat really *had* written her those love letters, so she had sent one to Lizzie to read for herself. It sat there on her lap, tempting her to open it and to make her misery complete. It was tied with pink ribbon and the ink was faded and pale and Lizzie's fingers itched to unfold it and see the words that her husband had written to another woman, a woman he had loved. She touched the faded ribbon and tried to resist the urge to unfasten it.

She would not read it. She would *not* torment herself.

She flicked the letter off her lap and onto the path, where a passing lady skewered it with her parasol tip and walked on without even noticing. It gave Lizzie some satisfaction, and when large drops of summer rain started to fall and the ink began to run she felt even better. Soon, she thought, Priscilla's love letter would be no more than pulp. Except that there were no doubt plenty more where that had come from.

She walked home through the rain and ran into the house, soaking wet, to find that Nat had returned for luncheon and was standing discussing household matters with Mrs. Alibone in the hall. Both of them stared at her, with her bedraggled hair and drenched gown, and Lizzie burst out laughing at their identical looks of surprise and disapproval.

"Madam is an Original," Mrs. Alibone said to Nat, in tones of disapproval as Lizzie scampered past, up

the stairs to change. "My former mistress the
Duchess of Cole had very particular ideas on the
behavior of young ladies—"

"I would not take Her Grace as a model of good
behavior," Lizzie commented over her shoulder. "She
tended to try to *murder* those she disapproved of,
didn't she? Something of an overreaction…"

She laughed as Mrs. Alibone drew herself up as
though she had starch in her spine.

That evening Lizzie and Nat went out to a
musicale at the assembly rooms. Alice and Miles
were there and various other members of Fortune's
Folly society, and Lizzie smiled until her face ached,
and chatted, and laughed but later she could not
remember a single thing that she had talked about.
Priscilla Willoughby sat across the room, dazzling in
pale pink, and smiled at Lizzie like a fat cat that had
eaten a particularly delicious saucer of cream, and
when Lizzie got home there was another love letter,
this time tied with scarlet ribbon, waiting for her.
Lizzie put it on the fire and went to bed.

She woke in the night with a low pain aching in
her belly and she knew at once what it meant. Six
weeks without her courses and she had started to
think, started to hope, that she might be expecting a
child. Her mind had tiptoed around the edges of the
thought because she had still been afraid to face it
head-on, but alongside the anxiety had been flickers
of excitement and tiny sparks of expectation as each

day had passed. Now, though, the hope and the excitement were extinguished in one huge flood of despair. It came from nowhere, ambushing Lizzie with its force and power, racing through her in an unstoppable tide, until she had to stuff the pillow into her mouth to prevent herself from crying aloud. The tears were flooding down her face and she pressed herself deep into the warm embrace of her bed, seeking comfort blindly. Nat was in the chamber next door—he had not come to her room that night—and a part of her wanted to run to him. She wanted so much the comfort he could give her. She wanted him to know instinctively that she needed him and to come to *her*. But the door remained obstinately closed and Nat's absence only seemed to underline the distance between them, and Lizzie's stubborn refusal to let others see her grief prevented her from seeking him out.

She stayed in bed the next day and the one after, pleading a sore throat, which was something that conveniently could not be disproved. Nat took one look at her wan face and said he was sure she was right to rest, and kissed her cheek and went out. He brought her flowers that evening, rich red roses from the gardens that smelled heavenly and made her want to go outside into the fresh summer air. He seemed anxious for her but Lizzie felt too tired to talk. She was puzzled, for her courses had never interfered with her life before—they had been trifling inconven-

ient things, but she had never experienced this lassitude. She fell asleep with Nat sitting beside her bed
and awoke in the middle of the night to find him gone.

On the evening five days later when Lizzie finally
got up out of bed, Nat took her to the subscription
ball, evidently hoping it would lift her spirits. Lizzie
drank too much and danced three times with John
Jerrold and tried not to mind that Nat partnered Priscilla Willoughby, who looked stunning in amber silk.

"You look blue-deviled, Lizzie," Alice said to her the
next day as they shared a cup of tea at the Pump Rooms.

"I have the headache," Lizzie confessed. "I had
too much wine again last night."

"Why?" Alice asked bluntly.

Lizzie turned her teacup around and around in her
hands. She had been asking herself the same
question. "It makes me feel better," she admitted
after a moment. "I feel so *sad,* Alice, and I do not
understand why. The wine takes the edge of the pain
away, at least for a little."

"And then you wake up feeling worse," Alice said.
She shook her head, exasperation and sympathy
mixed in her gaze. "Lizzie, you are in grief. You are
mourning for Sir Montague and for all the things that
you have lost. Be gentle with yourself." She leaned
forward. "Have you told Nat how you are feeling?"

Lizzie shook her head slowly. "I told him I had a
sore throat."

Alice's expression twisted. "Lizzie—"

"I'm not pregnant," Lizzie said suddenly. The words tumbled out of her, impossible to quell once she had started. "I'm not pregnant, Alice, and I wanted to be so much. I did not realize how much I wanted a baby until I knew there was not to be one." She knotted her fingers together. "I thought it would be a terrible thing to happen, but now that it has not…" She stopped as a tear plopped into the dregs of her tea.

"Oh, Lizzie," Alice said. Her tone was so soft. She put a hand over Lizzie's clenched ones. "Lizzie, I am sorry. I was not sure, that day at The Old Palace, that it was what you truly wanted."

"Neither was I." Lizzie sniffed, scrubbing at her eyes with a furtive hand so that the other tea drinkers in the Pump Rooms would not see her tears. Her unhappiness felt like a shard of glass wedged in her throat. "I wanted it so much, Alice," she said. "I still do. And at least then there would be something binding me to Nat." She looked up and met the arrested expression in Alice's face. "Don't look at me like that," she said. "I know you and Miles are blissfully happy, but not all of us are so blessed."

Alice squeezed her tightly clasped hands. "You and Nat were friends not long ago, Lizzie," she said. "What happened?"

"It all went wrong when I fell in love with him," Lizzie said sadly. "I don't know why, but I cannot talk to him now. He feels like a stranger." She bit her lip.

"I should never have married him. I knew it would be a disaster."

"Talk to Nat," Alice said. "Tell him how you feel—"

"No!" Lizzie straightened up. "I can't, Alice," she said more quietly. "Am I to tell him I love him and lose my pride as well as everything else?"

"Pride is a cold comforter," Alice said. She sighed sharply. "Truly I think Nat is almost as big a fool as you. He must be the only person in Fortune's Folly who cannot see that you are in love with him. I am inclined to give him a piece of my mind!"

"Don't!" Lizzie grabbed her hand. "Please, Alice. Don't. Leave it to me." She looked away. "I will talk to him in my own good time. I am not ready yet. My feelings are too raw."

"All right." Alice looked at her and sighed again. "But *please* be careful, Lizzie. You frighten me. So much has changed for you recently. It is no wonder you feel cast adrift." She looked at her. "What are you going to do for the rest of the day?"

"I have no idea," Lizzie said. The hours stretched before her, empty and dull. What had she done with her time before she married? For a terrifying moment she could not even remember.

"Lady Waterhouse. Lady Vickery." Priscilla Willoughby had paused beside their table and was now looking down her perfectly proportioned nose at them. "How charming to see you both here." She bared her teeth is a smile. "And how well you have fitted into local society, Lady Vickery. But then of course—" she flicked an imaginary speck from her gloves "—Lady Membury once told me that you were the cleverest maid she had ever employed." And she nodded and moved on.

Lizzie was halfway out of her seat, consumed with rage and disgust, her own concerns forgotten, when Alice grabbed her arm.

"Lizzie, no!" Alice hissed.

"I have had enough of that spiteful bitch!" Lizzie said.

"Yes," Alice said, her hand tightening on Lizzie's arm, "but a fight in the Pump Rooms is not the answer." She pulled her friend back down into her chair and poured another cup of tea. Lizzie, shaking with fury, was astonished to see that Alice's face was quite calm and her hand quite steady.

"I do not know how you can be so serene," she began, then stopped as Alice met her eyes and she saw the bright fury there was there.

"I am not," Alice said, "but I refuse to give Lady Willoughby the satisfaction of seeing that she has angered me. She wishes to provoke me into an ill-bred display simply to prove her point. Well, I will not oblige her."

"No," Lizzie said, subsiding. "Of course you are right."

"Revenge," Alice said, very precisely, "is far better than an overt display of anger."

Lizzie sat forward, her attention caught. "What did you have in mind?" she said.

"I HEARD THAT LADY WILLOUGHBY sent her apologies tonight," Alice whispered to Lizzie in the interval at the *al fresco* concert on Fortune Parade that evening. Miles and Nat had gone to fetch refreshments and she and Lizzie were sitting beneath an awning in the warm evening sunshine, and listening as the orchestra tuned up for the second half of the performance.

"She claims to be suffering from a headache but the servants say she has contracted a dreadful skin complaint. Apparently she itches, and the…um…intimate areas itch the most. It is the latest *on dit.*"

"How awful," Lizzie said, shuddering. "Do they have any idea what could have caused it?"

"No," Alice said. "It is quite a mystery." She examined her programme. "Oh good, the Bach cantata is next." She lowered her voice again. "I have heard, though, that the juice of the Buckthorn Alder can be very itchy if it is accidentally rubbed against the skin."

"I heard that, too," Lizzie said, nodding to Lady Wheeler and Mary as they passed by on their way to their seats. "Particularly if it is accidentally absorbed into one's undergarments."

"But of course that could never happen," Alice said, smiling angelically as Miles and Nat rejoined them, "for that would necessitate the juice getting into the laundry water and how could that be?"

"Only by the most extraordinary accident," Lizzie agreed. "Perhaps if she had received a gift of something like lavender water that she believed was from an old admirer…" She cast Nat a sideways glance under her lashes but he was talking to Miles and fortunately not attending. "Did they say how long it was likely to be before Lady Willoughby recovered?" she asked.

"Several days, I believe," Alice said, shaking her head.

"Really?" Lizzie said. "How terrible." Her eyes met Alice's and they smiled, conspiratorial as a pair of schoolgirls. It felt good to be wicked, Lizzie thought; good to take revenge on Priscilla Willoughby, who so richly deserved her comeuppance. She doubted that Priscilla was the sort of woman to be routed for long, however. It would take more than a bottle of doctored lavender water to vanquish her. Like the evil witch in the fairy tale she would surely be back for revenge.

Lizzie glanced at Nat and tried to erase the knowledge of his love letters to Priscilla from her mind. It had all been a very long time ago, she told herself. Nat might not love *her* but he no longer loved Priscilla, either. He could not. Nevertheless her jealousy of the woman who had once held her husband's heart was difficult to ignore. All those letters, all those declarations of love, all the words and the emotion that she wanted and was denied…The music started again and Lizzie fixed her gaze on the orchestra and tried not to care too much.

THE FOLLOWING DAY NAT had left the house before Lizzie had even woken up.

"His lordship has been called away on urgent family business," Mrs. Alibone murmured, when Lizzie came down for breakfast. "He did not wish to wake you but asked that I let you know he hopes to be back this evening."

She slithered out of the room like a snake leaving Lizzie feeling fretful and cast down. Why could Nat not have taken her with him to Water House? It was several years since she had seen his family. Was he ashamed to have married her? He had been absent so often lately that they barely felt married anyway. And why had he not left her a note rather than leaving a message with Mrs. Alibone, whom she hated? The housekeeper, with her sharp tongue and prying gaze, made her feel as though she was a prisoner in her own home.

Lady Wheeler and Mary called that morning, full of barely concealed curiosity as to how the investigation into Sir Montague's murder was proceeding. Lizzie thought that Mary looked dreadful. Her face looked drawn and sallow, her body was twitchy, fidgeting, utterly unable to keep still whilst her mother gossiped and chatted and accepted a second cup of tea.

"One wonders if Sir Thomas will be next," Lady Wheeler said fretfully as she stirred in three spoonfuls of sugar. "I am hoping no one will murder him, for he has been quite attentive to Mary and it would be a feather in her cap to catch him and become Lady Fortune."

"Tom is hardly a suitor I would wish on any of my friends," Lizzie said. "If I tried for a week I doubt I could name a single good quality that he possesses."

"Well at least Mary would be wed," Lady Wheeler said, with a sharp look at Lizzie that suggested that since *she* had managed to secure an Earl she should be a little more understanding of a mother's ambition. "Ever since Lord Armitage's defection Mary has been sadly out of spirits," Lady Wheeler continued, "moping around, sighing and sobbing, until it quite tries my patience—"

There was a clatter as Mary dropped her teaspoon against the china cup. Lizzie saw that her hands were shaking and her brown eyes were full of tears.

"Mama—" Mary whispered.

"I hear that Sir Thomas has also called on Miss Minchin," Lady Wheeler said, ignoring her daughter's anguish, and speaking of her as though she were absent rather than sitting next to her, "so Mary has a rival there, I suppose, though Flora is only a banker's daughter rather than Quality."

"I think it is probably the quality of Flora's fortune that appeals to Tom rather than her breeding," Lizzie said, rising to her feet. She smiled at Mary who managed nothing more than a grimace in return. "I pray you will not get your hopes up, ma'am," Lizzie continued. "Now that my brother has discovered, like Monty before him, that he can fleece his villagers for all manner of taxes I doubt he will bother to tie himself down in wedlock. He is not temperamentally suited to it."

"Well, it is most inconsiderate of him," Lady Wheeler said, taking the hint at last and moving toward the door, "especially when there are so few eligible gentlemen left in town. For what are we to do with Mary now?"

"Leave her in peace, I suggest," Lizzie said, pressing Mary's hands as they parted in the hall. She watched Lady Wheeler and her daughter walk away down the tree-lined avenue, Lady Wheeler's bonnet bobbing as she lectured her daughter and Mary dragging her feet and falling behind like a recalcitrant child.

When Sir Montague had first introduced the Dames' Tax, Lizzie remembered, Lady Wheeler had been one of the most vocal opponents, objecting to Sir James's attempts to buy a suitor for his plain daughter. That had all changed when Lord Armitage had jilted Mary; it was as though she was damaged goods now and her mother could not get rid of her quickly enough. There were a lot of unhappy people in Fortune's Folly as a result of Sir Montague's revival of the medieval taxes, Lizzie thought bitterly. So many of the things that had happened since the previous summer were a direct result of his money-grubbing ways, not least his own death.

Nat had not returned by the afternoon, nor sent

any message, so Lizzie went out riding alone, over the moors and down toward Fortune Hall. She wanted to see her old home, even though she knew it would leave her aching with a nostalgia for the way things had once been before Monty had had his head turned by money and Tom had proved himself such an out-and-out scoundrel. There had been a time when they had all rubbed along together well enough, yet something had gone wrong along the way and now Monty was dead and Tom had gone to the bad and even as she looked at the ancient manor house drowsing in the sun, Lizzie knew that that part of her life was over for good.

She was turning away to take the track for Fortune's Folly village when Tom stepped out of a field gate on her left and startled her so much that she pulled on Starfire's reins and the mare almost reared as a result. Lizzie calmed her automatically as Tom leaned casually against the gate and looked up at her, a smile that was not quite nice curling his lips.

"Well, if it isn't my cardsharp of a little sister," he said. "What brings you in this direction, Lizzie?"

"I was just taking a ride," Lizzie said. "How are you, Tom?"

"I'm better than some, certainly," Tom said. He straightened. "Priscilla Willoughby for one. She asked me to give you a message, Lizzie."

Lizzie raised her brows. "Lady Willoughby is a friend of yours, is she? I might have known." She tilted her head on one side. "I imagine the two of you would deal very well together, with so much malice in common."

"We have an arrangement," Tom said indifferently.

"Is she to become the next Lady Fortune, then?" Lizzie asked, with perfectly calculated innocence.

Tom laughed. He put a hand on Starfire's bridle and stroked the horse's nose gently. It was one of the odd things about Tom, Lizzie thought, that he adored his dogs and his horses and yet was without compassion when it came to people.

"I hardly think so," he said. "I am not wealthy enough to tempt Priscilla and I am not sure I wish to marry such a slut anyway." He looked up. "Don't play games with her, Lizzie. She's much more experienced than you are and she could hurt you badly."

"And you are warning me out of the goodness of your heart?" Lizzie asked. She found she was not unduly shocked to hear that Tom and Lady Willoughby were lovers. She remembered John Jerrold saying that he suspected that Priscilla was a great deal less respectable than she pretended to be. She wondered if Nat knew. Most probably he did not. In his mind Perfect Priscilla was probably pickled forever as the flawless, ideal wife. And Lizzie knew she could never tell Nat the truth because it would merely look like jealousy talking.

Tom laughed again. "Hardly that." He looked up at her, narrowing his eyes against the sun. "There are things you don't know, Lizzie—things about that oh-so-worthy husband of yours. That's what I want to tell you."

Lizzie's hands tightened involuntarily on the reins and Starfire side stepped. Tom grinned to see his barb strike home. "Your Achilles' heel," he said softly, "your love for the undeserving Earl of Waterhouse." He shook his head. "You're a great girl, Lizzie—I admire you, I really do. In so many ways we are so alike, but you are too, too naive."

"Don't bracket me with you," Lizzie said. "I may be wild, Tom, but I'm not a callous, heartless *bastard.*"

"More fool you," her brother said calmly. "You've given your heart to the wrong man, Lizzie."

"You're boring me with all this talk of love, Tom," Lizzie said. Her heart had started to thunder. She felt mortified. The thought of Tom and Priscilla Willoughby laughing over her innocent love for Nat, perhaps as they lay in bed together, made her feel sick. How had Tom known? Could everyone see how she felt? Were her emotions too transparent, her vulnerability evident to everybody? Everybody except Nat…

"What are you going to tell me?" she said, affecting ennui so that Tom should not see how much he was upsetting her. "Is your big piece of news that Nat was once Priscilla Willoughby's lover?"

As soon as the words were out she wondered if Tom was actually going to tell her that Nat was still Priscilla's lover and she felt a lurch of horror and a fresh wave of sickness engulf her. But Tom was shaking his head.

"I'm sure she would wish it," he said, "but no. I'll spare you that torture at least, Lizzie." His eyes were full of mocking amusement as he dealt out scraps of malice like playing cards.

"What I was going to ask," Tom said casually, "was whether you knew that Cousin Gregory Scarlet paid Nat to marry you?"

Lizzie stared at him whilst the sun poured down through the shifting leaves and the birds sang and she could not seem to hear them properly because there was a buzzing in her ears.

Paid to marry you… Paid to marry you…

"A dowry," she said, through stiff lips.

Tom was shaking his head. "A bribe, Lizzie. You know how stuffy Cousin Gregory is. He had heard you were becoming much too much like our mother." He paused. "The drinking, you know. You have a reputation for it. And the flirtations with unsuitable men… Very undignified and unbecoming to the ancient and great name of the Earls of Scarlet."

"You're a fine one to talk of conduct unbecoming," Lizzie said. She felt cold, skin deep, bone deep.

A bribe…Nat had been bribed to marry her…

"It's different for men," Tom said complacently. "I won't be labeled a drunken doxy."

"No," Lizzie said, "just an arrogant, insufferable, hateful *sot*."

Tom laughed with the pleasure of hurting her. Lizzie knew he was enjoying it. She could see it in his face and yet she seemed powerless to resist his provocation.

"You'll have to do better than that if you want to retaliate against me," he said cheerfully. "At least I won't be bought and sold like a piece of meat as you were." He stepped closer, staring up at her. "Cousin Gregory *sold* you, Lizzie, with an extra few thousand to sweeten your dowry, and Nat Waterhouse *bought* you because he needed the money."

Lizzie had heard enough. She dug her heels into Starfire's side and turned the horse so sharply that she knocked Tom flying. Lizzie pulled back and Starfire reared and for one satisfying moment Lizzie saw the genuine terror on her brother's face as the horse's hooves came down toward him. At the last moment she turned again so the horse pirouetted in the most perfect piece of dressage. Tom scrambled to his feet, swearing horribly, and Lizzie looked down at him.

"I never understood your need to hurt people, Tom," she said. "We were close once, you, and me, and Monty. Where did it all go wrong?"

She did not wait for his reply. She rode off toward Fortune's Folly and left Tom standing in the bridle-way staring after her. She could feel the venom in his look and her heart bumped against her ribs with the effort not to cry.

Bought and sold like a piece of meat...

A bribe…

A drunken doxy, just like our mother…

Gregory Scarlet had not wanted anything to do with her from the moment that he had inherited from her father and now all he cared about was preserving the good reputation of the Scarlet name. And Nat had agreed, for the money… For the money… The words drummed in her head with every beat of Starfire's hooves.

When she got back to Chevrons she rubbed Starfire down herself and fed her. Being in the stables with the horses soothed her. It was one of the few things from her past life that was a constant. The house was quiet when she went in. A supper for one was laid on the table in the dining room.

"Lord Waterhouse returned whilst you were out, my lady," Mrs. Alibone said. "He is dining at the Oyster Club tonight and said not to expect him back until late."

Nat was out. Of course he was. He was always out, the husband who had been bribed to marry her. He was working, or he was visiting his family, or he was with his friends…Lizzie felt sick with misery that Nat did not choose to spend his time with her. But then it was money and duty that had forced them to wed, not love.

She stripped off her riding gloves and slapped them down on the table. The decanter on the sideboard seemed to beckon to her, the wine glowing red in the evening sunshine. One little drink would take the edge off her misery.

A drunken doxy, just like our mother...

With a sudden violent sweep of the hand she sent the decanter tumbling onto the floor. It smashed into the skirting board and broke, spilling wine across the carpet. Mrs. Alibone slid back into the room so swiftly Lizzie wondered if she had been lurking outside the door polishing the keyhole.

"Madam!"

"An accident," Lizzie said. "I do apologize for the mess. I'll tidy it up—"

"Madam!" Mrs. Alibone sounded even more outraged at the thought of her mistress cleaning. "You certainly will not!"

Lizzie sighed. "Very well. Thank you, Mrs. Alibone." She glanced at the table with its lonely dinner setting. "Pray tell Cook not to bother with dinner. I shall go out."

Mrs. Alibone raised her brows. "Out? Madam, you cannot! It is not the Done Thing!"

"Yes, I can," Lizzie said. "I am going out without my husband. Again. Shocking, is it not?"

And she ran up the stairs to get changed.

CHAPTER ELEVEN

"I WILL BE MAKING your cousin Mary an offer of marriage tomorrow morning." Tom Fortune lay sprawled in his chair in the study at Fortune Hall. His shirt was hanging loose and his trousers were unbuttoned. He was enjoying the ministrations of Priscilla Willoughby's skilful mouth and equally clever hands and was feeling very mellow. Being pleasured by a veiled woman was proving extremely erotic. Priscilla had refused to let him either see her or touch her because the skin complaint she was suffering had left her with a terrible rash. Tom thought it hilarious that Lizzie had apparently inflicted such humiliation on his vain mistress. Priscilla seemed to find it less amusing. In fact Tom suspected that the only reason she was here and was prepared to indulge his vices as usual was because she wanted something from him in return.

"I tried to seduce Mary," he continued. "I wanted to make sure she would be obliged to wed me."

"What happened?" Priscilla's mouth brushed his cock in the lightest and most tantalising of touches, her cunning little tongue circling him, flicking and delving. Tom shivered with enjoyment.

"She ran from me like the startled virgin she is," he said. "I do believe she was terrified. Stephen Armitage cannot have had her when they were betrothed. Or perhaps he did—perhaps that was why she took fright."

Priscilla's mouth tugged on him and he groaned. "At least you were spared the appalling tedium of having to make love to her," she murmured. "Do you think she will accept you?"

"I'll make sure she does," Tom said. His mind was starting to splinter with pleasure. He really did not want to talk, could not talk. But Priscilla kept accompanying her attentions with questions; questions it was becoming more and more difficult for him to concentrate on.

"Did you speak to your sister?" she asked, fondling him, stroking until he thought he would burst. "Did you?" Suddenly she bit him, not quite gently.

"Ow! Yes!" Smarting, Tom almost pushed her away, but already she was soothing the hurt, laving it away with her tongue and he started to relax again as renewed pleasure swept away the pain. "I told her about Waterhouse being paid to wed her," he gasped, shifting in his chair to aid Priscilla's movements. "She was very distressed, though she hid it well."

"Good." Priscilla rewarded him with the subtlest and sweetest of caresses. "She is an evil little witch and she deserves to suffer for what she did to me."

When Tom had first heard about the doctored lavender water he had been filled with admiration for Lizzie—and contempt for Priscilla in believing for a moment that Nat Waterhouse would have sent it. Now, though, as Priscilla urged him to the most exquisite climax, he was not inclined to do anything other than agree with whatever she said.

"I think," he panted, "she is suffering very much indeed."

"Good," Priscilla said again and he heard the satisfaction in her voice and thought she was smiling as she teased him over the edge, and he came with a triumphant shout and the release rolled over him leaving him spent and almost—almost—regretful that he was to marry Mary rather than her cousin.

NAT HAD BEEN DISAPPOINTED not to see Lizzie before he had come out. Mrs. Alibone had said that she had gone riding and Nat had been glad of it for he knew that riding was one of the things that made Lizzie very happy. He wanted her to be happy and manifestly she was not. He could not understand why things seemed so different from how they had been before he and Lizzie wed, but evidently they were and it was his task to discover why and to solve the problem. That was what he had been doing from the first: solving the problem of Celeste's disgrace, solving the problem of Lizzie's lost reputation, protecting his family, trying to make all well again because he cared deeply for them all and, devil take it, dealing with problems was what men *did*. It was the most damnable thing that everything seemed to be going to hell in a handbasket rather than sorting itself out. His father was dangerously ill, Tom Fortune was circling and threatening further black-mail, Lizzie was grief-stricken and seemed wilder by the day and under the circumstances the July meeting of the Oyster Club, a most exclusive gentlemen's dining club with very restricted membership, excellent food and ample wine, was exactly what Nat needed to help him forget for a few short hours that the rest of his life was in chaos.

He reached for his glass. They served wine in half pint glasses at the Oyster Club and that always loosened men's tongues. It was Nat's task, along with Dexter and Miles, to listen for anything that might throw some light on the Fortune murder case for they were lamentably short of leads. No one appeared to have seen or heard anything on the night that Monty Fortune had died, other than a vague rumor of a masked woman seen flitting about the village. There had been the argument between Monty and someone else several nights before his death but again, no one had seen the other person or could identify them. They were making little progress, and yet in cases of this kind something usually gave in the end. It was a matter of patience and endurance, rather like his marriage.

Further down the long table, Nat could see Dexter and Miles talking to various acquaintances. The Club was eclectic, membership comprising local businessmen, professional men and gentry. The food arrived, the famous oysters that gave the Club its name followed by a prime beefsteak. Nat started to relax and tried not to think about Lizzie, left at home. For some reason the image made him feel edgy. The last time he had left her alone in the evening she had gone out and almost gambled away the Scarlet Diamonds. The village was still talking about it. It was surely impossible that she could do anything else even remotely as outrageous but he was painfully aware that they had never really discussed the matter properly, had not really talked about anything of importance in the last few weeks because Lizzie seemed so locked in her grief that he could not reach her and he knew he had used his work as an excuse not to try as hard as he should…

Some sort of disturbance was taking place at the other end of the room. Servants were seen scurrying in all directions, diving for cover. He heard masculine voices exclaim:

"I say! Lady Godiva!"

"What ho! What a filly!"

Men were standing now, craning their necks to see, raising their glasses in a toast. The dazzling lights of the chandeliers shone in Nat's eyes and he blinked, completely unable to believe what he was seeing.

A woman on horseback was coming up the sweeping staircase. The horse's hooves made no sound on the thick red carpet and the soft jingle of its harness was the only noise as the whole banqueting hall fell silent. The woman was young and she sat very tall and straight in the saddle, moving gently with the motion of the horse. There was a little smile curving her lips and a wicked spark in her green eyes. Her long titian hair tumbled in glorious array over her shoulders and down to her waist. Her white thighs gripped the horse's side as she urged it up the staircase.

Nat's brain refused to accept the evidence of his eyes.

She was stark naked.

Her lissom, pale skin looked like alabaster. One small but perfectly rounded breast peeked from beneath the cascade of her hair, the nipple pink and pouting from the ministrations of the cool night air. The other breast was hidden, but the auburn strands of her hair seemed only to emphasize its tempting curve. Her hands were holding the reins in her lap covering what little was left of her modesty.

Nat heard the men around him draw in their breath sharply as they saw what he saw. And what he saw was his wife, the new Countess of Waterhouse, and she was completely nude, displaying herself in all her wanton beauty in front of the assembled company of the Oyster Club.

Nat's first response was complete denial. This

simply could not be Lizzie. Not even she would do something so outrageous, so scandalous. The room spun about him and he closed his eyes for a moment, but when he opened them and the world steadied, Lizzie was still there and she was still very, very naked in front of forty extremely appreciative gentlemen. She was riding along the corridor now, toward the big balcony windows and there was a very indiscreet rush of men in her wake.

Swift on the heels of Nat's disbelief came shock, sharp and sickening, and a mixture of fury and mortification. Men were smacking their lips now, eyes bulging from their heads, the coarsest of jests on their lips. *Coarse jests about his wife.* They were looking on *his wife* with lust. No doubt they all wanted to ravish her senseless. And Lizzie herself, provocative, triumphant Lizzie, was smiling at them alluringly, enjoying the admiration and the attention.

Nat watched as Lizzie approached the open doors of the balcony window. It was a good twelve-foot drop to the ground and a ripple of apprehension spread about the room as the assembled company took in her intention.

"Thirty guineas says she will make it!" One enterprising gambler declared, slapping his coins down on the table.

"Fifty against!"

The crowd jostled for the best view.

Nat pulled himself together and strode toward his wife. "Elizabeth!"

His voice was perhaps a little less authoritative than he might have desired, whether from anger or shock or a combination of emotions. Whatever the reason, Lizzie ignored him completely and walked the horse up to the edge of the balcony.

There was a moment's pause and then they jumped, horse and rider united in a most elegant and perfectly executed leap down to the street. Nat—and everyone else—was afforded the most perfect view of Lizzie's pert, rounded buttocks and the quickest, tantalizing flash of the crease between her thighs. A concerted sigh ran through all the men in the room, and then the place erupted into chaos as they abandoned the landing and ran down the stairs to see if both horse and rider had survived the jump. Nat ran, too, down the staircase and out into the warm, damp night, torn between fear and an anger so intense he had never experienced it before. Men were pushing and shoving to get a view and as Nat ruthlessly cut his way to the front of the crowd he saw Lizzie trotting demurely away down the street. The lamplight gleamed on the pale skin of her bare back and buttocks and on the lovely curves and hollows of her body. The crowd burst into spontaneous applause.

"I say! How marvelous!"

"Splendid creature!"

Nat felt the relief rip through him followed swiftly

by ungovernable rage. He saw Miles approach him and then his friend put a hand on his arm and started to speak but Nat did not seem able to hear him. He shook Miles off violently and set off down the street in the direction that the horse had gone. He could still hear the sound of hoofbeats echoing through the night air.

She had gone too far this time.

The blood roared in his ears. What had he been thinking to leave Lizzie alone again? How could he have been so foolishly smug and complacent as to think that she might sit quietly waiting for him, when she was no doubt bored and lonely and so like a child throwing a tantrum she had to do something completely outrageous? This was Lizzie Scarlet, the wild, headstrong, *wilful* miss who was no more likely to change and reform than her gray mare would turn to a roan gelding. Nothing could excuse this behavior— not Lizzie's grief nor her misery nor her anger. The truth was that she was spoiled to the bone and she was never going to change. She had made him a laughingstock and proved publicly that their marriage was a sham and a debacle.

The anger threatened to devour him whole. How many years had he known Lizzie? How many times had she pulled a trick that was, if not as appalling as this one, then disgraceful and scandalous and undisciplined? When she had been no more than Sir Montague's naughty little sister it had not mattered. He had laughed, and shaken his head over her wildness whilst thinking privately that she was a hoyden who had been dragged rather than brought up. Now, suddenly, it mattered terribly. Everything was different because she was his wife.

Nat found that he was running down the Fortune Street, following the faint, fading rap of hooves until he came to the mews at the back of Chevrons. His breath was coming in short, sharp bursts. His blood fizzed with rage and tension. He stormed into the stables and came up short to find Lizzie there, calmly rubbing her horse down. She was wearing a loose dressing robe now, though her feet were still bare, and the fact that she was clothed now only seemed to incense Nat further. For some reason he had expected her to run and hide from him, and her blatant refusal to back down, to accept blame, to beg his forgiveness for her dreadful behavior, was the last straw. And in that moment he realized with appalled horror that he was hugely, hopelessly and unbearably aroused. He looked at the saddle lying on the floor and thought of it pressed between her thighs, and barely managed to repress his groan.

He grabbed her by the shoulder and spun her around. She stood there, the brush in one hand, her face set and pale. In her eyes was a sparkle of rage that met and matched his.

"Aren't you going to congratulate me?" she said pertly. "It was the most perfect jump. Starfire—" she patted the horse's neck "—is all spirit and no fear."

All spirit and no fear.

Nat realized that he was almost too insane with rage and arousal to speak. He took Lizzie by the shoulders and pushed her roughly ahead of him out of the stall and into the hay store next door. The door of the stall banged behind them and the horse shifted. Nat caught sight of one of the grooms out in the yard, his face a picture of shock and speculation. No doubt he had seen Lizzie ride in, naked and shameless. Nat did not know why that should worry him particularly when every other gentleman in the county had just seen her displaying herself with abandon, but somehow it did. He slammed the door of the store-room in the groom's face, shot the bolt and turned to his wife. He grabbed the neck of her robe and wrenched it from her so that she was once more standing naked in front of him.

"And you think that *this* is the appropriate attire for riding?" His voice shook so much he could barely force out the words. "And in front of every one of my friends and acquaintances?"

Her chin came up. She made no attempt to cover herself. Once more her bright auburn hair covered her shoulders and tumbled over her provocative little breasts and she put her hands on her hips. "No doubt they envied you," she said, her gaze going to the immense bulge in his pantaloons.

"No doubt they thought you a whore and wanted to have you on the banqueting table," Nat said. The mere thought of any other man possessing her—or even wanting to possess her—drove him to insanity. "Was that what you wanted?"

The fury sparked again in Lizzie eyes. She threw the brush at him. He ducked as it sailed over his head.

"Bastard!" she said. "I hear my cousin bribed you to marry me. All that talk of honor and saving my reputation and *caring* for me—" Her voice broke. "Oh, I knew you needed the money, too," she finished bitterly. Her breasts were rising and falling rapidly with each gasping breath she took. "At least you were honest about that. But you had my dowry for that. You did not need for Gregory to *sell* me to you, as well—"

Nat made a grab for her, but she slithered from his grip, lithe and slippery, and snatched the riding crop that was on the table. She held it out toward him like a weapon.

"Don't touch me or I'll hit you! I mean it!"

"Lizzie," Nat said. "Please…" He made a desperate final grab for his control. "Can we talk about this?"

In response she brought the crop down on his arm, the pain so jarring he caught his breath.

"Keep away from me!"

"All right," Nat said, the fury whipping through his blood. "If you want to play it like this."

He did not recognize the jumble of lust and fierce violence and frustration within him. It felt as though he had been propelled far beyond his normal self by feelings and emotions that were completely uncontrollable and absolutely alien to his nature. He grabbed the end of the crop and used it to drag Lizzie toward him. She wriggled her arm free again and brought the crop down hard against his buttocks. The sensation, the pleasure and pain, burst through his body in an explosion of sparks. His cock jutted fiercely. He groaned. She did it again, with a wicked flick of the wrist and he froze as even more intense feelings racked him. A third time and he almost came where he stood. He tore the crop from her hands and snapped it in half, throwing the pieces into a corner. She did not take the opportunity to run away. She stood in front of him, her eyes and the tilting smile on her lips, taunting him.

"I warned you," she said.

"And I'm warning you." Nat was panting. "Parading yourself before all those men...I am the *only one* who can have you."

She shrugged an insolent shoulder. "That's all you care about, isn't it—the sex and the money. Well, if you want me you'll have to take me."

Even as he reached out to her she whirled away from him and ran for the door. She was quick, but now he was quicker. He caught her by the upper arms and spun her around so that her bare back was against the rough brick wall of the store. He yanked her head back with one hand tangled in the silken tresses of her hair and ground his mouth against hers and in return she bit his lip hard and he tasted blood.

This was madness, this frenzied, desperate need he had for her. He knew it and the fact that it was so far removed from his usual rational demeanor filled him with equal measures of despair and arrant desire. He did not understand why he felt driven by the need to tame her but he grabbed one of the leading reins from the table and looped it about her wrists, dragging them above her head and securing the leather over a jutting metal hook. The expression in her eyes when she realized that he had restrained her was feral. She kicked out at him but he brought his body in close to her, trapping her flailing legs between his thighs. She writhed and wriggled now to no avail.

"Lizzie," he said. They were close, staring into each other's faces, her breasts touching his chest as they both panted for breath. And then that impudent smile twitched her lips again.

"Nat," she said. "How far would you go?"

"As far as you," Nat said. "Further."

The dare was in her eyes. "You think so? Try me. Test me. Take me."

Her words snapped the last of Nat's control. He ran his hands down her body, over the breasts that had so tormented him with their pert, pouting beauty when she had flaunted them in the face of every man in Fortune's Folly.

Take me...

Now at last he could pinch and squeeze and suck

on her until she cried out and arched to his mouth, satisfying himself with both her submission and her eagerness. He could part the silken softness of her thighs and find the slick center of her and feel the way that her body closed about his marauding fingers just as it would squeeze him to an excess of pleasure and lust. He could run his thumb over the nub of her and revel in the way that she twitched and jerked in her bonds, and the way in which he could demand this response from her and she would give all she had because she was as desperate as he.

"You should not have provoked me," he said against her mouth whilst his fingers still invaded her, sliding, stroking. "You did not understand what would happen."

Her eyes were a slumberous green from sensual arousal now, her lashes a dark flicker against her cheek, her lips parted on each needy breath.

"Oh, I understand this well enough," she said. "It is the only thing between us that I do understand." She writhed. "Finish me. Please. I don't mind begging."

Nat shook his head. "Consequences," he said. He twisted his fingers inside her a little and heard her gasp.

"I'll come anyway," she said, "just to spite you."

"And then you'll come again," Nat said, kissing her in such gentle counterpoint to his words, "and again until I say you can stop."

She did come then, against his hand. And again, still restrained, at the insistence of his lips and tongue, and then he could wait no longer and unfastened her bonds and tossed her down into the pile of hay. He held her with one hand whilst he freed his shaft with the other. He lowered his mouth to hers again and she kissed him back, as insatiable as she was angry, her hunger as violent as his own. He was so hard by now that he thought he might explode, simply shatter. She pulled up his shirt, scoring his back with her nails, biting his chest and shoulders. There was no gentleness in her touch. She wanted revenge and it hurt. And when she dug her fingers into the stinging marks that the crop had made on his buttocks he spread her and plunged into her with hot, ruthless strokes and came immediately, shouting her name. Lizzie screamed and her body arched and convulsed about him. It was over in seconds.

Afterward, when he had recovered a modicum of strength, Nat wrapped her in the tattered remnants of her gown and carried her into the house. Her body felt soft and compliant in his arms, her head against his shoulder, her eyes closed. The edge had gone off Nat's anger now but he felt bruised and tired yet still unsatisfied. He hunted that satisfaction and fulfilment all night long, seeking oblivion in Lizzie's body, driving her to wild peaks of pleasure, making her climax again and again until she was spent. He woke her simply so that he could touch her at will and do whatever he wished with her pale, tantalizing body. She did not refuse him once. He lay with his shaft buried deep within her, hard and hot, for several hours, not moving, resisting the twitch and spasm of her body about him as though determined to show he could resist the power she held over him. He felt as though he was in a dream in which he pursued something so elusive that it was forever within reach and yet it slipped away from him just when he thought he had captured it. Even when he took her for the final time the pleasure overwhelmed him only to ebb away and leave him exhausted and empty, deprived of whatever it was he sought.

Nat fell asleep trying to puzzle out what it was that he was searching for and awoke as the summer dawn broke into the room in all its shimmering golden glory. He turned instinctively to search for Lizzie's warmth and found the bed empty. The corresponding barrenness inside him seemed to deepen and grow. He felt at the same time scoured clean of the anger of the previous night and yet even more hollow and lonely than he had before. And he felt shocked. Shocked with himself and appalled at what he had done. He could not escape the thought that his marriage, for all its extremes of physical pleasure, was a complete disaster in other respects and he did not know what to do to put it right. He did not even know where to start.

Where was Lizzie?

Nat's apprehension started to increase. Last night... Last night he had been intolerably angry with his new wife, so furious and possessive and distraught that he had taken her and used her. He had probably frightened her or given her a disgust of him. Lizzie was wild, his perfect physical match; she aroused in him emotions that he had never dreamed he possessed and that made him forget to be gentle. He had been so incensed that he had made no allowances for her relative youth and lack of experience.

Guilt twisted his gut. She had run from him now just as she had after that first night in the folly. On the thought he got up, grabbed his dressing robe and went to the door that connected their rooms. It was locked.

"Lizzie?" He rattled the handle. "Lizzie!"

He went out into the corridor and was about to try the other door into Lizzie's room when he heard a step behind him.

"May I be of assistance, Lord Waterhouse?"

Mrs. Alibone was standing in the corridor behind him, wearing a long black dressing gown of formidable respectability, a candle in one hand. "If it is locked I could fetch the spare set of keys," she continued. Her eyes were bright with prurient excitement and suddenly Nat felt sick.

"No," he said. "Thank you." He was not having the housekeeper intruding into Lizzie's room and perhaps finding her distraught, in floods of tears. It was bad enough that the entire household knew that Lizzie had ridden out naked the night before—and that when they returned he had ravished her in the stables. There would be plenty of talk without providing a sequel. Suddenly, despite his anger the previous night, he felt desperately, feverishly protective of Lizzie.

"Thank you, Mrs. Alibone," he said pointedly, when the housekeeper made no attempt to leave, "you can go now."

Only when Mrs. Alibone had slid silently away did he turn the handle. By now he was shaking. The door was not locked, but Lizzie's bed was neat, turned down for the night but untouched.

Nat snatched his clothes, dressing haphazardly in shirt and pantaloons, and managing—just—to drag on his boots without the assistance of his valet. He ran down the stairs, through the waking house and out into the garden.

Where was Lizzie? Where would she run?

Almost as soon as the words formed in his mind he saw her, sitting on the wooden swing under the wide spreading branches of an ancient apple tree. She was swinging very slowly backward and forward. Her head was bent and the early-morning sun burnished the deep auburn strands of her hair, setting them alight. She wore a bright yellow gown that looked fresh and pretty. Nat felt some strange sensation squeeze his heart as though it were clenched tight inside a fist.

She had not run from him after all. Despite everything she was still here. The relief overwhelmed him.

He moved toward her across the dew-drenched grass. A blackbird sang in the tree above her head. The scent of roses was on the air. Then Lizzie looked up and the misery he saw in her green eyes made Nat's heart clench again, this time in shock, for it was stark and painful to witness.

"Lizzie," he said. "Sweetheart—"

She stood up and let the rope of the swing slip from her hand.

"This has to stop, Nat," she said. "I cannot bear it any longer."

CHAPTER TWELVE

LIZZIE HAD WOKEN before the dawn, when the very first call of the birds had broken the quiet of the night and the very first rays of the sun had barely started to lighten the eastern sky. She had been profoundly glad that Nat had not stirred when she slipped from the bed. She had known she had to get out of the house, into the fresh air, to breathe, *to think.*

In the peace of the early morning she had sat in the garden and thought about the disaster that was her marriage. She had been so angry with Nat last night for his mercenary acceptance of Gregory Scarlet's bribe and even more so because he had not told her about it, and he had been equally angry with her for her wildness and her outrageous behavior. They had been pushed as far apart as the poles. That such mutual fury had erupted into equally mutual desire had not surprised her in the least. That was the way that it was between herself and Nat.

That was the only thing there was between herself and Nat.

And it was not enough for her.

Oh, she knew that sex without love was possible. Hundreds, thousands of people had sex without being in love with one another and evidently Nat was one of those people who had no difficulty in separating out the two things. She was not. And now, finally, it had broken her heart and she knew she could never do it again.

She looked at Nat now as he approached her across the grass. He was in no more than shirt and breeches and he looked casual and disheveled, as though he had pulled on his clothes carelessly. The breeze flattened his shirt against his muscular torso and ruffled his dark hair. He looked troubled and harried, and the love she had for him pounded through Lizzie with every beat of her pulse. She knew it was a catastrophe to feel like this but she could not help herself. She could not deny her love or fall out of love with Nat simply because he was unable to return her feelings.

Last night she had wanted to be able to provoke him and to know that she could rouse a response from him. She had done so. But this morning she faced the hard truth that it was not the response she wanted. She wanted to know him properly, to feel as close to him emotionally as she was physically. She wanted his love, and he could not give that to her. Each time they made love it became more difficult for her to hold back her feelings because although she could respond to him and take pleasure—great pleasure, she admitted—in the act, it left her feeling cheated and desolate, more acutely aware than ever that outside their bedroom they barely spoke.

"This has to stop, Nat," she said. "I cannot bear it any longer."

She saw the expression of bewilderment deepen on his face. "I don't understand," he said.

No. And she could not explain to him, not completely, because in doing so she would lay her feelings beneath his feet and he would crush them, not deliberately, for she was sure that he would never seek to hurt her on purpose, but simply because he could not match her love for him.

"I'm sorry," she said. "I am sorry about last night. I was very angry and upset to discover that you had taken money from Cousin Gregory to marry me. It made me behave very badly."

Nat rubbed his forehead. "I am sorry, too," he said. "I treated you very badly. Your anger seems to fuel mine and then it is madness between us."

Lizzie chose her words with care. "I think that we need to get to know one another better," she said. "We have barely spoken since we wed. It feels as though we are strangers to one another now. And until we have resolved our difficulties I feel we should not sleep with each other again."

The look of bewilderment on Nat's face was replaced by a rather comical look of horror. If Lizzie had not felt so wretched she might even have laughed.

"Not sleep with one another?" he repeated.

Trust a man to pick up on that point first, Lizzie thought. "Not have sex with one another," she elaborated. "A sex ban," she said, warming to her theme, "like the Lysistrata in Ancient Greece. No touching, no kissing until we know one another better." Her classical education had been somewhat neglected—in fact, her entire education had been somewhat neglected since governesses had not stayed long at Scarlet Park and even less time at Fortune Hall—but she had a vague recollection of a play in which the women had withdrawn their sexual favors.

"Lizzie, we have known one another for nine years," Nat said. "It is not as though we are strangers to each other."

And you do not really know me at all, Lizzie thought, nor do I know you. She started to walk slowly across the lawn toward the house.

"I realize that," she said, "but for almost all our acquaintance I was no more than Monty's little sister to you, and you…"

You were like a hero to me.

He had been. Nine years older and with all the glamour that age and experience could bestow, he had always seemed out of her reach.

"There is a vast gap between the friendship we had before," Lizzie said, "and being husband and wife."

"Many people who marry are practically strangers to one another when they wed," Nat said. "It is accepted."

Lizzie thought of Flora Minchin. Flora and Nat had been virtual strangers who would have wed and perhaps Nat would have been more comfortable with a wife he did not need to know well. All he had wanted was someone who was rich and could one day fulfill the role of Duchess of Waterhouse with aplomb. Instead he had got her, rich, it was true, but a complete hoyden.

"I know," she said. "Unfortunately I cannot live like that." She looked him in the eyes. "It makes me unhappy to give myself to you with such abandonment and yet to feel so remote from you the rest of the time," she said. "It feels wrong to me. I need to know you better, Nat. I need time."

I need to try to make you love me…

She trembled a little at the thought. Perhaps she was mad even to imagine that she could turn his caring and his desire for her into something deeper and more profound. She did not know; all she knew was that she owed it to herself to try and that she was determined that she would give them this chance.

"I understand that you might need time to adjust to your new situation," Nat said. "This is strange for you and new, and you are young and have experienced so much loss lately…" He stopped, frowning more deeply. "If I hurt you last night…"

Lizzie knew that he thought she was shocked at

the physical demands he was making on her and so she was withdrawing because she needed time to come to terms with them. In an odd way, although he had misunderstood her reasons, she loved him all the more for trying to give her what she wanted even when he did not understand.

"You did not hurt me," she said, "but I do need some time. I am sorry. It is true that I am in mourning and I feel very angry and resentful all the time and that is why I go a little mad and do such scandalous things…" She stopped. She knew that one day soon she would need to talk to him about all the pent-up anger and frustration and misery that was inside her or it would poison everything. This morning her hurt was too fresh and new to try, and she felt so weary, but she would explain as best she could very soon.

"Will you do it for me, Nat?" she appealed. "Will you try to know me better, do things together, talk to one another?"

She could see that he still did not understand why she needed it to be this way but that he could also see how passionately it mattered to her. He took her hand and she tried not to shiver with hope and longing.

"Very well," he said. "I know you are angry and unhappy." The lines about his eyes eased as he smiled a little. "Indeed I would have to be blind not to have noticed and I am sorry that I have been angry, too, and not more patient with you."

Lizzie felt almost winded with love for him in that moment. "You would have to be a very complaisant husband indeed not to be infuriated by my behavior," she whispered, and he smiled at her again, looking tired and sad, and she wanted to soothe that sadness away.

"Would you like to go riding with me later—take a picnic, perhaps?" Nat said. "We could make a start on getting to know one another better."

"I should like that very much," Lizzie agreed, smiling with dazzling pleasure. A tiny seed of hope was unfurling in her heart, so new and delicate that she was almost afraid to put too much trust in it.

Nat's thumb moved gently over the smooth skin on the back of her hand. "But this idea of not touching," Nat continued. "Perhaps you could reconsider?"

Lizzie looked up at him. The soothing movement of his thumb and the warm clasp of his hand on hers were very seductive. She was tempted to compromise. But that way lay danger and weakness. In no time they would kiss and then they would make love again and she would be back where she had started having lost the chance to win the thing that she so desperately desired, Nat's love.

She removed her hand from his. "I am sorry," she said. "No compromises." Despite herself, her voice came out a little huskily from the effect of his proximity. Nat heard it and immediately his eyes narrowed to a predatory gleam.

"You will be the one who breaks the terms first," he said softly.

"No, I will not," Lizzie said.

"Yes, you will because you have no patience."

Perhaps, Lizzie thought, he knows me better than I imagined. But I will show him.

She smiled into his eyes. "I'll wager I do not."

Nat smiled straight back at her and Lizzie felt her head spin. This was different. This was new. Her husband was flirting with her. Nat Waterhouse, whom she had known since she was eleven years old, who had viewed her as the rather troublesome little hoyden whom he was always extracting from scrapes, was actually flirting with her.

This is the bit we missed out, Lizzie thought suddenly. We never had a courtship. We went straight from a rather strained friendship to an even more strained marriage and there was no time to adjust. But now we can change that…

Suddenly she felt light-headed with excitement.

Nat took her hand again and kissed the palm and Lizzie snatched it away from him. She could feel the imprint of his lips on her skin and curled her fingers over the place where the kiss had been. "You are cheating already!" she protested.

"I'll wager you lose, sweetheart," Nat said. "I will see you at breakfast." He strolled away across the grass and Lizzie watched him go, her heart suddenly lifting. He had never called her sweetheart before that morning. He had probably never thought of her in that way. Of course Nat had no idea that she was gambling on far more than he was, on the chance of his love, but suddenly she thought this wager with her husband might prove a great deal more fun than she had imagined.

"So," Laura Anstruther said, "you rode naked into The Granby Hotel, you quarreled passionately with Nat—"

"I'm guessing that you then made love even more passionately," Lydia put in slyly.

"And now you are refusing to sleep with him again until he falls in love with you," Alice finished.

"That's about the sum of it," Lizzie said. She looked around the circle of her friends. "Well? Do you think I am mad?"

They were sitting in Laura's library later that morning and the summer sun was streaming in through the long windows. Alice and Lizzie had been into the village and brought back the news and gossip for their friends and now they were taking tea, all except Lydia who was eating a pickled egg.

"I can't help it," Lydia said defensively, catching Lizzie's grimace as she reached for the jar, "I developed a taste for them a few months ago and now I cannot stop. It's not my fault—being *enceinte* has given me a liking for all manner of strange food."

"The vinegar smells horrid," Lizzie said.

"It tastes wonderful," Lydia said, beaming as she popped another egg into her mouth.

"No, you are not mad," Laura said to Lizzie, patting her hand, "but I do think you are very brave in risking your heart like this. I'm surprised that Nat agreed," she added.

"Well of course he thinks that I am shocked by his demands on me," Lizzie said, coloring a little. "And he did not precisely agree. He sees it more as a wager and thinks I will lose."

"And meanwhile he will be falling in love with you," Alice said.

"If he does not—" Lizzie began. She had not allowed herself to think what might happen if she set out to win Nat's love and failed. Presumably life would feel as desolate as it did now, only worse.

"He *will*," Laura said. "You have had men falling at your feet for years, Lizzie."

"And the one that I want, my own husband, is indifferent to me," Lizzie said. "There's some irony in that."

"Nat is not indifferent to you," Laura said thoughtfully. "He cares deeply. He has always been there for you, Lizzie, for as long as you have known him. What he has not done yet—" she paused thoughtfully "—is to let that regard for you grow into love. But I think he is close and now that you have changed the rules of the game, well…" She smiled. "We shall see."

"There is a horde of people approaching up the lawn," Lydia commented, peering out of the library window. "Whatever can they want? There is Mrs. Broad, and Mrs. Morton from the dressmakers and the haberdasher and the milliner and the florist—"

"And Mrs. Lovell the solicitor's wife, and Mrs. James the doctor's wife, and my mama, and the servants from Fortune Hall—" Alice said.

There was a thunderous crash at the front door as the first of the visitors applied themselves to the knocker, then there was a babble of voices and then Carrington, Laura's aged butler, staggered into the library followed closely by about forty people.

"A number of ladies from the village wish to speak with you, Mrs. Anstruther," Carrington shouted, over the tumult. "There is Mrs. Broad and Mrs. Morton and—"

"Pray don't feel you must announce everyone, Carrington," Laura said hastily as the butler looked as though he was about to expire with the effort. She raised her hand.

"Ladies, please!" The room fell obediently quiet. "What may we do for you?" Laura added.

"You've had the news from the village?" Mrs. Lovell asked, quivering like a greyhound. "We've only just heard—Spencer, Sir Montague's valet, has been found murdered!"

Lizzie gave a gasp. She exchanged a look with Laura. "That is terrible," she said. "I am so sorry—"

"No one liked him very much anyway," Mrs. Broad said, pushing to the front of the crowd. "He

was always full of airs and graces. But the word is
that someone mistook him for Sir Thomas and
murdered him by mistake."

Lizzie could not quite repress a laugh. "Oh dear,
I see. Poor Spencer."

"But that's not why we're here," Mrs. Broad said
bluntly. "We need your help. Sir Thomas is a
complete bastard, begging your pardon, milady, and
we have to stop him. He's only been the squire for
two minutes and he's eaten my chicken and he's
taxing the shopkeepers to raise money to buy all his
fancy clothes and pay for his fancy women—" Here
there was a rumble of agreement and discontent from
the shopkeepers of the village. "And we thought Sir
Montague was bad, but Sir Thomas is worse! Why,
he's levying a tax on *death* now, taking half our
goods when we die. None of us can afford to live and
now we can't afford to die, either!"

"Then it seems in our interests to protect and
support one another and to make sure that no one else
dies for a start," Lizzie said.

"Aye," Mrs. Broad said darkly, "unless it is Sir
Thomas. I'll string him up with my bare hands, so I
will!"

Once again there was a murmur of anger and discontent from the villagers and Lizzie remembered
Dexter saying that before he was murdered, Sir
Montague had received death threats and had been
in danger. Clearly Tom had not heeded the example

that had been made of Monty and it was tempting simply to allow the villagers to lynch him. Lizzie sighed. She supposed that Nat would not approve of mob justice, nor would Dexter, or Miles for that matter, despite the fact that they all detested Tom, too. And in her heart of hearts she did not want Tom to die, cad though he was.

"What are we to do?" Mrs. Morton asked. "This cannot go on."

Lizzie looked at Laura, who was smiling gently at her. "Alas there is very little that I can do in this state," Laura said, gesturing toward her hugely pregnant belly, "but I think that you will take up my mantle admirably, Lizzie."

"I'll help you," Alice added. "On behalf of Laura and Lydia, and everyone else…"

Lizzie looked at Lydia, who was sitting with quiet dignity in her chair, Lydia who more than anyone deserved revenge on Tom. "Do it, Lizzie," she said.

Lizzie looked back at Laura again. Laura nodded slightly.

"All right," Lizzie said, suddenly feeling the weight of responsibility. "The first thing I am going to do is to write to the Prince of Wales to see if he can intervene in this matter of the ancient laws. He was a friend of my father and so he may be disposed to help us—"

"The man's a fool," Mrs. Broad said trenchantly.

"That's treason," Mrs. Morton pointed out.

"It's still true," Mrs. Broad said.

"Ladies," Lizzie said, holding up her hand, "it may be true and it may be treason but if the prince can help us that is good enough for me."

Several people muttered their agreement.

"To get a response will take some time," Lizzie continued. "So in the meantime I suggest a series of…" She paused. "Countermeasures against my brother which will, I hope, stop him in his tracks for a little while. Meet me at the river at four this afternoon and we shall begin."

"What on earth do you plan to do, Lizzie?" Alice said when the ladies had filed out with a pledge to meet later and Carrington had tottered in with more refreshments for the four of them.

"I mean to hit Tom where it hurts," Lizzie said. "What are his favorite things?"

"Clothes and women," Lydia said.

"Quite," Lizzie agreed. "His wardrobe and his collection of pornography." She turned to Laura. "Do you know if Dexter and Miles are occupied today? I would rather not be interrupted in what I plan to do."

"If Spencer has indeed been murdered then I imagine they will both be very busy indeed," Laura said. "Poor man—terrible enough to suffer the fate of murder, but to be murdered by mistake?" She sighed. "Anyway, I am sure the coast is clear."

"What are we going to do?" Alice asked.

"We are going to break into Fortune Hall," Lizzie

said. "We are going to steal Tom's clothes and his pornographic books and we are going to destroy them in full public view." She laughed. "We are going to make him suffer for what he has done to everybody."

CHAPTER THIRTEEN

IT WAS A VERY HOT afternoon. Four o'clock saw Nat strolling through Fortune's Folly village with Miles Vickery, discussing the latest development in the murder case.

"We're very little further forward," Miles was saying. "The murder of Spencer must surely be linked to that of his master and the gossip that he was murdered by mistake for Tom could well be true, but once again no one saw anything except for another mysterious sighting of a masked woman last night."

"At least we know it wasn't Lizzie," Nat said, lips twitching, "unless she combines murder with naked riding."

"Yes…" Miles cleared his throat. "Um…I hope that everything is all right between the two of you?"

"Perfectly, I thank you," Nat said. A few hours ago, he thought, his response might have been very different. Now, however, he had cause to hope.

"Because every man who was there last night views Lady Waterhouse with the utmost admiration and respect," Miles continued.

"Doing it too brown, old fellow," Nat said.

"Well," Miles said, "they view her with…ah…appreciation and admiration. She does have the best seat on a horse of any woman in the county," he added slyly.

"That's more like it," Nat said. He laughed. He found that he was looking forward to seeing Lizzie later and taking a picnic out onto the hills. They would talk. He would explain to her about Gregory Scarlet's contribution to her dowry and he would try to understand the anger and grief that drove her and then, perhaps, their marriage might not be such an unmitigated disaster after all.

"I wonder why all the shops are closed," Miles said, staring around at the shuttered windows along Fortune Street.

"I heard that Tom Fortune was taxing the shopkeepers heavily," Nat said. "Perhaps this is their way of protesting."

"And what is that crowd doing on the bridge?" Miles said. "What on earth is going on?"

"There's a fire!" Nat said, scenting smoke on the air.

They quickened their steps and found themselves on the bridge over the River Tune. The crowd was good-tempered and allowed them to push their way through. Miles leaned over the parapet and the breath whistled between his teeth.

"Hell and the devil!"

Nat was a second behind him and it took him a

moment to see what was happening. On the river-bank, Mrs. Broad and Mrs. Morton were tending to a bonfire, feeding it with sheets of paper from a large folio. Meanwhile in the river it looked as though someone was doing their washing, for piles of clothes were floating on the water. They were caught on the stones of the riverbed, they adorned the overhanging branches of the willow trees and they flapped in the current like banners. Those items that broke free were floating away under the bridge and some enter-prising villagers were scooping them up at the other end and making off with them.

"Those are good-quality garments," Nat said, spotting a gray velvet jacket and a red-and-gold em-broidered waistcoat as they bobbed past. "A bit showy for my taste, but surely too good to throw in the river."

"That depends on why you would be destroying them," Miles said, grinning. A piece of charred paper from the bonfire fluttered past and he made a grab for it. "I say, look at this!"

Nat squinted at the page. It carried some lurid il-lustrations and some even more explicit text in French. "That… That looks like a dildo!" he splut-tered, pointing at one of the pictures. Immediately someone in the crowd snatched the paper from Miles's hands and pored over it and the pitch of ex-citement seemed to rise even higher.

"Tom Fortune's collection of pornographic

writings," Miles said, trying not to laugh. "Oh dear, I know he spent a lot of money on that folio." He pointed. "Look. I think we have found the perpetrators of this outrage."

Nat looked. In the river shallows, their skirts hitched up to their waists, the water lapping about very shapely legs, stood Lizzie and Alice. They were laughing together. Lizzie's head was thrown back and her red hair tumbled from its ribbon and she looked exhilarated and very happy. Nat's breath caught to see the vivid excitement in her face. He glanced at Miles, who was watching Alice with a little smile playing about his mouth.

"What are we going to do?" he asked.

Miles cocked an eyebrow. "Join them," he said. He pulled off his jacket, unfastened his stock, passed them to a helpful bystander and ran down to the river.

That had not been quite what Nat had meant. Vague thoughts of reading the Riot Act, dispersing the crowd and rescuing Tom's clothes if not the pornography, had been jostling in his mind with the thought that what Lizzie had done was very probably illegal. Then he saw Miles leap into the water and grab Alice about the waist and kiss her with a great deal of enthusiasm. The crowd cheered and Lizzie tilted her head and looked up at the bridge and her eyes met his.

For a long moment they stared at one another and Nat could see apprehension creep into Lizzie's eyes and all the joy seemed to drain from her and she started to wade clumsily toward the riverbank. Nat had an odd feeling inside then and it seemed of prime importance to reach Lizzie and reassure her and put that irresistible smile back in her eyes. He climbed quickly onto the parapet and the crowd gasped and Lizzie turned and stopped, looking at him wide-eyed as he teetered on the very edge of the bridge.

And then he jumped and the last thing he thought before he fell was to wonder just how deep the river was, and that it would probably have been a good idea to check first.

LIZZIE GRABBED NAT AS he rose, spluttering, to the surface, and dragged him into the shallow water. Her heart was pattering with a combination of nervousness and shock.

"What are you doing?" she squeaked, anxiety for him making her sound as shrill as a fishwife. "Are you mad? You could have killed yourself!"

Nat was laughing. "It's a hot day and I needed to cool down." He pushed the soaking hair back from his face and caught her about the waist, holding her close to him. She could feel the heat of his body through his drenched clothes and the beat of his heart against hers. Relief filled her that he was unhurt and with it a strange weakness that made her legs tremble. Nat tightened his grip and bent his head to kiss her. Lizzie held him off with her palms against his chest.

"No! Remember we have an agreement!"

Nat glanced up at the bridge where the crowd was cheering and whooping. "Damn the agreement," he said. "You'll disappoint our audience and they are so proud of you. *I* am so proud of you." He gave her a brief, hard kiss, then drew back and looked at her, his gaze intent on her face. His eyes were blazing with triumph and possession and it made her feel weaker still.

"Nat—" she began, but the words were lost as he kissed her again, this time with a thoroughness that had the crowd shouting approval and left Lizzie utterly shaken. She clenched her fingers in his soaking shirt and held tight as the world spun.

"This isn't like you," she whispered when his lips finally left hers. "I thought you would be angry with me. I have committed an offence against the law. You do understand that, don't you?" Her brow creased as Nat simply smiled at her. "What has happened to you?" she whispered.

Nat silenced her, kissing her for a third time until she forgot the crowd, forgot that they were standing in a river, forgot everything except for Nat. It felt different, though she could not quite explain how, but there was excitement in it as well as gentleness, and an eager anticipation. His hands were warm on her through the drenched gown and the sun was hot and the crowd loud and Lizzie thought her head was going to burst with the blazing sensation of it. When Nat let her go he touched her cheek gently and his gaze moved over her face like a caress.

"Remember that we are to go out riding together this evening," he murmured. "I promise to behave." He looked down at his soaking pantaloons and laughed. "I suppose I had better go and change."

He splashed off through the shallows and Alice came over to Lizzie, her blue eyes alight with amusement. "Well! If that is what happens when you deny Nat your bed I think I might even try the same thing with Miles!"

"I thought he would be angry that we had broken the law, but he said that he was proud of me," Lizzie said, watching Nat as he hauled himself up onto the bank. His hair was sleek and dark with water and his clothes clung to his hard, masculine body and merely looking at him made her feel very hot and bothered.

"Miles once said that when you deny yourself something you really want, you only end up wanting it more," Alice said. She gave Lizzie a speculative look. "You have taken away Nat's certainty, Lizzie. You have changed the rules. It is making Nat think, and making him work for what he wants." She laughed. "It's about time. Don't give in. Bring him to his knees!"

"I will," Lizzie said, thinking of the evening ahead and feeling a burn of anticipation. "I won't give up now."

THAT EVENING THEY RODE up onto the hills and spread their picnic on a blanket beneath an ancient oak tree that sheltered the remains of an old shepherd's hut. They talked and Nat preserved a scrupulously respectable distance from Lizzie whilst at the same time never taking his eyes from her for a moment. There was a tense thrill in the pit of Lizzie's stomach as they talked, a prickle of eagerness along her skin, an excitement that seemed very new and achingly sweet and that made it seem inordinately difficult for her to concentrate.

"I have written to the Prince of Wales about the problem with the Fortune's Folly medieval laws," Lizzie said, as she sat looking at the view across the hills. "He was a friend of my papa and so I hope he will help our cause." She rolled over onto her stomach on the rug and propped her chin on her hand. "I discovered a document in Laura's library that relates to the Charter of the Forest. It was written soon after Magna Carta and it supports the rights and privileges of the common man against his lord and it struck me that if we can invoke it against Tom we might be able to overturn the Dames' Tax and all the other taxes—" She stopped, for Nat was looking at her with a very whimsical smile on his lips.

"What is it?" she demanded wrathfully.

"You," Nat said. "Now that you have a cause you are like a woman inspired—"

Lizzie slapped at him. "Don't laugh at me!"

"I'm not," Nat said. "I've thought for several years that you needed—" He stopped.

"Needed what?" Lizzie said curiously.

"Something to do, I suppose," Nat said. He laughed. "Some focus for all that untrammeled energy and vitality you have. It is no wonder that some women have the vapors out of sheer frustration at the constrained nature of their lives."

"Society is so foolish in what it approves of as appropriate or not in a woman," Lizzie agreed. "I have always found it intensely annoying."

"I had noticed," Nat said wryly.

"I had not expected you to feel like that," Lizzie said, plucking a blade of grass and chewing it. "I mean I did not think you would want me to be occupied other than as a conventional wife and mother. I thought you had very decided notions on the role of your wife and that I do not exactly conform to them."

"I can change my attitude—even if I am stuffy and old-fashioned," Nat said. He sounded rueful.

"You are not always so conventional and proper," Lizzie said. "Sometimes you are equally as wild as I."

Their gazes locked, Nat's dark and heavy with sudden desire. The heat sizzled through Lizzie's blood, scalding her.

Kiss me, taste me, touch me…

Awareness, vivid and intense flared between them. Lizzie found she had already moved closer to

Nat on pure instinct and need alone, and hastily drew back. This was no way to go on if she was to stick to her resolution.

"I suppose that when I have a home of my own I will be able to grow into the managing female I was always destined to be," she said quickly.

"I know that you do not like Chevrons very much," Nat said, surprising her. "I should have consulted you about where we lived, I suppose. I confess that I did not think of it. All I could think of was that I had to marry you, save your reputation, get you away from Fortune Hall and from Tom and—" He stopped abruptly.

"You wanted to rescue me," Lizzie said softly. "It is what you do."

Nat looked at her. There was gentleness in his eyes and something else, something that looked oddly like confusion.

"I suppose I always have done," he said slowly, "and yet there is more to it than that, Lizzie…"

Lizzie held her breath and waited, aware of the silence, aware of the warm breeze through the summer grass and aware of the hammering of her heart. Had Nat's feelings for her started to change, as Laura had predicted they would? Was he beginning to see her differently, to see beyond the need to protect and defend to a love that was greater than that, all encompassing, taking heart and soul? There was certainly an arrested look in his eyes as he watched her but when he did not speak she rushed in to fill the silence, too nervous to let it lie between them.

"I sometimes think that the Fortune family must be cursed," she said with a little shudder. "Monty murdered and now Spencer as well, supposedly in mistake for Tom, and Tom himself only a hairsbreadth from madness…"

"Tom isn't mad," Nat said, a harder tone entering his voice. "He is no more than a dangerous scoundrel who has been given too much license to misbehave." He caught Lizzie's hand and turned it over to press his lips against the vulnerable skin of her wrist. "I feel I owe it to you to catch Monty's murderer, Lizzie," he said. "And I admire you very much for what you are doing in standing up to Tom. So do the people of Fortune's Folly. Someone had to take your brother on and who better than you?"

"Because I am equally badly behaved?" Lizzie said.

Nat laughed. "Because you are the only one with the nerve to match him."

Once again their gazes held. Lizzie's pulse raced against the touch of Nat's lips and his expression tautened as he felt her tremble. He leaned forward to kiss her and she rolled away from him.

"Oh, no, you don't. Keep back! You promised not to try to seduce me."

Nat laughed again, ruefully this time, and released her. "All right. You're safe with me."

"I doubt it," Lizzie said, feeling delightfully unsafe, "but I trust your honor as a gentleman."

Nat groaned. "A pity."

"We are talking," Lizzie said. "*Please,* Nat."

Nat's expression sobered. He turned on his side so that he could look at her properly. "I know," he said. "There is much to talk about." A frown touched his brow. "Last night you accused me of taking your cousin's money as a bribe to wed you."

Some of the bright pleasure went out of Lizzie's day. "Tom told me," she said, haltingly, looking away from Nat and out across the vast bronze and green expanse of the moors. "He said that Cousin Gregory paid you to marry me because he thought I was a disgrace to the Scarlet name and wanted rid of me."

Nat shifted uncomfortably. "It wasn't really like that, Lizzie."

"Did he give you money?" Lizzie pressed. "Did he, Nat?"

When Nat looked up and met her eyes she already knew the answer.

"He did," she said tonelessly, "and you didn't tell me."

"It wasn't like that," Nat said again. "Lizzie, sweetheart—" He reached for her, but let his hand fall to his side as she turned her head away. "Gregory suggested he should add to your dowry, that is all," he said. "God knows, he has done nothing for you since becoming Earl of Scarlet."

"So he thought to make everything right with money," Lizzie said bitterly, "and ease his conscience." She sat up suddenly, fiery and indignant. "Did he say that I was a disgrace to the Scarlet name?" she demanded. "Did he say I was like my mother?"

"No!" Nat said. "If Tom told you that then it was only his malice." He caught her arm. "Don't listen to Tom, Lizzie," he said. "Whatever he tells you he is only trying to hurt you. He takes the truth and twists it with his spite. Promise me you won't listen to him."

"All right," Lizzie said. She was puzzled at the tone in Nat's voice. For a moment he had sounded almost desperate. "I know Tom is a liar and a scoundrel," she said. "I'll try not to let him hurt me again."

She felt Nat relax. He slid his hand down her arm to entwine his fingers with hers and she did not move away this time. The evening sun poured down on them, warming Lizzie's skin, making her sore heart ease a little and helping her feel content for the first time in weeks.

"Nat," she said slowly.

"Hmm?" Her husband made a sleepy sound of enquiry.

"If ever anything like this happens again," Lizzie said, "will you tell me? You arranged the wedding and chose us somewhere to live and you make all these plans without reference to me but I am your wife now." She smiled. "I know that many men do not see the need to consult their wives on any matter, but I do not take kindly to that."

"I had noticed," Nat said. He sat up. There was a rueful light in his dark eyes. "I am sorry," he said. "This is new for me, too, sweetheart."

Lizzie touched his cheek. "In return I promise I will try not to react so badly to things in future by gambling away a fortune or taking my clothes off in public."

Nat gave a strangled laugh. "Perhaps if you could discuss that with me first as well…"

"Yes," Lizzie said. She allowed him to draw her down into the circle of his arm and lay with her head pillowed comfortably on his shoulder.

"You need have no fear for your virtue," Nat whispered against her hair. "I only want to hold you."

"I am not sure that I have any virtue left after all the things that we have done," Lizzie admitted softly. She wriggled closer into his embrace and lay listening to the strong beat of his heart.

"Ah, Lizzie…" Nat's fingers brushed the hair gently back from her face, twining the soft auburn curls about his fingers. "Don't say that. In so many ways you are the sweetest, bravest and most admirable woman."

"And you are evidently quite deceived in my character if you think so." Lizzie held her breath. There was a note in Nat's voice she had never heard before, a mingling of tenderness and admiration and something else she did not yet dare name as love.

"Don't say that," Nat said again. He did not smile. "I saw you looking after Monty the night he returned so drunk from the Wheelers' dinner." His mouth set in a thin line. "I have often thought how little you have been spared by Monty and Tom—" His tone hardened still further, "And your parents. Things you should not have had to see or endure...All the people who should have cared for you and instead they hurt you and left you to fend for yourself." His arms tightened about her. "It offends me deeply."

"That was why you were always trying to protect me, wasn't it," Lizzie said softly, glancing up at his unyielding face. "Do you remember when I first came to Fortune Hall and Tom was always teasing me and you stood up for me even though I knew it irritated you because you were so much older and really did not wish to be bothered with a tiresome little hoyden..."

Nat laughed. "Even then you had more courage than either Monty or Tom. Do you remember when they made you walk along the edge of the battlements and you did it without a murmur, even though you were terrified of falling? And then Monty tried and almost fell in the moat?"

"Serve him right," Lizzie said. "He always was a bully." She sighed. "It was kind of you to tolerate me following you around like a shadow." She turned within the curve of his arm and pressed her lips to the line of his jaw. "You are a kind person, Nat Wa-

terhouse. You are always seeking to help people—"
She broke off as she saw a flash of undeniable pain
in Nat's eyes.

"What is it?" she said.

"I don't always succeed," Nat said.

Lizzie frowned. "I don't understand."

There was silence for a moment. Held close
within Nat's embrace, Lizzie could sense tension in
him and some kind of conflict, deep and painful. She
pressed closer, wordlessly offering comfort with the
warmth of her body and the touch of her hands and
after a moment Nat let out a sigh.

"I had another sister," he said. His voice had a
rough edge. "Celeste had a twin. She died."

Lizzie was shocked. In all the time that she had
known Nat, she had never heard mention of another
sister. He had not talked of her. Neither had his
parents nor Celeste. Lizzie kept very still and quiet,
waiting for Nat to continue, hoping that at last he
might see her as a person he could confide in and
draw strength from rather than another responsibility,
another burden he had to carry.

"She was called Charlotte," Nat said. "There was
a fire at Water House one night when the girls were
about six years old. I saved Celeste." He cleared his
throat. "I could not save Charley, too."

"Nat," Lizzie said. She could hear his pain now,
as raw as when it had first struck. It was an echo in
Nat's voice and it was in the taut way in which he

held her hard against him. "I had to choose," he said. His voice was so low now that Lizzie could barely hear him. "I tried to carry both of them but they were terrified, too frightened to keep still. Charley slipped from my grasp. I had to let her go to save Celeste." He shook his head a little, a lock of his hair brushing Lizzie's cheek as he moved. "Even now I can remember the lick of the flames at my back and the heat of the banister under my hand and the smoke in my throat, so thick and choking. It was such a long way down the stairs…" He stopped. "I tried to go back for Charley but they would not let me. They said that I would die, too."

Lizzie did not speak. She knew that nothing she could say could soothe him. There were no words. She held him close and felt the evening sun envelop them in its warmth and gradually she felt Nat relax a little as that unbearable tension seeped from his body and the tightness of his arms eased about her and he pressed his lips to her hair as though he would never let her go.

"I failed, Lizzie," he said. "I never want that to happen again."

"You saved Celeste," Lizzie said, looking at him. "That was no failure."

"Which is why I cannot—" Nat bit off whatever it was he was going to say and although Lizzie waited with unaccustomed patience, he did not speak again.

"You cannot…what?" Lizzie asked after a moment.

"Nothing." For a moment Nat's gaze was blind. "Just…don't make me out to be more honorable than I am, Lizzie."

He turned his head and gave her a lopsided smile. Despite the reassurance, Lizzie felt chilled. It felt as though despite opening his heart to her he was now keeping something back. A distance had opened between them. Perhaps, she thought suddenly, he resented the situation that his honor had placed him in when it had obliged him to marry her.

"That first night we were together," she said, her voice falling. "When we were in the folly… It was all my fault. I should never have provoked you so."

"You did not understand what you were doing," Nat said, a little roughly. "I did. It was my fault, not yours."

"I did know," Lizzie said honestly. "At least I knew in theory if not in practice. I pushed you too hard. I did it on purpose. I always go too far."

"You do seem to have a talent for it," Nat agreed, but his voice was gentle. Out of the corner of her eye Lizzie saw his lips curl in a smile that made her stomach drop with longing.

"In my defence," she added, "I had no notion that you had such an odious habit of losing your temper."

Nat laughed. "You have known me for years, Lizzie," he said. "You must have known I am notoriously short-tempered."

"I never really noticed it before," Lizzie confessed. "Oh, I knew that you could get angry with me sometimes, but I also knew that if you became all cross and stuffy with me you would come round eventually because—" She stopped. She realized that she had almost said:

"Because you loved me," meaning it in the sense of the acceptance and easy tolerance that had characterized their relationship previously. She had taken Nat's friendship for granted. With a pang of misery she realized how much she had lost when she had blown that relationship and all its certainties apart.

"Because we were friends," she amended. She sighed. "Oh, Nat, I am so sorry. I have been so thoughtless and careless and as a result everything has changed and sometimes I *wish*—" The vehemence in her tone startled her. "I wish that matters were back the way they were before and we could have that uncomplicated friendship again."

Nat loosed her and sat up, and she immediately felt cold as the evening breeze tiptoed gooseflesh along her skin. The sun was sinking now, pink and gold in the western sky, but suddenly the air was chill.

"Do you?" His voice was neutral, his expression unreadable. "We can't go back, Lizzie."

"I know," Lizzie said. She clasped her knees to her chest, curling up for both comfort and warmth. "I know," she said again. "It is merely that so many things have changed for me and I miss the old certainties."

Suddenly she jumped to her feet, wanting to banish the blue devils before they spoiled the evening.

"There are some things that are the same as they were before," she said. "I can still ride better than you." She jumped up onto Starfire, laughing down at Nat as he scrambled to his feet. "I'll race you back home."

She won, but only just.

Nat kissed her good-night at her bedroom door that night. He trapped her against the panels of the door and held her with the press of his body against hers and she could feel his arousal and the control he was exerting over himself and the knowledge of her power was more heady than the best champagne.

"You'll break first," Nat said, against her mouth. "You know you want me and you have no patience to wait for the things you want."

"I will *not* give in first," Lizzie said. "You underestimate me. And you are cheating again," she added, as his mouth trailed teasing kisses along the line of her throat. "You are not supposed to kiss me or even touch me."

"I can compromise," Nat said, easing back from her, "but only so far."

Lizzie lay in bed and looked at the connecting door between their two rooms. She thought of the insight Nat had given her into his past and the terrible burden he carried about his sister's death. He must know in his own mind that he had saved Celeste's life and yet in his heart there would always be the reminder of the impossible choice; he could not have saved both girls at once and so he bore the guilt for the one he had failed. It seemed the most desperately, damnably unfair weight for a man to bear.

She wondered what else Nat had been going to tell her. Perhaps it had been something else to do with Celeste. Perhaps she should have pushed him a little, made him talk? But it had taken him nine years simply to tell her what had happened at Water House that night. She could not force him to confide more, not now when everything was so fragile between them. Despite Nat's withdrawal she still felt a spark of hope that he was starting to see her differently. She did not want to spoil matters by giving in to her usual haste and impatience.

Lizzie stared hard at the connecting door. She knew it was not locked tonight and that it constituted the most terrible temptation but she had not come this far to give in on the first night. She could excuse herself, of course, if she did choose to go to him— she could argue that after Nat had laid his emotions bare she was offering him her comfort and love. Yet although she ached to be in his arms some spark of stubbornness held her back. They had started to build something different, something stronger between them. She would not undermine it now.

To her surprise she slept well and woke feeling refreshed and happy. Nat's haggard face and surly bad temper at the breakfast table, in contrast, suggested that he was feeling neither.

"Did you not sleep well, my love?" Lizzie said, bright as a daisy, as she poured the coffee.

Nat scowled. "Not a wink."

"I am sorry," Lizzie said.

"I doubt you are," Nat countered. He slapped his newspaper down on the table with unwonted force. "I am going out." He glared at her. "Not because I want to, but to keep my hands off you, madam wife."

He had thought that she would succumb. Lizzie felt hugely pleased with herself. "Be sure to be here later to escort me to the subscription ball," she said sweetly, "or I may have to ask someone else." She popped a cherry from the fruit bowl into her mouth.

Nat's gaze dropped to her lips. He scowled. "I'll be here."

"Oh good," Lizzie said and she tilted her face up for an oh-so-chaste kiss on the cheek, and smiled as her husband slammed out of the house in a very bad mood indeed.

"EVERYTHING ALL RIGHT, old fellow?" Dexter Anstruther asked mildly as Nat joined him at The Old Palace ten minutes later. "You look as though you had a rough night."

"I'm perfectly fine," Nat snapped. "Why is everyone so damnably interested in my welfare at the moment? First Miles, now you—" In truth he felt the complete opposite of fine. Hours of lying awake confidently expecting Lizzie to come through the connecting door had been superseded by hours of surprise and chagrin that she had resisted followed by hours of struggle to subdue his bodily impulses. If Lizzie would not weaken and come to him then he was damned if he would give in and go to her. She had wanted this ludicrous sex ban anyway and he was all of two days into it and feeling as primed as a callow youth with no self-control. It was ridiculous. It was embarrassing. He had gone for months without a woman before he married Lizzie and now he did not appear to be able to last a single day. She was driving him mad—in a different way from the usual.

Yet, despite his physical torment Nat found he had other images in his mind now, not simply the deeply tempting ones of making love to Lizzie. He remembered Lizzie in the river, laughing joyously with Alice as they destroyed Tom's fine clothes, taking revenge on him on behalf of the people of Fortune's Folly; he saw her racing ahead of him on Starfire, her hair flying in the breeze, skilful, fearless, the best and most breathtaking rider in the county. And he remembered Lizzie curled up against him on the picnic rug, his arms about her and his cheek against her hair as he did the one thing he had never imagined he could ever do and shared with her his deepest regrets and misery over Charley's death. He had felt so close to Lizzie then, drawing strength and comfort from her instead of seeing her always as a duty, someone to be protected along with his parents and Celeste. His entire perspective had shifted in that moment as he acknowledged that Lizzie's courage and generosity of spirit was not simply there for her friends or her unworthy brothers but that she had blessed him with it, too. It felt strange, it felt unfamiliar, but it was warm and loving and he had felt cold for so long…

"Dexter," he said, shifting slightly in his chair. "This marriage business…Devilish tricky, don't you think?"

"Devilishly so," Dexter agreed, without a single betraying quiver of his lips.

"What's the secret?" Nat pursued.

"Damned if I know," Dexter said. "I've been doing it less than a year. Communication, perhaps," he added thoughtfully. "Honesty," he added.

Nat shifted again. *Honesty…*

He had not told Lizzie about Tom's blackmail of him over Celeste. He had almost blurted it out last night when they had been so intimately entwined, heart to heart, but something had made him draw back. It was too soon. Lizzie's emotions were so tangled at the moment with loss and grief that Nat was sure any further proof of Tom's cruelty and vice could only make her feel a great deal worse. And though they were growing closer, he and Lizzie, talking and sharing secrets, he still felt that she had to be protected from Tom. He had to take care of her. He could not risk damaging the delicate, precious steps that he and Lizzie were taking. When she was stronger he would tell her. But he could not do it now. It would hurt her too much.

Nevertheless, Nat found that it made him feel uncomfortable to be keeping secrets from Lizzie, especially now when they were drawing closer in a different way that he could not quite define. The picture of wild Lizzie Scarlet that he had had in his mind for so long, Monty Fortune's little sister, was becoming overlaid with another. Not the silken temptress who had seduced him that first night, nor the scandalous Lady Waterhouse who was the talk of Fortune's Folly. This Lizzie defended the people in the village when Tom rode roughshod over their rights. This Lizzie had not run from him when they had quarreled so badly but had stood her ground. This Lizzie was a force to be reckoned with, growing to be a woman whom Nat could suddenly see would have all of Laura Anstruther's impressive authority one day. This Lizzie was admirable and courageous as well as lovely and seductive...Again he felt an abrupt shift in perspective, as though he were seeing Lizzie with different eyes. The memories of nine years fell away and with that came an equally sudden and overwhelming surge of feeling that had nothing to do with wanting her in his bed but was a tangle of love and protectiveness and sheer blazing joy that she was a part of his life...

He was still gasping at the physical shock of it when there was a sharp tap at the door and Miles walked in. Nat jumped and became aware that Dexter had been watching him with quizzical amusement. He wondered what on earth had been showing on his face.

Miles's news, however, gave him no further time to consider his feelings. "There's a lead," he said briefly. "An anonymous tip-off about the masked woman seen in the village on the nights that both Monty and Spencer were murdered. The message was left for me at Drum this morning. Dinmont said that a maidservant delivered it."

"Anonymous?" Nat said, frowning. "That could be nothing more than spite."

"I know," Miles said, unfolding a note from his breast pocket and handing it to Dexter, "but even so, we cannot ignore it."

Nat watched as Dexter read the note, glanced at Miles and then dropped his gaze to the paper again. There was an odd silence.

"What is it?" Nat said. "Who do they say it is?" He had a strange premonition. "Not Lizzie?" he said. Shock, anger and protectiveness engulfed him, over-whelming in its power. He felt stunned with the force of his feeling for her.

But Dexter was shaking his head. "No," he said. "It's not Lizzie. It's Flora Minchin."

CHAPTER FOURTEEN

LIZZIE WAS CROSSING the street on her way from Chevrons to visit Laura and Lydia at The Old Palace when she saw the small crowd that was gathered outside Mr. and Mrs. Minchin's townhouse. Previously it had troubled Lizzie slightly that she and Flora were such close neighbors now. They had never been friends—indeed, Lizzie had always thought that Flora was the most irritating pea-brained creature imaginable, a feeling she could now admit a little shamefacedly might have sprung from a certain jealousy. Even so, when she saw the crowd she almost hurried past. Then she heard the screams from inside the house, a sound that was easily defined as Mrs. Minchin having the vapors, and despite herself she paused.

"What on earth is going on?" she asked Mrs. Lovell, who was one of the many people milling on the steps outside.

"Flora's the one who murdered Sir Montague and Spencer, his valet," Mrs. Lovell said importantly, her face alight with excitement. She loved a good scandal. "She was the masked woman! Only fancy! They've come to arrest her now—Lord Vickery and Mr. Anstruther and your husband."

Lizzie screwed her face up. "Flora a *murderer?* Don't be absurd. She couldn't kill a fly!"

Mrs. Minchin's screams intensified, then one of the maids came running from the open door of the house wailing and wringing her hands in her apron. "Please will someone fetch the master?" she cried. "Madam is in hysterics and they're taking Miss Flora away and I don't know what to do!"

"Oh, this is ridiculous!" Lizzie hurried up the steps, grabbed the maid by the arm and hustled her back into the house, slamming the door in the faces of the avid crowd. Inside, the sounds of Mrs. Minchin's screams were so penetrating that they echoed off the walls. "Get the stable boy to fetch Mr. Minchin," Lizzie said in the girl's ear. "Run along now. Quickly!"

"But the mistress—" the maid began.

"I'll deal with her," Lizzie said. She went into the parlor. Mrs. Minchin was sitting on the sofa, her bulk quivering with every scream. Another maid was waving burnt feathers ineffectually under her nose. Lizzie pushed her out of the way and slapped Mrs. Minchin's face. Mrs. Minchin's blue eyes, so like Flora's own, opened wide and then she gulped and fell completely silent.

"Smelling salts," Lizzie said, grabbing them from

the table and pressing them into the maid's hand. "Make her lie down and then fetch her a cup of tea when she is calm."

"Flora!" Mrs. Minchin wept, trying to rise.

"I'll help Flora," Lizzie said, pushing Mrs. Minchin back down on the seat. "Don't worry. Everything will be fine. I promise." The matron collapsed into tears.

"She'll be all right now," Lizzie said, squeezing the maid's arm. "Sal volatile, then tea."

She hurried out of the room. There were voices in the drawing room and as Lizzie ran down the corridor, Dexter emerged through the doorway with Flora following him. Flora's face was utterly blank, a terrible white mask, her blue eyes fixed and staring. As Lizzie watched, Flora stumbled over the edge of the carpet and almost fell. Lizzie rushed forward and grabbed Flora's cold hands in her own, steadying the girl.

"What on earth do you think you are doing?" she said wrathfully, steering Flora back into the drawing room and turning like a tigress to confront Miles and Dexter and Nat. "Can't you see she's terrified? Let her sit down!" She steered Flora to a chair and gently eased her into it. "Why did you all have to come and frighten her?" she added furiously. "One of you would have been quite sufficient!" She chafed Flora's hands. She could feel the other girl shaking. "It's all right," she said, in an undertone. "Don't be frightened."

Flora's scared blue eyes fixed on her face. "I haven't done anything wrong."

"Of course not," Lizzie said stoutly. She drew up another chair and put her arm about Flora.

Nat touched Lizzie's shoulder. "No one wants to frighten her," he said softly, "but she won't tell us where she was on the nights in question, Lizzie."

"Well, go away and leave me with her, then," Lizzie said. "Give me five minutes. Go and make some tea or something. I am sure Mrs. Minchin could do with it."

Nat smiled at her and for a second Lizzie felt something tug deep inside her.

"Thank you," Nat said softly.

"Now, Flora," Lizzie said as Nat shepherded the others out and closed the door gently, "I am sure you haven't done anything wrong, but if you won't explain what you were doing that night, I can't help you." She paused. "Have you been slipping out at night, Flora?"

There was a pause and then Flora gave a little jerky nod of the head.

"So you did go out," Lizzie said, keeping her voice very steady. "Where did you go?"

Flora bit her lip and did not reply. She looked stricken and miserable.

"I suppose," Lizzie said gently, "you went to meet a man?"

Flora's gaze came up sharply to meet hers. "I wasn't...I didn't..." Her face crumpled. "It wasn't what you think," she said, her voice strengthening.

"The first time, I went to ask him to marry me but he turned me down. Then—" she hung her head "—I went just to…just to see him really. I *needed* to see him, but he sent me away."

Lizzie caught her hand. "You're in love with someone who doesn't love you back," she said, swallowing a very hard lump in her throat.

"Yes," Flora said. She sighed. "It hurts."

"I understand," Lizzie said, with feeling. "Who is it, Flora?"

The other girl didn't reply, her blue eyes sweeping Lizzie's face as though weighing whether she could trust her.

"Listen," Lizzie said quickly. "I know that you and I have not been friends, Flora, but I do want to help you. We need to persuade this person to vouch for you or you might be arrested—" She felt Flora shudder. "If you tell me who it is," she said carefully, "I'll speak to him and I am sure he will help you." She was not actually sure at all, but what else could she say? At the least, the man, whoever he was, could not be married if Flora had gone to propose to him, a feat which gave Lizzie a great deal of respect for her. She wondered who on earth could have turned down Flora and her fifty thousand pounds.

"It is Lowell Lister," Flora said with a gulp before bursting into tears. "I can't help it, Lizzie," she added, crying all over Lizzie's spencer, as Lizzie hugged her closer, "I love him so much and he won't marry me because he doesn't want my money—"

"He must be the only man in Fortune's Folly who *doesn't* want to marry an heiress," Lizzie said. "He probably loves you, too, but thinks he is being noble. The idiot," she added.

Flora gave a little hiccuping giggle and sat up. "Oh dear. And now he will think I am trying to entrap him." She squeezed Lizzie's hand. "Will you speak to him and explain? He likes you."

"I'll ask Alice to speak to him," Lizzie promised. "Lowell thinks I'm spoiled—and he could be right," she added fairly, "but Alice is lovely and will help you and Lowell respects her. Everything will be all right, Flora."

"Mama and Papa won't like it," Flora said. "My reputation is ruined—"

"Not if Lowell marries you," Lizzie said.

"But he is a farmer and they are such snobs," Flora said with a sigh.

"He is also the brother-in-law of a lord," Lizzie said, smiling. "I think that is the bit they will be concentrating on." She urged Flora to her feet. "Do you want to go and lie down?"

"No," Flora said, straightening up. "I must go to Mama." She gave Lizzie a spontaneous hug. "Oh, Lizzie, thank you. I didn't think I liked you—" Her eyes filled with tears again.

"Go on," Lizzie said, laughing. She pushed Flora out the door and watched her scurry down the corridor and into the parlor to her mother. Nat and Miles came out of the dining room and Lizzie grabbed Miles's arm.

"Could you send to fetch Alice? I need her to speak to Lowell."

Miles and Nat exchanged a glance. *"Lowell?"* Miles said.

"Flora loves him," Lizzie said, lowering her voice. "He is the one she has been slipping out to see."

"Why didn't she tell us?" Nat said.

Lizzie gave him a speaking look. "Oh please—her reputation?"

"I'll go and find Alice," Miles said. He smiled at Lizzie. "You are a miracle worker."

He went out, and Nat caught Lizzie's hand and drew her back into the drawing room. "Thank you," he said softly. "That was very kind of you, Lizzie. I didn't think you even liked Flora."

"I didn't," Lizzie said. She looked up into his dark eyes. "I was jealous of her," she whispered. "What you said that night in the folly was true, Nat. I was spoiled and envious and I wanted you for myself. I can see that now."

Nat's hands tightened on hers. He drew her closer. There was an intent look in his eyes that seemed to make the world spin. "Lizzie," he said. "Your honesty is very humbling—"

"What the devil is going on here?" Mr. Minchin burst into the room. "There's a restless crowd outside and my wife and daughter crying all over one another in the parlor and I hear some rumor that Flora is to be arrested—"

"There's nothing to worry about at all, sir," Dexter, at his most deferential, appeared behind him. "We believe that some malefactor laid false evidence against Miss Minchin, but it is all sorted out now."

"I'll have the law on them!" Mr. Minchin swelled alarmingly.

"We are the law," Dexter said smoothly, "and we will deal with it, sir."

Mr. Minchin's gaze fell on Lizzie and his high color died down a little. "I hear you were the one who sent for me, ma'am," he said gruffly. "Tended to my wife and daughter, too. I must thank you."

"A pleasure," Lizzie said. She freed herself from Nat's grip, very aware that he was watching her all the time. "Perhaps you should go and comfort them, Mr. Minchin? I know they will be grateful that you are here." She put a hand on his arm. "I think that you might also start to come to terms with the fact that you are likely to have Lowell Lister as a son-in-law," she added gently. "He's a very good man."

"Lister?" Mr. Minchin gave a start. "He's a farmer!"

"A rich and very well connected one," Lizzie said brightly.

"Lister," Mr. Minchin said again, his tone of voice altering. "A *gentleman* farmer. Yes, I see. I wondered what was wrong with Flora."

"It should be all right soon," Lizzie said. She smiled at him warmly.

"I can't see Flora as a farmer's wife," Nat said as Mr. Minchin bustled off to the parlor.

"She'll manage," Lizzie said. "She is nowhere near as stupid as she looks."

The door crashed open and Lowell strode in, followed by Alice and Miles.

"That was quick," Lizzie said.

"I found him in the street," Alice said. "He had already heard the rumors of Flora's arrest and was on his way here."

Lowell ignored them all, walked straight into the parlor, and without a word grabbed Flora and started kissing her.

"And that," Lizzie said, laughing, "is how a Yorkshireman deals with these situations." She turned to Nat, Dexter and Miles. "You had better go and find your informant. For my part—" she shot Nat a look "—I would ask Priscilla Willoughby. She is a troublemaker and she, too, has been creeping about the streets at night, so I understand. And while you are at it," she added, "you could ask her to give Tom an alibi for the night of Monty's murder. I think you'll find it was Priscilla he spent the night with, not Ethel." And she smiled with enormous satisfaction to see Nat's expression of blank astonishment.

THERE WERE TWO *on dits* at the Fortune's Folly assembly that evening. First there was Miss Flora Minchin's betrothal to Lowell Lister. The happy couple were present that night, danced a scandalous four dances with each other and could barely take their eyes from each other.

"Mr. and Mrs. Minchin seem very satisfied with Flora's choice," Lizzie said mischievously to Alice as they watched the newly betrothed pair in the quadrille. Flora and Lowell were so busy staring into each other's eyes that they were a step behind everyone else. "Can it be that you have already done a great deal of work in smoothing things over with them, Alice? I know Mrs. Minchin was dubious of the connection until you and Miles stepped in to point out the benefits of the match."

"We did what we could," Alice said, lips twitching. "I love my brother a great deal and hope he will be happy, but I do not envy him his snob of a mother-in-law."

"I think Flora and Lowell will deal together extremely well," Lizzie said. "She really is a remarkable girl—she gives the impression of being quite, quite stupid and yet she has extraordinary resolve."

"Lowell is totally besotted," Alice said, shaking her head. "I never thought to see him like this. He told me that he fell in love with Flora the first time she came to High Top on the day her wedding was canceled. He was absolutely determined to refuse her because of the disparity in their situations, but as soon as he heard she was in danger of arrest he realized what a fool he had been. Even so—" she sighed "—I do think Flora will have some difficulty in adapting to life as a farmer's wife. She has lived a pampered life. It won't be easy for her."

"What about the other *on dit?*" Lizzie said, her eyes sparkling. "Poor Lady Willoughby—such a sudden and unfortunate departure from Fortune's Folly!"

Lady Wheeler had paused at their table a moment earlier, Mary in tow, to say that Priscilla Willoughby had been called away most urgently on family business.

"Such a dreadful pity," Lady Wheeler had fluttered. "Dear Priscilla was having the most splendid stay here in Fortune's Folly."

"So we had heard," Lizzie had said sweetly. "Lady Willoughby's nighttime excursions were becoming the talk of the village!"

Lizzie had seen Mary's gaze jerk up to hers at the words, but Mary had not spoken and Lizzie had thought that she looked even more pale and sick than she had before.

"Who would have thought that illness would strike Lady Willoughby's family so abruptly?" Alice agreed now. "Did Nat say anything about his interview with her?"

"Only that he was glad she was leaving," Lizzie said. "I asked him if he were utterly disillusioned that his paragon of virtue had turned out to be a strumpet instead."

"Lizzie, you did not!" Alice clapped a hand over her mouth.

"Yes I did," Lizzie said unrepentantly, "and he said that he had not cared for her in years and would rather have a wilful minx to wife. So I think—" she cast her eyes modestly down and traced a finger over the struts of her fan "—that my plan may be working."

"It sounds as though it may," Alice agreed.

"So then I told him that was merely a line to persuade me back to his bed," Lizzie went on, "and he said—"

"Enough!" Alice said, holding up her hands.

Lizzie laughed. "All right. Where can Miles and Nat have got to with those ice sculptures? They will be quite melted." She scanned the room, catching sight of Mary Wheeler, who was speaking to Viscount Jerrold but looking as miserable as sin.

"Poor Mary," she said. "What can be the matter with her? Do you think she is ill? She looks ever more sickly by the minute."

Nat and Miles returned at that moment and placed a bowl of strawberries and ice before their wives. The ice was indeed melting in the heat of the assembly rooms and Lizzie pushed at it unenthusiastically with her spoon.

"Come and dance with me, since you have no interest in the dessert I specially procured for you," Nat said, smiling.

"Dancing is another thing like card-playing at which you are indifferent to bad," Lizzie said, pretending to sigh as they took their place in the set of country-dances, "but as I am your wife I feel I have to comply. It is my duty."

"You seem less than eager to do your wifely duty in other ways," Nat pointed out with an expressive lift of his brows.

"And you accuse *me* of a lack of patience!" Lizzie marveled. "Truth to tell, I enjoy making you wait. It means that you talk to me more."

"I enjoy talking to you," Nat said.

"You sound surprised," Lizzie teased. "We were friends once, Nat. We used to talk a lot."

"Yes," Nat said, and Lizzie could hear a shade of discovery in his voice, "but not like we do now. It feels different. I feel different…"

The movement of the dance took her away from him then and Lizzie felt as though she was as light as thistledown. Everything was changing; she could feel it in the air and the tingle in her blood.

She danced only once with John Jerrold, who remarked whimsically that the next *on dit* would surely be how unfashionably in love Lord and Lady Waterhouse were with each other.

"I seem to have missed my chance," he drawled.

"You never had one, Johnny," Lizzie said pertly, but his words warmed her. It was true that Nat had seldom shown much desire to dance with her in the past; he had sometimes squired her to the assemblies but had had little interest or aptitude for the dancing. Now, though, he danced with her several times and showed no desire to leave her side in between. It was extremely pleasurable to have his undivided attention, to feel him watching her, to exchange the lightest and briefest of touches with him, touches that shimmered through her whole body leaving her breathless and happy.

It was raining later when they came to leave, steamy summer rain that made the cobbled square in front of the assembly rooms smell of dust. Sir James and Lady Wheeler were bemoaning the fact that they had walked to the ball.

"I had no notion that it was going to rain this evening," Lady Wheeler said, looking as though she was taking the weather as a personal affront. "James does not have even so much as an umbrella to protect us with and our evening cloaks will be soaked—"

"Here, take my umbrella," Lizzie said, holding it out to Mary, who was nearest and was standing huddled in the doorway. "Nat and I will manage perfectly well without—" She stopped at the look on Mary's face. The girl was shaking and white and as Lizzie impatiently waved the umbrella at her she recoiled as though it were a snake.

"You know, don't you?" she whispered. Her eyes were huge and terrified. "You're trying to trap me!" And then she gathered up the skirts of her evening gown in both hands and ran away down the darkened street, the soles of her evening slippers slapping in the puddles.

"Mary!" Lady Wheeler called. "Mary, come back here at once! You'll ruin your gown! What on earth is she about?" She turned to Sir James. "What has got into that girl lately?"

Lizzie turned to Nat. "What was that about?" she said blankly.

"Lizzie, let me see that," Nat said abruptly, taking the umbrella from her hands and holding it up to the light. He shot her a look. "Is this yours?"

"No," Lizzie said, puzzled. "It belonged to Monty. I took it with me when I left Fortune Hall. It unscrews here—" she pointed to the chased silver engraving around the handle "—and I think he kept a brandy flask inside. You know what Monty was like…Oh!"

She stopped as Nat turned the silver band at the neck of the umbrella and it came apart in his hand. Lady Wheeler screamed and recoiled, much as her daughter had done only a moment before, for protruding from the handle was a knife, long, wickedly pointed and stained with blood.

"No!" Lizzie said, comprehension breaking over her with the force of a storm. "Mary!" She caught Nat's sleeve. "Why would she murder—" She broke off in stunned disbelief. "She *cannot* have done!"

Nat was staring down the darkened street in the direction that Mary had run. Lady Wheeler was screaming and looked as though she was about to faint and people were rushing from the assembly room doors out into the road to see what the commotion was all about.

"I have to find her," Lizzie said suddenly. Her heart was pounding. She felt dizzy. "I need to know what happened."

"No! Wait!" Nat grabbed her tightly. She could feel the tension in his hands as he held her. "Don't go," he said. "It could be dangerous."

"But this is *Mary*," Lizzie argued. She did not want to believe it. "Mary couldn't hurt a fly, least of all Monty! This must be some terrible mistake, or else it was an accident. I need to find her, help her—"

"No," Nat said again. "Lizzie—"

Lizzie slid out from beneath Nat's hands and sped off down the street.

"Lizzie!" Nat bellowed. She could hear his running footsteps behind her, but she did not check. She had to find Mary. Could it have been her friend who had taken Monty from her, the brother who was so vain, so selfish and so monumentally dislikable, and yet whom against the odds, Lizzie had loved? Could Mary really be the culprit? Of course, she thought wildly, Mary had not known, had not understood, how important Lizzie's small family had become to her when she had lost so much. She had hidden her affection for Monty and Tom well beneath a laughing veneer that made light of their faults when really she had had such a tenacious fondness for them because they were all she had had…She ran, driven by anger, driven by loss, her grief suddenly as wild as an animal tearing at her chest.

The rain was harder than she had thought, stinging her cheeks, whipping the hair into her eyes, blinding her. The night was thick with cloud and hot, as though they were being smothered under a blanket. Where had Mary gone? Lizzie dived down an alleyway toward the river, hearing Nat crash into something behind her and swear ferociously. And then suddenly she saw the slight, hurrying figure before her in the fitful light of the street lanterns.

"Mary!" she shouted, and the figure turned and Lizzie saw the pale blur of her face and the wide staring eyes, before Mary ran to the edge of the bridge and disappeared into the chasm of water below.

CHAPTER FIFTEEN

"MARY! NO!" Lizzie ran down to the river, stumbling in the darkness, her feet slipping on the wet stones. She could see a shape in the water, tossed on the current like a piece of wood, a face, an outstretched hand… She plunged into the river, gasping as the shock of the cold water hit her, buffeted by the current, the mossy stones slipping beneath her feet as she stretched desperately to reach Mary. She grabbed at her, caught her arm and pulled with all the strength she had. The sodden material of Mary's gown ripped beneath the clutch of her fingers but then they were out of the grip of the current and they landed in a panting heap on the wet stone at the side of the river. Mary was as slack as a doll, as though all the strength had suddenly left her. And with it went all Lizzie's furious anger and misery, leaving nothing but numb despair.

"Why?" she said. "Why did you do it, Mary?"

Mary looked up. Her face was dull, wet and pale. "It was his fault," she said.

"Whose fault?" Lizzie wanted to shake her. "Monty's?" she demanded.

"Stephen left me because of him," Mary said. "It was all his fault. He brought that trollop back from London and Stephen left…" Her head was bent, the water dripping from her dark hair in rats' tails.

Lizzie frowned, shaking her head in disbelief. "You blame *Monty* for Stephen Armitage jilting you? What madness is this? Lord Armitage ran off with a courtesan—"

Mary's face crumpled into excruciating pain and misery. "It was his fault," she repeated. "He brought her here."

There was, Lizzie supposed numbly, a desperate sort of logic to Mary's thinking. It was true that Sir Montague had brought Louisa Caton, Miles Vickery's former mistress, from London in an attempt to sabotage Miles's betrothal to Alice. Instead of forcing Miles and Alice apart, Monty's actions had ruined Mary's future for it was *her* fiancé who had run off with the lightskirt. But to hold Monty to blame…

"He ruined my life," Mary said now. "I loved Stephen with all my heart." She looked up, her eyes suddenly bright with anger. "And then he had the audacity to propose to me himself!"

"*Monty* did?" Lizzie was dumbfounded.

"We quarreled about it," Mary said. "I went to Fortune Hall to beg him not to make me a formal offer because I knew that my parents would insist that I take it. But Sir Montague only laughed at me and on the night of our dinner he renewed his attentions. So I knew I had to do something to prevent him from asking my father's permission…"

"So you killed him," Lizzie said dully. She rubbed her forehead hard. A headache was building behind her eyes. "And Spencer?" she said. "What had he done to hurt you?"

"I thought he was Tom," Mary said, emotionlessly. "I made a mistake."

"And Tom had done…what?" Lizzie pressed. Mary's reasoning seemed both mad and ruthless at the same time. She had lost her judgment, almost lost her mind, and yet she sounded so sane. It was terrifying.

"He wanted to marry me, as well," Mary said simply. "He tried to force himself on me. He disgusts me." She shuddered. "And I know that Stephen will come back for me in the end, you see. I love him and I know he will give up that lightskirt and come back…" Mary stumbled to her feet. Her eyes were closed, her expression glazed and she seemed totally unaware of her surroundings. She took a step backward, missed her footing, and even as Lizzie reached out to grab her the water claimed her for a second time. Lizzie's hand met empty air and by the time she had scrambled to the edge of the river, Mary had already gone. Lizzie ran out into the stream, careless for herself, careless of the danger, but there was no sign. And suddenly she found herself in danger of losing her footing, too. The river ran fast and deep beneath the bridge and the roar of it was in her ears and she could see nothing but the black shifting mass as it tumbled past her. For one brief, terrifying moment she teetered on the edge, feeling the current trying to snatch her away, and then Nat caught her arm in an unbreakable grip and half carried, half dragged her into the shallow water and out onto the bank. She was breathing in sobbing gasps and clung to him, her arms about his neck, and although she could not see his face she could feel the seething anger in him but something else in his touch, as well.

"I'm sorry," she said. Her breath was coming in sobbing gasps. "I could not save her. I was not quick enough." She turned her face into Nat's neck and breathed in the scent of him and the deep reassurance and strength that went with it, and felt safe at last.

She felt the anger in Nat melt away as his arms tightened about her and he buried his face against her wet hair.

"Oh, Lizzie." His voice was muffled. "You will never stop, will you? You will never stop doing these mad and willful and *dangerous* things." But though he shook her, he was gentle, and she knew he was exasperated but there was anguish and relief in his voice and in the way he held her.

"I had to try," she repeated, teeth chattering, her whole body convulsed with shivers as Nat carried her up the bank and onto the street. "Even though she killed Monty and Spencer. She told me, Nat…" She shuddered again. "They both wanted to marry her, Monty and Tom, but she was so desperately in love with Stephen Armitage that she could not bear it. She thought Armitage would come back for her." She turned to look over Nat's shoulder and for the first time saw the lanterns and heard the voices of people down by the river. Miles came up and Nat said: "Any sign?" But Miles shook his head and his face was grim.

"I'm taking you home now," Nat said.

Alice came with them. By the time they put Lizzie to bed she was shaking and shaking with what felt like a fever. The lights were too bright and swung about her head like fireworks. She felt as though she was burning up.

"She's taken an ague, my lord," she heard Mrs. Alibone saying to Nat, in tones of the deepest disapproval, "and what can one expect, jumping in the river like a hoyden? Fine behavior for a countess! First that disgraceful incident with the horse and now this...I was never so shocked in my life! I am not sure that I can work in a household where such things go on!"

"Then I suggest that you find employment elsewhere, Mrs. Alibone," Lizzie heard Nat say in clipped tones. "No one speaks of my wife like that."

"I think it is shock and reaction," Lizzie heard Alice say, after Mrs. Alibone had bustled off to pack her bags, buoyed up on a wave of righteous indignation. "Lizzie is as strong as an ox."

"I'll stay with her," Nat said. Lizzie thought he sounded anxious and she wanted to reassure him, but her limbs felt weighted in lead and her head so heavy she could not lift it, could not speak.

She knew that Nat was true to his word. She knew that he was there through all the fever and the nightmares that followed when she dreamed of her mother running away down the corridors of Scarlet Park, and of Monty striding across the gardens of Fortune Hall that had once been his pride and joy, when she saw Tom's mocking face before her eyes and she thought she heard a baby crying, and she cried out herself in her anguish of all she had lost. She sensed Nat beside her and knew that she spoke to him and heard him reply, though afterward she could never recall what they had said. But his presence comforted and calmed her and eventually she fell into a deep sleep.

On the third day she woke feeling better, clear-headed and hungry, and found Alice sitting in the chair beside her bed.

"Nat will be so sorry not to have been here," Alice said, closing the book she had been reading and putting it aside on the table. "He has stayed with you the whole time, Lizzie. I do not believe he has slept at all. He only left you today because he needed to talk to Dexter and Miles to tie up the loose ends of the case."

"I know." Lizzie smiled drowsily. "I know he was here. I felt it." She wrinkled her brow a little trying to remember. The images were faint but the feeling of warmth, the confidence in knowing that Nat had been with her, persisted. "I spoke to him, I think," she said, "though I do not remember the words…"

"You told him how sad you were not to be carrying his child," Alice said, after a hesitation. "He asked me about it, Lizzie, and I had to admit that I knew. I think he was shocked both at the depth of your distress and the fact that you had not spoken to him about it." She stopped.

"It was wrong of me to hold so much back." Lizzie turned her head and looked at Alice's troubled face. "Yes, I told Nat so little of how I was feeling—about Monty's death, about our marriage, about the baby…I kept it all bottled up inside me but it was like an explosion—as fast as I pushed it down it jetted up again. All the anger and the grief and the unhappiness had to find a way out." She looked at the bars of sunlight moving across the ceiling above her bed and felt a deep peace. "I don't feel like that any longer," she said. "It has all gone now." A shadow touched her heart. "I do not suppose there is any news of Mary?"

"None," Alice said, standing up. "I am so sorry, Lizzie."

"I tried to help her," Lizzie said. Her voice caught. "Even though she had taken Monty from me. She was so hurt, Alice, so damaged and twisted and unhappy." She shivered. "I did not know love could be so destructive."

"I will go to fetch you some food," Alice said. "Now Mrs. Alibone has left I am afraid that the house does not function with anywhere near the same efficiency, but it is nice not to have her sinister presence lurking behind every door!"

After Lizzie had eaten the soup and bread that Alice brought she made her friend go home, for she thought that Alice looked exhausted. She lay a little longer in bed, watching the shadow patterns on the wall, and thought about how much Nat must care for her to have sat by her bedside and how she hoped deep in her heart that he loved her. She was sure she had felt his love for her; felt it in his presence beside her, heard it in his words, experienced it in his gentle touch.

Tonight, she thought. Tonight I will go downstairs and we will dine together and talk, and I will tell Nat I love him. Perhaps she had already told him when she had been in her fever. She was not sure, but she wanted to be honest with him and tell him openly of her feelings now. And the more she thought about it the more she hoped, stubbornly, optimistically, that Nat really did love her, too, or at least that there was the chance that what he felt for her would grow and mature into love. Just as her love for him had changed from the childish infatuation of her youth, so she was almost sure that Nat's feelings for her had also undergone a change in the past week or so. She clung tenaciously to the belief and felt her faith in him like a spark of fire spreading warmth through her body.

After a little while she slipped out of bed. She chose her gown with particular care, shivering a little with sensual anticipation as the green silk slid over the crisp material of her bodice and petticoats. Her skin seemed alive to every touch, anticipating Nat's hands on her later. They would talk and then they would make love, and this time it would be different, with all that wild passion transformed into something even more blissful because of their deepening feelings.

The maid arranged her hair, restraining the auburn corkscrew curls with a silver clasp. Lizzie dismissed the girl, took one final glance at herself in the looking glass, drew a shawl around her shoulders and was about to go downstairs when she heard the front door open and the sound of voices in the hall.

"Must you trouble me with this now?" That was Nat, his voice cold and hard and very angry. "I've told you, Fortune, that you will have no more money from me. It stops here."

"My dear chap." Lizzie recognized Tom, smooth, amused, in a parody of an English gentleman. "Nothing was further from my mind. Your little sister's shocking secret is safe with me, I assure you. I am sure she and your parents have suffered enough—and indeed, you have paid handsomely for her indiscretion, have you not?"

Lizzie froze, willing the stairs not to creak beneath her feet. The shock blasted through her body leaving her weak. Tom had been *blackmailing* Nat—and Nat had *paid* him? She could not believe it. Not Nat, who had always been dedicated to honor and integrity. Nat would never pay a blackmailer. He would see him damned first. It was not possible. And yet, and yet…Lizzie's mind spun. Tom had made some reference to Nat's sister Celeste. Tom must have ruined Celeste, debauched her perhaps, and was threatening to make the news public. It had happened before, with Lydia. Perhaps Celeste might even be pregnant, which would account for why she had been hidden away at Water House these months past. And of course under the circumstances Nat would pay to keep Tom quiet and preserve Celeste's secret. What choice did he have if he was not to parade her disgrace before the world and destroy his sister's reputation and his parents' lives? It was no wonder, Lizzie thought, that Nat hated Tom. But why had he not told her? Had he not trusted her to keep the secret of his sister's scandal?

With a sick feeling of dread and a bleak sense of disappointment Lizzie remembered the moment when Nat had confided in her about the fire that had taken Celeste's twin and his own guilt that he had not been able to save her. Was this the secret Nat had been keeping from her? He had come so close to telling her, but then he had drawn back. Lizzie felt a dull pain spreading through her at the thought that Nat had hesitated to trust her.

But Tom was speaking again and Lizzie leaned

closer over the banister, straining to catch his words even as her heart thundered so loudly she was afraid it would give her away; even when she was not really sure that she wished to hear any more.

"No, it is not Celeste who concerns me now," Tom was saying. "It is Lizzie. I have noticed—we all have—how tragically fond she has become of you, Waterhouse. It won't do, old chap. It won't do at all, not when you married her under false pretences."

"I don't know what you mean." Nat's voice was clipped, furious. "What are you insinuating?"

Lizzie heard Tom's voice grow louder. He must have moved closer to the door. Each word was now devastatingly clear.

"You haven't told Lizzie, have you?" Tom said. "You haven't told her about my blackmail because that would necessitate explaining to her that you married her for her fortune simply so you could pay me."

"Lizzie knows that I needed money," Nat snapped. "I made no secret of it."

"But not that you took her and her money for revenge," Tom said softly.

"That's nonsense and you know it." Was that a thread of hesitation in Nat's voice now? Lizzie heard his tone change and felt the icy trickle of fear down her spine.

"Is it?" Tom said smoothly. "I don't think so. You saw the opportunity to pay me back for my black-mail, didn't you, Waterhouse? You knew that under the Dames' Tax I would get half of Lizzie's money if she did not wed before September. That is my right as Lord of the Manor. So you snatched Lizzie from under my nose, stole her dowry from me and then used it to pay me off!" He laughed. "That is the sort of unprincipled trick that I would pull. I almost admire you for it, except that you swindled me of my fair share of Lizzie's cash, damn you."

There was a silence, a long, damning silence. Lizzie waited for Nat to refute her brother's words, for surely they could not be true. Nat would never have used her to get revenge on Tom. She could see now that he had needed her money to pay Tom and protect Celeste, but surely he had acted out of honorable motives.

And yet he had not told her about the blackmail. He had not trusted her.

The words slithered like cold, black poison through her mind and with another pang of icy grief she remembered Nat's words to her that evening of the picnic, when he had begged her not to listen to Tom, not to believe anything Tom said…

Tom had been the one to tell her the truth about Gregory Scarlet, a truth Nat had kept from her. And now she realized that Nat had been afraid because he had known Tom might tell her the truth about her marriage, too. Nat had promised her that there were no more secrets, but now there was this. He had lied.

Nat had paid Tom off using her dowry.

The thought left a bitter taste in her mouth.

She felt cold and doubting, not wanting to disbelieve Nat's integrity and yet suddenly facing the fact that he was not the man she had thought him.

"You must not tell her," Nat said, and Lizzie felt sick and dizzy to hear the words that confirmed Nat's guilt. "You must *not* tell Lizzie, Fortune. I don't want her to know the terms of our agreement. Not ever." He sighed "What do you want this time for your silence?" He sounded tired.

Lizzie sagged against the banister, her fingers clenched tight on the smooth wood. So it *was* true. She would never have believed it if she had not heard Nat's words for herself. But it was true. Nat had seen her as his opportunity to revenge himself on Tom. He had just admitted it. That was why he had not confided in her about the blackmail—because she would have realized he had paid Tom with her dowry. She would have realized that he had used her.

Lizzie sat down heavily on the stairs. In the beginning, when she had seduced Nat and he had offered her the protection of his name, she had been sure he had been acting out of honor. She still believed it now, though her faith in him was battered and tarnished. It was the same honor that had prompted Nat to protect Celeste and pay Tom's price. Nat was not a bad person; he was not like Tom, motivated by nothing but greed. But then Monty had died and Tom had refused his permission for the wedding and Nat had seen the most perfect opportunity for revenge. He had outwitted Tom by getting Gregory Scarlet's agreement for the match. He had taken Lizzie's dowry and in doing so not only had he denied Tom his share under the Dames' Tax but had also rubbed Tom's nose in it by paying him the blackmail money from his sister's fortune. It was neat, it was cunning, it was the perfect revenge. And she had been the instrument of it.

"I want the Scarlet Diamonds," Tom was saying. "They should have been mine anyway and it's the least you owe me for stealing my share of Lizzie's dowry. I almost won them off her that night at the gaming tables. So if you give them to me now I'll say nothing to her about the small matter of you using Lizzie and her dowry for revenge."

There was a pause and Lizzie realized that she was holding her breath in the hope that Nat would still refute the allegation and tell Tom he loved her, that he had married her because he cared for her and not to settle some score. But then Nat said:

"I cannot give it to you now. Lizzie is in the house—I need more time… Tomorrow…" And Lizzie's heart sank like a stone and she drove her nails into the palms of her hands to prevent herself from crying.

"Tomorrow, then," Tom said. Lizzie heard him laugh. "That seems a fair bargain, Waterhouse. We have divided Lizzie up, you and I, to our mutual satisfaction now. Bought her, sold her, split the money."

Somehow Lizzie got herself back up the stairs and into her bedchamber, closing the door with shaking hands. She felt cold through and through, teeth chattering, hands shaking as though she had an ague again.

Bought and sold, bought and sold...

What price now her pitiful hopes that Nat was starting to love her in the same way that she cared for him? She could see just how futile and sad her dreams had been. Her naïveté felt so painful. Nat might have cared enough for her to give her the protection of his name and wed her to save her reputation, but his prime desire had always been for her money and now she knew why. Blackmail and revenge...

She felt wretched and betrayed and she could not, she *could not* stay here and pretend she had not overheard that damning conversation, nor could she challenge Nat and hear him repeat the truth to her face and experience the hurt of it all again. It would destroy her. Her love for Nat had been ripped apart by what she had heard; it had been so devastated that she no longer knew how she felt.

She dragged out some writing paper and her inkpot but she was shaking so much that she spilt the ink across the skirts of her green gown and mopped it up clumsily with her handkerchief. Then she paused. What could she say? It all sounded so pitiful:

I have loved you for so long.

I wanted someone who loved me for myself alone.

Better simply to go with it all unsaid.

She knew she was running away again but this time she could not stop herself. She took nothing with her. She could not seem to think clearly enough to know what she needed to take. She heard Tom leave and Nat go into his study and she crept down the stairs and out to the stables and she took Starfire with no tack and rode off into the night, still in her green evening gown.

PART THREE

CHAPTER SIXTEEN

NAT WAS SHAKEN to discover how strong was the urge to go and find Lizzie as soon as Tom had left, to speak to her, to wake her even if she was sleeping. He knew he needed to tell her the truth at once before Tom had the chance to see her. Despite buying himself some time, he did not trust the man an inch.

Nat had begged for time from Tom not because he intended for one moment to give him the necklace, not because he wanted to keep the truth from Lizzie, but because he simply had to lull his brother-in-law into a false sense of security. He had to keep Tom away from Lizzie until he had the opportunity to tell her about the blackmail himself. Nat knew that Tom, in his cruelty and malice, would hurt Lizzie again, smash all the bright confidence that Nat had seen growing in her, trample her feelings in that hateful, careless way he had and destroy Lizzie's happiness all over again. The thought of Tom harming Lizzie, crushing her spirit, made Nat furious.

He could see now that he had been mad and misguided to keep the truth from Lizzie for so long. He had thought he was doing the right thing in protecting her. He had not told her because he could not bear to disillusion her even further about her brother; news of Tom's latest outrage and his extortion would surely wrench her to the heart. Nat had seen for years how much Lizzie had cared for Monty and Tom Fortune and felt angry and powerless in the light of their indifference toward their little sister. He had thought he could not add to Lizzie's disenchantment by telling her even more of Tom's sordid affairs. Yet now he could see only too clearly how his actions could be interpreted. Tom's corrosive, spiteful words seemed to be all that he could hear:

"We have divided Lizzie up, you and I... Bought her, sold her..."

Nat went to the table and poured himself a glass of brandy, drinking it down in one gulp. It was true that he had needed Lizzie's money to pay the blackmail but he had never for a single moment resolved to marry her just to thwart her brother. The idea was sick, twisted, but it had a kind of appalling logic. Under the Dames' Tax Tom would have been entitled to half of his sister's dowry. By carrying her off and marrying her against Tom's wishes, Nat had cheated Tom of that twenty-five thousand pounds. Then he had paid Tom with Lizzie's money. Oh, yes, Nat could see why Tom, with his warped and bitter mind would see his actions as no more than coldhearted revenge. But he did not care what Tom

believed. The only thing that mattered was what
Lizzie thought, and he had to explain to her, had to
make it absolutely clear in a way that proved that he
had never intended her to be an instrument of
revenge against her brother. Everything between
them was so new and so fragile. He would not let
Tom despoil it.

He paced the room. He loved Lizzie. He knew that
now with a clarity he only wished he had achieved
earlier. He had been a fool, so unutterably slow to
realize his feelings for her, so trapped by the way
things had always been that he had not been able to
see that everything had changed. He loved her gal-
lantry and her courage and the way that she was
maturing and growing into such a fine person. He
was so proud of her that it made his heart ache to
think of it. And he needed her, knowing that only
Lizzie with all her defiance and her stubbornness
and her spirit could fill his soul and banish the dark
that had been left by his sister Charlotte's death.

He saw that Alice had left him a note. She had
written that Lizzie had woken, had taken some food
and was resting. Nat had intended to go up to Lizzie
as soon as he had returned home, but Tom Fortune
had caught him just outside the house. Now, though,
he knew he could not delay. Lizzie might be weak
and tired after her fever, it was probably the very
worst time to add to her woes, it was certainly the last
thing he wanted to speak to her about when all he

wanted to do was to hold her and tell her he loved her, but the matter could not be put off a moment longer.

Nat went out into the hallway and looked up the darkened stairwell. Not a sound. The house was still and quiet. Premonition stretched his nerves tight. For the first time he realized that Lizzie might have come down whilst Tom was there and that she might have heard their conversation. Nat had been forced to invite Tom inside, being unwilling to have such a loaded discussion in the street, but now, belatedly, he could see how dangerous that move might have been. But surely if Lizzie had overheard she would have burst in, challenged them and demanded to know what they were talking about? That was Lizzie's way—to confront an issue not to run from it. Unless…Unless she had been so hurt and distraught to think that he had married her for no more than money and revenge that she had run from him. Gone without a word…

Even as the thought was in his mind Nat took the stairs two at a time and slammed open Lizzie's door. The room was empty and quiet with the candle burning down on the chest and a blank piece of paper and pool of ink on the dressing table.

Nat felt the shock and dread drive all the breath from his body. He ran through the quiet house, down to the stables where the groom said that Lady Waterhouse had ridden out ten minutes before and no, he did not know which road she had taken.

The breath pounded in Nat's chest and the shock and fear made his head ache. He had to find Lizzie. Where would she run? What would she do? She was barely recovered from her fever and should not be out riding about the countryside. He knew he had finally driven her away this time. In the past it had taken her so much strength and courage to stand and confront her issues. The only example she had ever had was of a mother who had run away from unhappiness and two brothers who indulged themselves indiscriminately.

Nat sent to Drum Castle, to Alice and Miles, and to The Old Palace, to Dexter and Laura, asking if they had seen Lizzie. It was far too late to pretend to his friends or indeed to anyone else that there was nothing wrong. He had made a terrible, monumental error in not trusting Lizzie with the truth sooner and he could only hope that when she had had a few hours to calm down she would come back and he could try to explain to her and they might begin anew.

That hope lasted as he rode out on all the tracks from Fortune's Folly, searching for Lizzie hour after hour. It lasted when he called at all the alehouses and no one had seen her. It lasted until he reached Half Moon House on the road to Peacock Oak, where the landlady Josie Simmons was throwing the last of the late night drinkers out into the darkness.

"Lady Waterhouse?" she said. "Yes, she passed this way a couple of hours ago." She jerked her head toward the stall where the horses were stirring. "Her mare is stabled there. She said she did not need her anymore. She went in a private carriage."

Nat frowned. "A private carriage?" There was no way that Lizzie could have made an assignation because she had left so abruptly. Unless... The doubt slipped into his mind and could not be dislodged. Unless she had been thinking of leaving him all along and her discovery of the bargain he had made with Tom had simply precipitated her actions. She could have sent word to someone as soon as she left.

"Meet me at Half Moon House..."

But he could not believe it. Not Lizzie, fiercely loyal, courageous, admirable Lizzie. Not when she had told him in her fever that she loved him, not when they had started to build a future, not when there was so much he needed to explain, so many things he wanted to say to her...

"She went with Viscount Jerrold," Josie Simmons said, extinguishing Nat's hope like the snuffing of a candle. "They took the road to the south."

LIZZIE SAT IN A CORNER of John Jerrold's traveling coach and felt lonely and wretched and betrayed. The curtains of the carriage were drawn and inside it was almost as dark as out. The track was bad and the journey slow, but Jerrold had wanted to make as much progress as they could that night. Lizzie had not asked him why he was leaving Fortune's Folly. She had barely spoken to him. When his carriage had pulled into the yard at Half Moon House she had scrambled in and begged to be taken wherever it was he was going, and had sat and shivered like a dog left out in the rain. Jerrold had asked no questions, had wrapped the blankets around her although their warmth seemed to do little to dispel her chill, and had passed her his brandy flask. She had drunk from it with gratitude and great appreciation, feeling the coldness in her bones ease a little although it seemed likely that the soreness of her heart would need more than the numbing of drink. This time, it seemed, not even the strongest brandy could dull the pain. It hurt too much.

"I'm leaving Nat," she had announced baldly at one point, and Jerrold had laughed and said that he had rather thought she was, and they had lapsed into silence again. He had not asked her why; perhaps, Lizzie thought, he did not care. She had thrown herself at him—for she had got into his carriage in front of the entire alehouse and fully aware that it would be the final ruin of her reputation—and he was not going to ask any questions. There was tension in his silence and in the way that he watched her. She knew what would happen when they reached the next inn and stopped for the night.

She waited to feel something. She was about to betray her husband, break her wedding vows and give herself to another man. Surely she should feel some guilt? Yet no feelings came. There was nothing. Nothing but cold, black emptiness. She felt as though she was floating, tiptoeing lightly but inevitably, toward disaster. Her mind was numb. What did it matter what she did now? Nat did not love her and nothing else seemed remotely important. She had lost him. He had never truly been hers to lose. Gregory Scarlet had been right when he had said she was like her mother. Like the Countess of Scarlet she had pinned everything on her one true love, gambled and lost. Like her mother she would run away with second best—with a man who wanted her even if he was not the one she wanted.

They finally stopped in Keighley at the Crossed Hands. The inn was busy but the landlady, seeing quality, made a private room available to them at the top of the creaking stair. Lizzie sat down on the bed, realizing as she caught sight of herself in the mirror what a shocking fright she must look. She had no cloak or bonnet, her hair was awry and the diamond clasp long gone, and her gown was ripped and stained. She wished she cared but she looked at her reflection and saw a stranger looking back at her.

"Here you are, my lord, my lady." The landlady's eyes darted slyly from Lizzie to Jerrold and back. "A nice cozy room for you. Shall I send up some food?"

"Just some wine, thank you," Jerrold said. Lizzie heard the chink of money changing hands. "Then you can leave us alone—and you have not seen us."

"No, my lord," the woman said. She dropped a curtsy.

The wine arrived quickly. Jerrold poured her a glass and Lizzie drank it down almost greedily but still she felt nothing other than a lassitude that stole all thought. It was too much of an effort to move, too much of an effort to do anything at all. John Jerrold came across and sat next to her on the bed. He took the glass from her hand and placed it on the table. She watched his movements and they seemed so slow, as though everything took so long to happen, her seduction unraveling before her eyes with agonizing detail. She could not feel, could not think. Jerrold kissed her. He was good at it. She had known he would be. She remembered that a month or so ago—was it so recently? It felt like an age—she had been tempted to go out onto the terrace at the Wheelers' house with John Jerrold to see if he was any good at kissing. And now she knew.

Yet still she did not feel anything. Jerrold turned her around so that her back was to him and put his hand beneath the fall of her hair, his fingers cool on her nape. Lizzie closed her eyes and thought of Nat tracing his fingers down her neck and down the curve of her bare back, and she shivered. Jerrold's hand had gone to the laces of her gown. She felt the ribbons give and the bodice ease, and then it fell apart and Jerrold's hand was on her bare skin and she thought of Nat sliding his hands over her body and suddenly her feelings came alive with such force that she gasped. The pain hit her so hard and so fast that she almost cried aloud in anguish. She grabbed the bodice of the gown to her breasts and spun around.

"I can't do this!" She stopped, looking at the expression on John Jerrold's face. "My God," she said slowly as she saw the look in his eyes. "Neither can you."

Jerrold's expression eased into rueful amusement. "Actually I think I could," he said, "but I'll allow it is more difficult than I had thought."

"I love Nat," Lizzie said. She gulped in a breath. "Whatever he has done, I still love him. I'm so sorry, Johnny." She felt stricken, desperate. "I did not mean to be a tease," she said painfully. "I don't know what happened to me, but I can't make love with you because I cannot bear to betray Nat. I love him so much."

"I think I knew that really," Jerrold said wryly.

"Fasten my gown up so that we can talk," Lizzie said, spinning around again. "I cannot hold a conversation like this."

"A pity," Jerrold said, the amusement returning to his voice. He tied her laces. "I could definitely have done it," he added, his hands lingering on her bare shoulders. "Damn it, Lizzie…"

Lizzie slapped his hands away. She felt wretched with misery over Nat but at the same time a small spark of spirit had kindled inside her. It made everything hurt like the devil but at least she was feeling again.

"It's too late for that," she said. She looked at Jerrold, at the fall of his fair hair over his brow and the wicked light in his narrowed eyes and she sighed. "You make the perfect rake, Johnny, but I cannot let you seduce me." She put her head on one side. "Nor do I think your heart is really in this. Tell me what was so difficult for you. Was it because I'm married?"

Jerrold laughed. "That's never stopped me before." His smile vanished. "No, it's nothing to do with you. You're beautiful and I like you very much and I thought that I wanted you, but—" He stopped and ran a hand over his hair. "Devil take it, Lizzie, I think I'm in love, too, and it is the most damnable thing."

Lizzie's eyes grew huge. "You're in love with Lydia!" she burst out. She pressed a hand to her mouth. "I thought that you liked her when first she came to Fortune's Folly last year. Oh, that is bad, for Lydia will never give you a chance. She has been so hurt by Tom I doubt she will ever trust a man again." She broke off. "Sorry," she said. "That isn't very helpful."

"No," Jerrold said, "but it is accurate." He picked up his wineglass. "I have been trying not to kill your brother for months," he added conversationally. "It is very difficult, for I hate him more than any man on earth."

"There's a long queue," Lizzie said. "You'll have to wait your turn." She sighed. "Don't give up on Lydia. When we go back to Fortune's Folly I'll help you—" She stopped dead.

"You're thinking," Jerrold said, "that you can't go back. You have run away from your husband and by now everyone will have heard that you are with me and that you are ruined."

"Yes," Lizzie said. "And I am thinking that although I love Nat with all my heart, he does not love me and nothing can change that."

"Tell me about it," Jerrold said, smiling at her. "Perhaps I can help. After all, we've got all night."

NAT'S HEAD HURT. His body hurt. Everywhere hurt. Even in the worst excesses of his youth he had not appreciated that alcohol could have such a devastating effect. Then he remembered that he had not taken any drink. As memory rushed in, irresistible and damnably painful, everything started to come back to him. He had lost Lizzie. Hurt and confused by his betrayal, she had run off with John Jerrold. The grief crashed through him again and he closed his eyes and wished for oblivion.

Oblivion did not arrive. Gradually Nat's senses started to register information, whether he wanted it or not. He appeared to be lying on sawdust and rough stone. The floor was cold beneath his cheek. There was a sour smell in his nostrils, a smell of damp and neglect. He could hear water dripping. He raised his head, groaned, and let it fall again. He could hear voices above his head. Someone said:

"For pity's sake, Waterhouse…"

It sounded like Miles Vickery.

Nat opened his eyes again and saw a pair of highly

polished boots. Definitely Miles. He wished his friend would go away.

Someone hauled him to his feet. Dexter Anstruther this time. Damn it, why couldn't they leave him alone? He blinked at them, squinting to get them in focus. His head was throbbing as though he had taken too much cheap wine. He tried to form some words.

"What time is it? Where am I?"

"It is eleven o'clock and you are in Skipton gaol," Dexter said. "You were arrested last night for breach of the peace." He pushed Nat down onto a wooden chair. Nat winced as various bruises and cuts made their presence felt.

"You'd better start talking and it had better be good," Miles said, his face tight and white with fury. "We've been looking for you everywhere after we got your message last night. What the hell are you doing here and what's been going on? Where's Lizzie? And why is Tom Fortune telling anyone who'll listen that he has been blackmailing you to the tune of twenty-five thousand pounds?"

"Because he has been," Nat said. "It's true." He put a hand up to his head. It seemed the only way to support it.

"You bloody fool," Miles said with blistering contempt.

"You were a blackmailer yourself once," Nat said bitterly. For a moment he felt so angry and violent that he almost considered knocking Miles down. But to lose his friends as well as his wife would only make him feel worse. It wasn't Miles's fault that he was telling him some long overdue home truths. And besides, he was not sure he could stand up straight enough to hit anyone.

"So?" Miles said coldly. "That does not make it right."

"Never mind that now," Dexter said, always the peacemaker. "We'll sort it out. We'll get you out of here, too. Nat." His voice changed, grew more urgent. "Where is Lizzie? Tom is also saying that she found out you married her for revenge and that she has left you. The *on dit* in the village is that she has run off with John Jerrold."

"It's true," Nat said again. "I was out all night looking for her, but I do not know where they have gone."

It was all coming back to him now. He remembered his anguished and exhausting hunt through the night, taking the road to Skipton, searching through all the inns and boardinghouses on the way in the vain hope that he would find Lizzie. No one had seen her; no one knew anything. As he drew a blank at each place so his despair had grown. Lizzie and John Jerrold…He could not bear to think of it. It tore him apart, ripped to shreds all the newly discovered love and tenderness he had for her. He had had no idea he could feel like this nor that it could hurt so very much.

By the time he had arrived in Skipton late the

previous night he had been almost beside himself with anguish and worry. He had found the town awake and feverish with the Goose Fair celebrations and had been in the Market Square when the night had erupted into a full-scale riot. The alehouses had emptied and more and more men had piled into the fight. Despite trying to calm matters, Nat had found himself plunged into a brawl and then ignominiously dragged off to cool his heels in gaol with the male-factors, a disastrous end to his night's search.

Nat grimaced. When Richard Ryder, the Home Secretary, heard what had happened he would be furious. It was perhaps a good job that he was planning to resign his post before he was sacked.

Dexter and Miles exchanged a look. Miles's face was still white and tight with fury. "I have known you a long time, Nathaniel," Miles said, and his eyes were so cold that Nat almost shivered, "and so I feel that I can say without fear of reprisal or contradiction that you are the most abject fool in Christendom."

"Miles," Dexter intervened, "is this really the time and place—"

"Damn right it is," Miles said. "He's an idiot and someone should tell him. Lizzie has no father—and only a poor excuse for a brother—to protect her, so I will take the role." He gave Nat a tight smile. "Yes, even I can see the irony of me preaching morality to others, but…" He took a deep breath. "None of us can keep silent any longer, Nat. You must be the only person in the *whole* of Fortune's Folly who has not realized that Lizzie has been in love with you for months and you have ridden roughshod over her feelings and emotions with a wilful cruelty that can only remind her of how little people have cared for her throughout her entire life!"

"I know," Nat said. "I know." He felt wretched. "I did not intend it to be like this," he added. "I've been trying to do the right thing. I love her, too."

"Then find her!" Miles bellowed. "What are you waiting for? Why are we even having this conversation? Damn it, man, get out there—"

"Don't shout," Dexter said. "You'll make his headache worse. Besides, we've got to get him out of gaol first." He looked at Nat. "Go and douse yourself under the pump in the yard. You look appalling. If Lizzie sees you like that she won't want you back."

He slapped Nat on the back and all Nat's bruises winced in response.

"Come on," Dexter said, not unkindly. "You have a wife to claim."

CHAPTER SEVENTEEN

"BACK ALREADY, EH?" Josie Simmons said, as Lizzie collected Starfire from Half Moon House that afternoon. "And wearing the same clothes as you were yesterday." She shook her head at Lizzie, her expression suggesting that she had seen any number of unfaithful aristocratic ladies come a cropper. "Your husband was here last night looking for you," she added. "I told him you'd gone with Lord Jerrold."

"How kind of you," Lizzie said. "I really do appreciate that."

"Whole village knows now," Josie said with what seemed to Lizzie to be grim satisfaction. "Never seen a man so distraught as Lord Waterhouse," she added. "Except perhaps Major Falconer when he thought Mrs. Falconer would refuse to marry him. Or Mr. Anstruther," she continued, "when he found out that Mrs. Anstruther had been a highwaywoman." She sighed massively and placed her hands on her hips. "Any road, he was proper upset was Lord Waterhouse," she said. "She's a bolter," I told him, "just like her mama. Sees a man and goes after him like a dog after a rabbit—"

"No, I am not," Lizzie said, jumping up onto Starfire's back. "A bolter runs away. She doesn't run back again."

"Aye well," Josie said, "you might be right there, milady. Hope your husband sees it that way. You'll be wanting to creep back meek and quiet and beg his forgiveness, I'll wager."

"I've never been meek and quiet in my life," Lizzie said, "and I am not going to start now."

She kicked Starfire to a gallop down the track to Fortune's Folly. She felt exhilarated, excited and dreadfully nervous, but through her anxiety and her desperation she clung on to the thought that Nat had been distraught at her disappearance. He had been searching frantically for her, according to Josie. That must mean that he cared for her a little even if he was angry, and believed she had betrayed him. She shivered. She would never be able to prove that she had not been unfaithful with John Jerrold. Nat would have to trust her, to take her word. She wondered if he was generous enough, strong enough, to do that.

The previous night Jerrold had helped her to see that running away could never be the answer. The truth might be painful; it might not be what she wanted to hear but Lizzie knew she had to be courageous and face it. So she knew she had to talk to Nat, to beg him to explain Tom's blackmail. In her heart there was renewed hope that they could finally lay all their secrets to rest and this time she would *not* let it be extinguished. She would fight for what she wanted. She was not like her mother. Nat was the one person she was no longer prepared to lose.

"I won't come with you," Jerrold had said to her as he had put her into a hired carriage in the inn yard that morning. "I doubt my presence would help soothe the situation and I have no desire for your husband to put a bullet through me." He had kissed her cheek. "I know I can trust you to explain to him that I behaved with honor. Be happy," he had added as he slammed the door and gave the coachman the order to move off.

Lizzie galloped down Fortune's Folly High Street, scattering the crowds like chaff, hearing the gasps of shock and speculation and seeing the scandalized faces of the crowd. So the news was already out. Josie had been right—gossip spread faster than the plague in Fortune's Folly and no doubt Tom would have fanned the flames by telling everyone she had run away just like her mother.

At Chevrons she discovered that Nat was from home and had not been back since the previous night. Her appearance at the house caused a minor sensation; her maid screamed on seeing her and threw her apron over her head

"Oh milady!" The girl gasped, "They are saying such terrible things about you! They say you ran off with a handsome lord and that you are a bolter just like your mama, and they are taking bets in the

Morris Clown Inn that Lord Waterhouse will divorce you! Your brother has staked a thousand pounds on it! Oh, milady!"

"Thank you, Clara," Lizzie said. "This is one bet I will ram down Tom's throat until he chokes on it." Even so, the nerves that had been tormenting her ever since she had set off home from the inn at Keighley did an extra large somersault in her stomach. Would Nat divorce her for her supposed adultery? The panic closed her throat. That was what had happened to Lady Scarlet and the shame and dishonor had been appalling. Lizzie had wept for her mother every day whilst the lurid court case was dragged through the newspapers and penny prints, each detail more sordid and humiliating than the last. She could not believe Nat would do such a thing to her.

In an agony of impatience and anxiety she dashed out of the house again. She simply could not sit at home and wait for Nat to return. She had to do *something,* so in the end she called at The Old Palace to see if Laura or Dexter knew where Nat had gone. There was no answer to her pull on the bell, though she could hear the jangle of it echo deep inside the building. Carrington the butler did not shuffle up to see who was calling. No one came.

Deeply disappointed, Lizzie turned to go and then, suddenly, the door was flung wide and Alice Vickery stood on the threshold. She looked hot, harassed and flustered and when she saw Lizzie her hopeful expression melted into one of deep disappointment.

"Lizzie! Oh, no! I was so hoping that you were Dr. Salter!"

"Alice," Lizzie said, catching her friend's arm, "please, I need your help. Do you know where Nat is? I *must* see him."

Alice did not respond immediately and Lizzie felt chilled. She had known that her friends must also have heard the gossip, but if they did not believe her innocent, if they would not help her, then all truly was lost.

"I know things look bad," she said desperately. "I know you will have heard terrible scandal about me, but I swear I did not betray Nat with John Jerrold! Oh, I was stupid and hurt and I behaved badly but I need to find Nat and tell him I love him and explain everything—" She stopped as Alice looked at her as though seeing her for the first time.

"Oh, Lizzie," Alice said, grabbing her hands, "I want to help you—of course I do—but I cannot do so now! There is no time. Laura and Lydia both went into labor some time ago and they are about to give birth and Dr. Salter is attending a confinement over near Peacock Oak and the midwife is with him, and lord knows how long they will be gone and in the meantime I am alone here with the servants and none of us know what to do!" She looked despairing. "We have boiled some water and found clean towels but what to do with them—" She shrugged hopelessly.

"Laura and Lydia have both gone into labor at the same time?" Lizzie repeated, so stunned by the news that she momentarily forgot her own troubles. "What are the odds against that?"

"I don't know!" Alice snapped. "I don't have time to calculate odds right now." Lizzie heard a wailing noise float down the stairs toward them, followed by the sound of Rachel, the maid, with an edge of hysteria to her voice, exhorting calm. "That's Lydia," Alice said. "Oh Lizzie—" Her blue eyes were frightened now. "What shall we do?"

"Where are Dexter and Miles?" Lizzie demanded, following her into the hall.

"They are out looking for you!" Alice said. "They found Nat in gaol in Skipton this morning. I have just had word from them. Apparently Nat had been searching for you all night and ended up in a brawl. Nat of all people! Anyway, I have sent Carrington out to fetch them back. Laura keeps asking for Dexter." She bit her lip. "Lydia has no one," she finished softly.

A sort of fatalistic calm took hold of Lizzie. She had absolutely no idea about childbirth, either, for its secrets were shrouded in mystery that was hidden from the uninitiated. A part of her wanted to leave Alice and to ride out to find Nat—Nat who had spent the entire night looking for her—but she knew she could not do that to her friends. They needed her now. Everything else would have to wait.

"Lydia has me," she said. "I am the baby's aunt."

She squared her shoulders. "Very well then, Alice. We shall have to deal with this ourselves." She gave Alice a little shake. "Laura has done it before, so she knows what happens—"

"I don't think that helps, judging by the things that Laura is saying in between the swearing," Alice said miserably.

"First we send for Josie Simmons," Lizzie continued firmly. "She used to be a midwife before she became the landlady of Half Moon House. Send Frank on a fast horse. He can take mine. I know he is the gardener, but he rides well. Then send someone for your mama, Alice. She is only next door and she has given birth to two children, so she must know what to do."

"Mama is hopeless in a crisis," Alice said, staring at her.

"Well, she will be good in this one," Lizzie said decisively. "I have a feeling she will do us proud. Go!" She gave Alice a little push and then when she had made sure that her friend had hurried off she turned toward the stair. As she put her foot on the bottom tread there was a scream from above that almost made her turn and run, then she stiffened her spine. She had lost so many people. She hoped she would not lose Nat, too. What was certain was that she *would not* lose Lydia and Laura, two of her best friends, through ignorance or folly or neglect. She would give her last breath to help them even though she had little real idea what she must do. She was praying very hard as she ran up the stairs, harder than she had ever prayed before in her life.

WALKING INTO THE Crossed Hands Inn in Keighley, Nat Waterhouse was assailed by the now familiar and deeply repulsive smell of ale and sweat. He doubted that he would ever want to drink a pint of beer again. He had seen the inside of every inn on the road from Skipton to Keighley and he hated the lot of them, but on the way he had picked up news of a traveling coach with two occupants, one of whom was a flame-haired woman of staggering beauty and he had known that it was Lizzie.

There was only one occupant of the taproom at the Crossed Hands, a man sitting in the corner by the window placidly drinking a glass of brandy and reading the newspaper. As Nat came in he rose to his feet.

"Waterhouse," he said. "I thought you would come."

Nat, dragging up every ounce of civilized behavior he could muster and finding it exceedingly difficult, just about managed not to hit him across the room.

"Jerrold," he said. He looked around. "Where is Lizzie?"

His mind was already conjuring up images, unbearable, intolerable pictures of Lizzie lying in bed upstairs, naked, sated and blissful, having shared a night of tempestuous passion with her lover. His fingers itched to take Jerrold by his immaculately tied neck cloth and murder him without further ado. He had played this moment over and over in his head, time and again, telling himself that if he really loved Lizzie and she wanted to be with Jerrold and not with him, he should let her go. Perhaps a more generous man would indeed free his wife so that she could be happy. But Nat was *damned* if he was going to let Lizzie go without a fight.

He waited in an agony of suspense for what seemed an hour and then saw the self-deprecating smile that twisted Jerrold's lips.

"Lady Waterhouse has gone back to Fortune's Folly," Jerrold said. "She didn't want to be with me. She has gone to find you, Waterhouse. Good luck," he added, ruefully, to the empty room.

Nat had already gone.

WHEN DEXTER ANSTRUTHER, Miles Vickery and Nat Waterhouse arrived at The Old Palace some three hours later, accompanied by an exhausted and tottering Carrington, they found the place in uproar. Dr. Salter and the midwife, Mrs. Elton, had only just arrived. Josie Simmons and Alice's mother, Mrs. Lister, were sitting on the stairs with the maids Rachel and Molly and Frank the gardener, and appeared to be working their way through the contents of their fourth bottle of brandy while the other bottles rolled empty on the flagstone floor below.

"Ah!" Josie said, lumbering to her feet as Dexter

ran into the hall. "Mr. Anstruther! Late again! Quick enough to do the deed—" she cackled, nudging Mrs. Lister "—but slow to wet the baby's head!" She waved the half-empty brandy bottle at him in salute.

"Laura?" Dexter said. "Is she—"

"She's fine," Josie said heartily, slapping him on the back so hard Dexter almost fell over. "Dr. Salter is with her now, but he says there are no problems. I did a grand job though I say so myself, and the ladies were splendid! Not a swoon in sight!"

Nat was looking around for Lizzie, but in the chaos of The Old Palace she was nowhere to be seen. He had already called at Chevrons to be told by the breathlessly excited maid that Lady Waterhouse had returned and had ridden out to look for him. Nat rather hoped that Lizzie was here or they would be chasing each other across the county for days.

He saw Alice coming slowly down the stairs toward them, a bundle in her arms. Her face was radiant. She smiled at Miles as though she had been given the sun and the moon and the stars and held out the bundle to Dexter.

"A son for you, Dexter," she said. "Congratulations."

Dexter was at her side in a second, drawing aside the swaddling clothes to touch the baby's face with a reverent finger. His son's tiny rosebud mouth opened and a loud wail emerged.

Mrs. Elton bustled forward. "Give him to me, Lady Vickery," she commanded, taking the baby from Alice and bending over to admire him. "The little lamb! My, look at the size of him! Poor Mrs. Anstruther. No wonder she is exhausted!"

Laura and Dexter's daughter Hattie rushed forward and Dexter swung her up into his arms.

"I've got a brother!" Hattie said importantly. "May we go and see Mama now, Papa?"

"Yes," Dexter said. "Yes, we shall go at once."

Nat could hear the catch in his voice and felt a rush of emotion. Devil take it, there was something about this childbirth business that quite unmanned him. He looked across at Miles to see if he was suffering the same problem, but Miles was kissing Alice and paying no attention to anything else at all.

Dexter and Hattie set off up the stairs and Josie turned to Nat.

"You'll be looking for your lady wife, no doubt," she said. "She's with Miss Cole. I don't know how the poor girl would have managed without her. Lady Waterhouse gave her the strength and the spirit to go through with it, I reckon—" She stopped.

Nat looked up and saw that Lizzie was coming down the stairs. Like Alice she was holding a small bundle in her arms and she had a huge smile on her face.

"I have a niece!" she said. She sounded so happy and so proud that Nat felt the emotion rip through him again. "She is the most beautiful baby!" She saw Nat and stopped dead.

There was a long silence. Lizzie's eyes were

enormous, her face suddenly pale. She came hesi-
tantly down the last few steps and Nat went across
to meet her. He could see that her eyes were
swimming with tears now. He remembered the
broken words she had whispered in her fever and the
desperate longing for a child that was in her heart.
He reached out and touched her cheek with fingers
that suddenly shook.

"I hear you were splendid," he said softly.

"I came back to find you," Lizzie said. Her voice
was shaking, too. She looked down at the bundle in
her arms. "I…Somehow I became diverted." She
smiled suddenly, dazzlingly. Nat's heart lurched with
love. "This is Elizabeth," she said shyly.

"Elizabeth?" Nat said. He felt his heart catch as
he looked down into his wife's face. "Lydia named
the baby for you?"

Lizzie nodded. "Elizabeth Laura Alice Cole," she
said.

The whoops from the hall behind them became
louder as Josie and Mrs. Lister and the servants
started their fifth bottle of brandy and with it a round
of elaborate toasts to the babies. Alice came over
and took the baby from Lizzie's arms.

"I will take little Beth back up to her mother and
sit with Lydia a while," Alice said, holding the baby
in the crook of her arm. She smiled at Miles.

"You are an expert already," Miles said, his eyes
gleaming as they rested on her and the sleeping child.

"Hmm. If you wish us to set up our own nursery, Alice, you need only say the word and I am at your service."

"Actually…" Alice said, blushing peony-red, "I think I might already—"

Miles caught her and kissed her hard. "Don't squash the baby!" Alice chided, as she emerged ruffled and even pinker from her husband's embrace.

Nat grabbed Lizzie's hand and pulled her through the door into the library. And suddenly it was quiet and it was just the two of them and the rest of the world was shut out.

"Lizzie," Nat said. His voice sounded rough to his own ears. He closed the distance between them until she was less than a heartbeat away. "You came back."

"Yes," Lizzie said. "Nat, I need to tell you—"

"Let me speak first," Nat said. He felt as though his heart would burst with everything he wanted to say to her, with all the love he had for her. "Please, Lizzie."

Lizzie waited. Her face was white. Nat could hear her breath coming quick and light.

"I don't care what's happened," Nat said. He felt as though he was teetering on the edge of a precipice, fearful that with a single wrong word she would be lost to him forever. But he had to say what was in his heart. "You came back to me," he said. "I love you. I don't care about John Jerrold. I don't care what happened with him. All I want is you, Lizzie."

"Nat," Lizzie said. She sounded shaken to her soul. "Oh, Nat."

"Don't say anything," Nat said, catching her hands and drawing her to him. He could feel them both shaking. "You must understand. I made a terrible mistake in not trusting you with the truth about Tom's blackmail and I am sorry for it. It was entirely my fault. I was trying to protect you, but instead I drove you away. But you must believe that I never sought revenge through you, Lizzie."

He gripped her hands tighter. "I want only you and I love you for yourself alone," he said. "When you were in your fever you spoke of love, Lizzie. You said that you wanted someone who would love you forever and would never leave you nor betray you." He sought her gaze with his. "I am that man you once spoke of, Lizzie. I am the one that you wanted, and if you trust me I will never hurt you ever again. I swear it on my life."

"Let me speak now," Lizzie said. The tears were running down her face, huge tears that plopped onto Laura's worn carpet, making the colors bright. "Nothing happened with John Jerrold, Nat." She gulped in a breath. "I only turned to him because I was so unhappy. Then I realized that I couldn't go through with it, I wasn't like my mother after all. I could not accept second best because all I wanted was you. The only man I ever loved was you." She freed herself, resting her palms against his chest and looking up into his face with candid eyes. "I realized then that I had to come back and talk to you," she said, "and find out the truth about Tom, because I could not throw away the most precious thing I ever had."

Relief and sheer, blazing joy smashed through Nat and then his arms went about her and he kissed her, pressing feverish kisses across her cheek and brow, until he found her lips at last and she gave a little sigh and melted closer into his arms. And then all was quiet between them for a very long time and not even the sound of the increasingly drunken revels outside the door could penetrate their happiness.

LATER, LYING COCOONED IN their bed in the aftermath of lovemaking and in the hot darkness of the Fortune Folly summer night, they talked. They lay as close as when they had made love. For a while they had both drifted from fulfilment into sleep but they awoke together and Nat held Lizzie with proud possession as well as love.

"I was such a fool not to tell you about Tom's blackmail," Nat said. "I only gave into it in the first place to protect Celeste and my parents, and because I could see no way out. I kept it from you because I wanted to protect you from this latest example of Tom's wickedness and instead I gave him the means to ruin our happiness."

"I suppose Tom seduced Celeste, the blackguard," Lizzie said. She was feeling so light and free, so blissful that nothing could touch her happiness now, and yet she still had space in her heart to feel Celeste

Waterhouse's pain. She rested her head on Nat's chest and felt the warmth of his body and his love envelop her. There were no doubts or fears now. They had banished them forever.

"I could not understand how a man like you could succumb to blackmail," she said, "but I can see that you had to protect your family."

"I thought so," Nat said. He shook his head. "Perhaps I was wrong in what I did. But Tom did not seduce Celeste, Lizzie. He found her in a compromising situation—a very compromising situation—with another debutante. He had witnesses, and such scurrilous and damning tales of what they were doing together that I..." He shrugged uneasily. "Well, it would have been the scandal of the season had it got out and I know it would have killed my father. I simply could not allow that to happen. I love my sister and I have to protect her."

"A woman," Lizzie said. She could see what Nat meant. Such things were never spoken of outside the brothels and bawdy houses of London. It was as though they did not exist, though everyone knew that they did. For such a scandal to take place in the *Ton* would have been the most shocking, the most outrageous piece of tittle-tattle for years.

"Poor Celeste," she said softly. "Poor, poor girl."

Nat drew her closer to his body and Lizzie stretched, luxuriating in the warmth and intimacy of their connection.

"In some twisted way I think I have been trying to make up for failing Charlotte all those years ago," Nat said softly, after a moment. "I felt that I could never allow myself to fail again. I had to protect everyone—Celeste, my parents and you, too." He cupped Lizzie's face in tender hands. "I thought that if you knew of the blackmail, of this latest piece of cruelty on Tom's part, you would be utterly destroyed," he said. "You had already lost Monty, scoundrel though he was, and even before you told me how you felt about your family, I knew that you cared deeply for your undeserving brothers. Love has no rhyme or reason—" He pressed a kiss on her hair, moving one hand softly over her tumbled curls. "And I could not bear for Tom to injure you even more. So I kept quiet, wanting to shield you from harm. And in the process I hurt you very much because of my apparent lack of trust in you. I am sorry, Lizzie. Will you accept that I never married you to revenge myself on Tom and that I wanted more than anything to care for you?"

Lizzie raised her hand to his lean cheek, feeling the stubble rough against her fingers. "I do accept it," she whispered. "I knew in my heart that you were honorable, Nat, but I felt so shocked and deceived when I overheard you talking to Tom."

"I was trying to buy time," Nat said, "so that I could tell you myself about the blackmail. I was terrified Tom would blurt it all out to you first and that you would misunderstand and hate me for it."

"I did," Lizzie said, "but not for long." She brought his head down to hers so that she could kiss him. "Enough of the past," she said gently. "We can let it go now."

They washed the memories away with kisses, soft and sweet. The drowsy press of Nat's body against hers was the most tender thing Lizzie had ever experienced. Nat brushed the hair away from her brow.

"Miles told me I was a fool," he whispered, "and he was right. I have loved you for so long, Lizzie darling, and I could not even see it. All I ever wanted was to care for you and protect you. I admired you. I was so proud of you and I could not see all my feelings were but facets of my love for you." He drew away a little. "I am sorry about the baby," he said gruffly. "I wish you had told me."

"It doesn't matter anymore," Lizzie said. "I can wait. Now I know I have you."

She remembered telling Alice she had wanted a child to bind her closer to Nat, but now that she knew his whole heart, that his whole life was hers, she felt strangely serene and patient. It was a new sensation. There was no hurry. She could see that now. Whatever came to pass, she had Nat beside her, and that was the only thing that mattered now. Perhaps in time she would be able to build the family she wanted; the one that she herself had been denied. She did not know, but she had Nat and he loved her and that was more than enough.

"Although," she added thoughtfully, moving her hand over the flat plane of Nat's stomach and down, "I do not mind trying to make a baby whenever you wish…"

Nat rolled over lazily, drawing her beneath him. His mouth moved from her lips to the line of her throat, gentle kisses that caressed her even as his hands roamed over her body worshipping every curve and hollow. Previously there had been nothing but passion between them and Lizzie had understood that, but this felt different. Now there was a need to give and give again with generosity and love. She felt it for Nat and knew he felt the same for her, and at last she experienced the depth and power of his love for her.

"I love you," he murmured as he slid inside her with infinite gentleness, "I will always love you, Lizzie. Lizzie," he repeated, "my love, my life."

"I love you, too," Lizzie said. She remembered all the times she had held back from telling him. Her pride had come between them. Her fear of the inequality in their feelings had kept them apart but now there was no more reason to hide and no more secrets to keep. She moved restlessly beneath his hands and her body quickened with the pleasure he could always give her but now it was love returned as well as pleasure given, deep and searing in its intensity.

"You're impatient still," Nat murmured, laughing, as he rocked within her, tantalizing and slow, and

Lizzie gasped and pulled him to her for a kiss that stole her soul. "Some things will never change."

"You are no better," Lizzie whispered, her skin slick against his in the heat of the night, the tide running strong between them again now, "though you pretend—the conventional Earl of Waterhouse, so proper, so passionless. I should have realized from the first when I knew what a terribly cross disposition you had. I should have known such temper could only be matched with such passion—" She broke off on another gasp as Nat moved again, his mouth at her breast now, shocking and sweet. The desire twisted within her, driving her higher. This time it was a matter of slow, shimmering, exquisite delight and afterward Nat wrapped her in his arms and held her and she knew she had come home at last. The nightmares were gone. The tragedy of her mother's lost love had at last been balanced by her love found.

"No more running away," Nat said. "I never want to lose you again."

"Why should I run?" Lizzie said. "My heart is here. It is yours. Now and forever."

EPILOGUE

September

IT WAS A FINE, sunny day in early autumn when the Prince of Wales came to Fortune's Folly to declare formally that the villagers were free from the curse of the Dames' Tax and the other medieval laws. The streets were bright with bunting. There was a fair on Fortune Row and a platform erected in the market square so that His Highness could address the crowd. He had seemed extremely pleased to make Lizzie's acquaintance again, commenting on how she had grown from the little hoyden he remembered from Scarlet Park into a remarkably beautiful young woman. As he had said it his eyes had lingered suggestively on her face and the bodice of her gown until Nat had decided that enough was enough and suggested with cold politeness that His Highness might like to address the crowd now. Thus recalled to his duty, the prince had made a stirring speech, talking graciously about the people of Fortune's Folly and their courage in standing up to the oppressor—an oppressor who now looked very much the worse for wear as he sat in the stocks with a cabbage leaf on his head and a broken egg oozing down his face—and how the ancient liberties and rights of their great country had come to their aid in a time of need. He quoted the ancient Charter of the Forest and how it defended the rights of the common man against their lords, and declared all the Fortune's Folly medieval laws null and void. People were cheering as they raised their tankards in a toast.

"To Magna Carta!" Someone shouted. "To the Charter of the Forest!"

"To old King John! Aye, and to the Prince of Wales!"

"And to Lady Waterhouse," Josie shouted, drinking to Lizzie, "for putting an end to our oppression!"

"So Fortune's Folly is free of tyranny at last," Lizzie said, trying not to laugh as she watched the village children take another enthusiastic shot at Tom in the stocks. "Oh dear, poor Tom. Should I put an end to his punishment now, do you think?"

"Not yet," Nat said. "People have a great deal of anger to vent on him first."

"Perhaps he will reform," Lizzie said hopefully. "Perhaps some good may come of this."

Nat laughed. "You are very generous, my love, and I know that against all the odds you do care for your brother and wish him to be happy, but…" He shook his head, "I think that on this occasion you may be asking too much if you expect Tom to reform."

"There are others I wish happy, too," Lizzie said sighing. "Sir James and Lady Wheeler…"

"Yes," Nat said. "It was brave of them to come today."

Lizzie thought that in the harsh, unforgiving glare of the sunlight Lady Wheeler looked so old and worn, as though all the life, all the hope and the joy had gone out of her. They had never found Mary's body and now George too had left them, gone to London to bury the memory of his sister's disgrace in a round of drinking and dissipation, if the gossip was to be believed.

"And then there is Lydia," Lizzie said, turning to look at her friend. Lydia was standing with Dexter and Laura, Hattie and baby Edward. She was dressed in lilac with a saucy matching bonnet and she was holding Beth in her arms. The sun was shining on her face and she looked so young and so happy as she smilingly answered a question Laura was putting to her.

"Lydia cannot lock herself away forever," Lizzie said with sudden passion, "and deny herself the chance of love."

"Well," Nat said, brushing his lips against her hair, "if what you told me is true, then John Jerrold will do his utmost to persuade her of that."

"She allowed him to speak with her and to kiss her hand earlier," Lizzie said, with a little giggle. "I suppose it is a start. He will have to be very patient with her and by nature I am not certain he is a patient man."

"If he wants her enough, he will be," Nat said.

"And now Alice and Miles are setting up their nursery," Lizzie said, "so that just leaves you and me…" She turned in his arms and raised one hand to his cheek. His eyes were full of love; love that was warm and bright and that Lizzie knew would grow stronger and stronger between them forever.

"What are we to do, Nat?" she whispered, raising her lips to his.

"You can kiss me for a start," Nat said, "and we shall go on from there."

Lizzie smiled at him. "And there will be no more secrets."

"Never again," Nat said. "The last of the secrets are told."

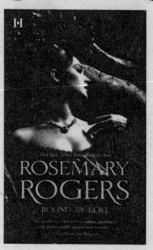

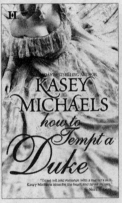
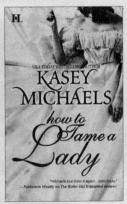

REQUEST YOUR FREE BOOKS!

2 FREE NOVELS
FROM THE ROMANCE/SUSPENSE
COLLECTION PLUS 2 FREE GIFTS!

YES! Please send me 2 FREE novels from the Romance/Suspense Collection and my 2 FREE gifts (gifts are worth about $10). After receiving them, if I don't wish to receive any more books, I can return the shipping statement marked "cancel." If I don't cancel, I will receive 4 brand-new novels every month and be billed just $5.74 per book in the U.S. or $6.24 per book in Canada. That's a savings of at least 28% off the cover price. It's quite a bargain! Shipping and handling is just 50¢ per book.* I understand that accepting the 2 free books and gifts places me under no obligation to buy anything. I can always return a shipment and cancel at any time. Even if I never buy another book from the Reader Service, the two free books and gifts are mine to keep forever.

185 MDN EYNQ 385 MDN EYN2

Name	(PLEASE PRINT)

Address	Apt. #

City	State/Prov.	Zip/Postal Code

Signature (if under 18, a parent or guardian must sign)

Mail to **The Reader Service:**
IN U.S.A.: P.O. Box 1867, Buffalo, NY 14240-1867
IN CANADA: P.O. Box 609, Fort Erie, Ontario L2A 5X3

Not valid to current subscribers of the Romance Collection,
the Suspense Collection or the Romance/Suspense Collection.

Want to try two free books from another line?
Call 1-800-873-8635 or visit www.morefreebooks.com.

* Terms and prices subject to change without notice. Prices do not include applicable taxes. Sales tax applicable in N.Y. Canadian residents will be charged applicable provincial taxes and GST. Offer not valid in Quebec. This offer is limited to one order per household. All orders subject to approval. Credit or debit balances in a customer's account(s) may be offset by any other outstanding balance owed by or to the customer. Please allow 4 to 6 weeks for delivery. Offer available while quantities last.

Your Privacy: Harlequin is committed to protecting your privacy. Our Privacy Policy is available online at www.eHarlequin.com or upon request from the Reader Service. From time to time we make our lists of customers available to reputable third parties who may have a product or service of interest to you. If you would prefer we not share your name and address, please check here. ☐

BOB09

NICOLA CORNICK

77389 THE SCANDALS
    OF AN INNOCENT   ___ $7.99 U.S. ___ $8.99 CAN.
77377 THE CONFESSIONS
    OF A DUCHESS   ___ $7.99 U.S. ___ $8.99 CAN.
77303 UNMASKED   ___ $6.99 U.S. ___ $6.99 CAN.
77211 LORD OF SCANDAL   ___ $6.99 U.S. ___ $8.50 CAN.

(limited quantities available)

TOTAL AMOUNT $ _____
POSTAGE & HANDLING $ _____
($1.00 FOR 1 BOOK, 50¢ for each additional)
APPLICABLE TAXES* $ _____
TOTAL PAYABLE $ _____
(check or money order—please do not send cash)

To order, complete this form and send it, along with a check or money order for the total above, payable to HQN Books, to: **In the U.S.:** 3010 Walden Avenue, P.O. Box 9077, Buffalo, NY 14269-9077; **In Canada:** P.O. Box 636, Fort Erie, Ontario, L2A 5X3.

Name: _____
Address: _____ City: _____
State/Prov.: _____ Zip/Postal Code: _____
Account Number (if applicable): _____

075 CSAS

*New York residents remit applicable sales taxes.
*Canadian residents remit applicable GST and provincial taxes.

HQN™

We *are* romance™

www.HQNBooks.com

PHINC0809BL